Canine Legends

Canine Legends

A Dog Agility Story

Marco Magiolo

Marco Magiolo

CANINE
LEGENDS
A DOG AGILITY STORY

MARCO MAGIOLO

Copyright © 2022 Marco Magiolo
All rights reserved.
Cover picture: Arrow / Flecha by Marcela Françoso
Edition 2

While this book is based on real events, names, places, and part of the timeline have been fictionalized solely for dramatic purposes and are not intended to reflect on any actual person or entity. Positive reviews from wonderful readers like you help other readers feel confident about choosing this book. Sharing your happy experience will be greatly appreciated.

For Arrow
(Para Flecha)
(2004 - 2018)

Some people say dogs are man's best friend. Who would have thought that one day dogs would change my life so much?
So many trips, places, cities. So many people, feelings, and experiences.
This is a story I like to describe as YEAR ONE. The first year entering a world that would be part of my life for many years to come.
It is a story about friendship, partnership, and love.
A story about winning and losing.
About Legends.
CANINE LEGENDS

1

THE FIRST COMPETITION

It was March 2006; I remember it very well.

An outdoor arena used for baseball and football practice, alongside a sports store that used to sell fitness equipment.

There we were, Arrow and I. Ready for our first official competition.

I was completely lost; I remember parking my car a few meters from the arena. From a distance, it was already possible to see several other competitors walking, exercising, and warming up with their dogs. A jump outside the track was being used for training.

I parked my car, turned off the engine. I was nervous. For a second, I didn't want to get out of the car. I looked at Arrow in the backseat, inside her crate, with those giant eyes, and wagging her tail like, "So, are we going or not?"

I got out of the car, just me, and started walking towards the competition area, praying to God to see familiar faces.

What was I waiting for? Everyone approaching me, introducing themselves and welcoming me? Of course not! People were there to compete, not to welcome every newcomer who showed up.

I approached the arena and that's when I heard Leo's voice shouting in my direction:

"Hey, Marquito!"

What a relief! Someone I knew.

Leo approached me with a big smile, opened arms and gave me a hug!

"What's up? Ready for your first competition?"

"Yes! Sure!"

"Where's Arrow?"

"She's in the car. I don't know where I'm staying yet. I was looking for a space for me!"

"Are you crazy?" said Leo. "Your place is already reserved in our tent!"

Leo pointed back to a giant tent, where all his students were staying with their dogs and crates. Another relief!

After having sat under the tent with Arrow already in her favorite place inside her crate, I approached the track's fence and began to observe the other competitors running.

It was my first competition so I would enter the beginner's category. But before that, the master's category was competing. I was ecstatic with what I saw. Amazing dogs. They were fast, agile, well trained, and the speed…. WOW! There was no doubt that Arrow and I had no chance against those people.

Leo approached me once more. He was doing everything he could to put me at ease. Years later, I would be able to see what he did for me. Not every trainer will help you like that. But Leo was on my side since day one. He was my trainer.

"Those guys are good, right?" Leo said smiling.

"Man, I don't know how they manage to do it so perfectly."

Leo gave me a smile and put his hand on my shoulder.

"Marquito, I've seen your training. It will only be a matter of time before you are competing against those guys. Trust me."

I completely ignored his comment. At that point I really did not believe it.

Leo was, without a doubt, one of the coolest guys I have met in this world. He was a Behaviorist with a specialty in canine sports. Highly respected in positive training even though some old-school trainers used to criticize him for believing that traditional negative training could bring better results. Back in the day when he was still competing, his dog had the fastest dog walk ever seen in competitions.

DOG WALK

###

It was time! The Beginners class is starting! My first competition!

"Ladies & Gentlemen, competitors!" announced the speakers, "Walking course for Beginner's category."

Walking course is the moment where competitors get to enter the track and check the course for the first time. We never knew what kind of course we would have to compete on until we were there. We had seven minutes to identify everything, think about a plan and leave. After that, it was warm up the dog and come back, but this time for the real competition.

My legs were shaking, heart racing and seven minutes to walk the course. In that moment you do not know what lies ahead, but you need to be ready anyway.

It's funny how weird life is. I perfectly remember that course, my first one. And today when I remember, I laugh at my nervousness. Basically, there were two straight lines, with jumps, tire, two tunnels, an A Frame, slalom, and dog walk. Simple, easy, no challenges! But to a handler competing for the first time, that looked pretty hard.

I walked that course with absolute concentration!

I closed my eyes, thinking, memorizing. Analyzing every

possible mistake, but also trying to think like Arrow, looking from her point of view.

The buzzer exploded in my ears! It was the end of the walking course!

"EVERYBODY OFF THE TRACK!" announced the speakers.

It was time!

Leo was outside waiting for me.

"All good?" Leo asked.

"Yes, yes!" I replied quickly.

I was so focused that I didn't talk to him much. I am sure he understood.

There were 26 beginner competitors that day. On the entry list I was eighth.

I put the harness on Arrow. As usual, she couldn't be happier. She came out of her crate all bouncing around, wagging her tail and playing. I took her to the side yard for the last pee before entering the track, and went to the line in the pre-track. Then the competition started.

Even today, I believe that the worst part in a competition is not walking the course, it is not the moment you step into the arena to start your run, it is not when you are running your dog. The worst part is the damn pre-track! Who invented that stupid idea?

The pre-track is nothing more than a line outside the track where competitors have to wait for their turn. The atmosphere is so tense! It feels like a bunch of people waiting in line to be murdered in a public square! How you deal with the pre-track is something very personal. Some handlers talk to their dogs, some handlers exercise, some just watch the competitors ahead entering the track.

I was focused on looking at the competitors ahead of me. I thought: "If I watch what they are doing wrong, maybe I can be ready for the tricky parts of the course".

The problem was, looking at the other competitors before me only made me more nervous. Out of seven teams ahead of me, five were eliminated. Every time someone was out, a thought crossed my mind: "You will eliminate! You will fall! It will be shameful!"

"Next team Marcus & Arrow," announced the speakers.

Well, there was no more time for nervousness. It was time! I stepped into the arena and looked ahead at the judge. Bad guy, arms crossed behind his back. The whistle blew, announcing I should proceed.

From the entrance of the arena to the starting mark it was approximately six meters. I remember walking as if I was on eggs shells. Limp legs, heart pounding in my temples, dry mouth.

I put Arrow on the starting spot.

"STAY!" I gave the command.

Harness off and I walked a few meters from her. PERFECT STAY! I looked at her. I remember those huge brown eyes staring at me as if to say: "Release me and run!"

"OK!" I said.

Then she came, jumping the first jump and giving 110%! That was Arrow! My nervousness? I don't know what happened, but it disappeared! A surge of adrenaline simply took over my body releasing strength and potential to my legs!

Arrow was overcoming obstacle after obstacle. Her bulging eyes and her gaping mouth, saliva flying everywhere just pushing me to run harder to finish that course as fast as I could.

I didn't have eyes or ears for anything else, didn't see anything that was going on outside the arena. I could hear absolutely nothing from the crowd screaming outside.

One of the crucial points was the dog walk. We had been training running contacts for months and until that point, I had not seen any other competitors doing running contact that day.

We reached the dog walk and I gave the command to Arrow, "RUN!", I screamed!

Arrow was so fast that while on the dog walk she passed me, running faster and without slowing down she reached the descent, pure speed touching the contact zone as she ran. It was so fast that for a split second I thought she was going to miss the next jump, she looked back probably wondering why I was so far behind.

I raised my arm:

"TUNNEL!!!" I yell, pointing to the next obstacle.

Without thinking twice, Arrow plunged into the tunnel at full speed, finishing that course with the last two jumps.

TUNNEL

When it was over, the first thing I did was hug her! And there I stayed for about five seconds, until I started to notice the screams coming from outside the arena. I didn't understand what had happened, and why those people were so loud.

I looked to the other side at the results screen, and there was a giant number 1 next to our name. Yes, we were first!

We left the arena because the next handler was getting ready to start his run.

Leo was outside at the exit gate waiting for us.

"MY GOD IN HEAVEN, what was that? What an incredible dog walk! And the speed! My God!".

Apparently, Leo was more excited than I was. At that moment I honestly had no idea if it had been good or not.

"It was good?" I asked.

"Jesus Christ, it was perfect!"

On the way back to our tent, one of the master's competitors walked on our side and in a deep voice said:

"Congratulations, great run!"

"Thanks!" I replied with full awkwardness!

"Hey, congratulations from Sany!" Leo said.

Sany was a member of the national team the year before and

he was the most important figure in Florida within the sport. But the day was not over yet, I still had another run to do.

###

After all the competitors ran, the final result came out. We were in third place. Two other competitors were faster than us.

How? I don't know, because I swear, I had probably run more than my body could offer. But two other people were still faster than us.

In local competitions the final results used to come from the combined result of two runs. So, we still had one more run ahead.

We had at least a 90-minute break until the next course, and after our first run, many other competitors from the Beginners category came to congratulate us, including Amadeus, a competitor who along with his dog Augustus, was considered the favorite and the best beginner that year. He was the one who had finished first in the first course.

###

Tension began to build again as the judge started preparing the course for the second Beginners run.

"Walking course for beginners!" announced the speakers.

Off we went, all 26 competitors walking the course for the second and final run of the day. Seven minutes!

Typical beginners' course. Multiple straight lines with two changes of direction. Nothing complex or too challenging. Front entry slalom, the easiest slalom entry you can find in Dog Agility. But for a bunch of beginning competitors, even that could be tricky.

In the second course, the last placed enters first, and the first placed enters last. That means that we would be the second to last to enter the track.

###

I went to sit outside the arena with Arrow sitting next to me, watching the first competitors entering the track. One by one, the dogs were having trouble finishing the course without penalties. There were bars on the ground, many dogs doing the slalom incorrectly, and silly eliminations on a quite simple course, without major traps.

Undoubtedly it ends up leaving you worried. "Is that course harder than I think?"

Thirteen teams to the end and we walked to the pre-track, lining up with the other competitors. Behind me, only two teams, second and first places, Amadeus and Augustus being the last team.

"On track Marcus & Arrow!" announced the speakers.

Another burst of energy and adrenaline, wobbly legs and nervous walking. During the ten seconds of walking between entering the track and the starting point behind the first jump, a thought came to my mind. "Don't let her run in front of you".

The big problem I saw while watching the other teams was dogs running in front of the handlers. With handlers staying behind, the dogs were looking back for reference, missing the obstacles ahead. If I could keep Arrow behind my line, I could complete the course without penalties.

STAY!", I put Arrow in the starting position, while removing her harness.

Immediately her eyes widened. Open mouth salivating and her breathing increasing.

"Stay ahead of her! Stay ahead of her!". That's what I told myself.

I put a lot of space walking up to jump number three. Something pretty daring for a beginner handler.

"OK!" I yelled from behind the third jump.

Arrow exploded with adrenaline, throwing her body over jump number 1 and running towards me. Immediately I launched myself toward the next obstacles, as Arrow chased me down the course!

"Stay ahead of her! Stay ahead of her!"

The slalom was approaching and for a second, I worried if she would enter properly, because she was so far behind me. I aimed at the slalom and yelled: "WEAVES!!!". I looked out of the corner of my eye as Arrow dove into the slalom in an absolutely beautiful way. I could have sworn I heard cheering from the stands, but honestly I was so focused on the run that I didn't even pay attention.

Two, three, four more jumps and... THE END!!!! Now I could hear the cheers and applause from the crowd. We got it! We finished without penalties.

Walking off the arena, Leo was there to congratulate us.

"Damn! What a run! What a Marquito debut!", Leo was euphoric!

Still catching my breath I tried to answer:

"Man, awesome! Wow! Incredible!"

When I was going to respond to Leo, screams of disappointment from the crowd caught my attention. I turned my eyes to the track to see that the team behind us had just been eliminated. The handler's frustration made me feel bad for her but that's when a thought popped into my head. "If the second place was eliminated, does that mean we're in second??" I turned to Leo and before I even asked, with a mischievous little smile he said:

"Well, your podium is guaranteed! Second at least!"

I didn't know how to react. Podium? In my first competition? Really?

I returned my attention to the arena when Amadeus and Augustus started their run. Fast and accurate they were overcoming the obstacles. Amadeus, despite being in the Beginners, was already an experienced handler. He was only in the Beginners because he was starting a new dog, however he had already competed for years with other dogs, including in the master's category. It was clear that he would win the competition, nothing could happen to take the first place from him... wait a minute!

That's when the unthinkable happened, Augustus left the slalom incorrectly, not making the last door, skipping to the next jump. Amadeus and Augustus were ELIMINATED!

I froze for a few seconds before processing the information! Leo put his hand on my shoulder:

"Congratulations! You just won your first official competition!"

Not knowing how to react to that situation, I started walking with Leo back to our tent, and on the way, probably fifteen people came to congratulate me! Other competitors and trainers would stop me and shake my hand, patting me on the back, for my first victory!

Twenty minutes later, I was on the podium lifting my first trophy with Arrow beside me on the day that would be imprinted in my memory for the rest of my life.

As I left the podium, Amadeus came to talk to me. When he approached, I was a little worried about what the most experienced beginner handler had to say to me. Gently he extended his arm offering his greeting.

"Congratulations, nicely done!" said Amadeus.

"Thanks!" I replied shaking his hand.

"You won today because I was trying to beat your time. Your dog is amazingly fast. I think I'll have to train harder to beat you!", Amadeus said smiling.

"I think I got lucky." I replied smiling back.

"No, luck has nothing to do with it. Your dog is very well trained. You deserved it."

Amadeus patted me on the back again and started walking away.

"See you next month." Amadeus said from afar.

2

FAMILY

I have no doubt Dog Agility filled a hole in my chest. Two years without my father by our side. It was 2004, two years before my first competition.

What my father did to our family left huge scars. Scars that I don't think will ever heal. Every month when I saw my mom getting ready to visit my dad at the Florida State Penitentiary in Bradford County, three hours away by bus, I felt a lump in my throat. I felt anger, I felt hatred for what my father had done to my mother, to my younger brother. I feel for them, not for my father.

"Why do you waste your time going there?"

"Your father made a mistake, and he's paying for it" my mother answered. "But he is still your father and deserves your respect. One day he will come back and our lives will continue, as before."

"Bullshit". That's what I thought, but I would never answer my mother that way. I was angry at what he had done. I hadn't gone to visit him since he was sent there, and my mother was always fighting with me about it.

"You need to go see your father." she said. "He asks about you every time, and why you never go with us to visit him. Your brother has been there several times."

My brother had been there several times because my mother made him go, and being a minor he couldn't refuse it. But it was I who used to hear my brother crying many nights or at bedtime, especially after coming home from visiting him.

"I'll go next month." That is what I always said, always looking for excuses to not go.

I often used Dog Agility as an excuse.

"I have training today." I said. "There is a competition this weekend and I need to rest." It was another excuse.

"This thing you do with your dog, is it more important than your father?" my mother replied.

Honestly, it was. Dog Agility was where I learned to put my anger, my competitive spirit, all my ghosts aside.

"No mother, it's not! I just need to be prepared.", another one of my excuses.

Talking about what happened that Tuesday morning June 2004 still hurts a lot, but I remember every detail.

My brother and I used to sleep in the same room and before 6 am my mother used to "invade" the room to wake up my brother, and prepare him to go to school. I could wake up a little later.

We were having breakfast around 6:45 in the morning and my brother already had his backpack ready to go to school. My mother served us orange juice. My dad already had his tie knotted and his pharmacist's uniform ready to leave for work.

The best memories I have of my father are from my childhood, when he used to find time to take me fishing.

We are Brazilian. My parents moved to Orlando when I was 10 years old, and my brother, just five. They came from São Paulo, looking for a better life and the American dream. My father was already a pharmacist in São Paulo, and got a work visa when he was hired to work as a manager/pharmacist in Florida.

We used to live near Windermere, in Orlando. When I was little, the expensive houses for the rich people that exist there today, were not there. It was just an open area with lakes where we could go fishing.

Because my father used to work so many hours a day, almost always seven days a week, if he had some time off we tried to make the most of it. Every minute was worth it. He used to rent a boat and we would go fishing in the middle of the lake in Windermere.

So many good memories.

That Tuesday morning things would take a horrible turn. Around 6:45 am someone knocked on the door. Three knocks, hard, like banging on the door.

My mom freaked out and nearly dropped the orange juice jar. My father dropped his napkin on the ground.

"What is that?" asked my father surprised, looking at the clock wondering who was knocking on the door at that time.

My dad got up and walked toward the door. I got up to follow him, but my mother held me gently. From the kitchen, we saw as my father opened the door, two police officers were outside.

"Mr. Machado?" one of the officers with a strong and intense voice, asked.

"Yes." my father replied, confused.

"My name is Investigator Porter. I have a warrant for your arrest."

An almost deadly silence hung in the air. I looked at my mom, who at that point looked more confused and scared than me.

My dad didn't say anything. He knew, he just knew. One of the officers grabbed him by the arm and began to read him his rights. Ten seconds later and my dad was handcuffed, looking at us with an expression on his face that meant a lot of things, but not surprise. He knew why this was happening.

"What is this?" my mother asked, scared and trembling.

"Miriam!" said my father while he was being handcuffed. "Don't do anything. Do not say anything. Call Walter, he'll know what to do."

3

THE SEARCH FOR MASTERS

Four months have passed since my first competition.

July 2006, and with the extreme heat at that time of year in Florida, the only possible places to practice Dog Agility were indoor locations. Florida has never had an abundance of indoor locations to practice Dog Agility.

If there was one of those perfect places to compete in the summer in Florida, it was Arcadia. The giant Fairgrounds that hosted horse and cattle events became the official site for Dog Agility between May and September.

Lots of grandstands, huge parking lot, snack bars, space for a crating area, and a good competition surface gave the place the perfect touch to host competitions.

Some competitors used to complain about the red clay surface, but I've never cared, and never had any problems during the years I competed there.

In the last three months I have actually achieved more impressive results than I could even imagine. Three competitions, two wins, and one second place. Amadeus and Augustus were my greatest rivals. The two times I won; they finished second. The only time I finished second, they won. It was clear that Marcus & Arrow and Amadeus & Augustus were the teams that drew the most attention in the Beginners category. But that day, something different was at stake.

No one has ever bothered to be champion in the beginner's category. In fact, staying a long time in the lowest category without being able to move up to the Masters, was actually more shameful than victorious.

During my first four months in that world, I heard of handlers staying in the beginners category for over 18 months. But I had other plans.

To move up to the master's category you needed three Qualifiers. Each run that you finish without penalties is considered a Qualifier. A penalty is when your dog knocks a bar, does not touch a contact zone on the dog walk, A Frame or seesaw, or even when your dog refuses an obstacle. Of course, elimination or not completing a course, is also not a qualifier.

Both Arrow and I, and Amadeus & Augustus had two Qualifiers until that day. The question was, who would go up first to the Masters category, and who would have to spend at least another month in the Beginners category.

###

I arrived very early that day. I remember waking up at 4:30 am because Arcadia was almost a two and a half hour drive from my house. I did not want to take the risk of being late.

Car parked, backpack on my back, Arrow on the leash beside me.

Unlike four months ago, now I was a little better known. Walking into the Fairgrounds, approaching the arena and bumping into other competitors, already earned me some compliments.

"Hey Marquito, how are you?" asked one of the competitors.

"I'm fine, and you?"

A few more steps, and we were at the place where our tent was already prepared, with the crates waiting for our dogs.

"Good morning Marquito, how is Arrow? Ready?", Taylor asked me.

"She's so ready!"

Taylor was one of the coolest people I've met in Dog Agility since I started competing. She was a lady in her 60s, very active and competing with her dog, Bowie. Some say that twenty years before, she was one of the greatest competitors in the country, with two appearances on the US National Team.

"Ah, you guys, that competitive spirit! Looking to get to the Masters." Taylor said smiling. "I've done my part. Now I just want to stick around in the beginners playing with my dog."

"You need to do what makes you happy, right?" I replied smiling.

"Truth! I hope you make it today!"

While I was arranging my things under the tent, I saw the figure of Sany Bastos in the distance. The most important Dog Agility competitor in Florida. He participated the year before in the Agility World Championship, getting into the finals. But unfortunately, he lost.

In the track, it was difficult to beat him. He used to teach Dog Agility in South Florida. But if you wanted to attend one of his classes you would have to invest about one hundred and fifty dollars an hour. For me, forget it. I was completely satisfied training with Leo.

At that moment out of the corner of my eye I saw Sany starting to walk towards me. Seriously? What could he want with me? Surely, he was just walking towards me by coincidence, to do something besides talk to me.

"Marquito!" Sany said with a strong but smiling voice.

"Hey, Sany!" I replied a little awkwardly.

"I heard that you could move up a category today."

"Well, let's see! You never know what might happen.", I was just trying not to look so awkward.

"I've been watching your last runs. I have to say, you and your dog have potential."

I froze for a second, thinking, "Is Sany Bastos praising my dog?"

"Thanks!" I replied shyly.

"With the right training it could go very well for you."

I had no reaction for a moment.

"Who is the breeder?"

"Arrow is from a herding dog farm." I replied.

"Ah, herding. She is not from a competition lineage. Sorry for that" Sany smiled in the corner of his mouth. "And also, training with the wrong guy. You will go up to Masters, but after that, I don't see much future for you."

An awkward silence filled the air. I didn't know what to say. The guy that I've always idolized, and even thought I wanted to be like one day, saying those kinds of things about my dog.

"Anyway, good luck!" Sany turned around and left.

I was completely still, fixated on my thoughts about what had just happened.

Seriously? Is that the guy I always used as an example? Saying things like that? No, it can't be. Who does that guy think he is?

"So, ready?" Leo approached me.

My silence continued for a few more seconds, and Leo understood what had just happened.

"What did Sany tell you?" Leo asked realizing that the short encounter with Sany had not gone well.

"That guy is an asshole!" I said.

"Welcome to the real world. I never wanted to say anything to you because I didn't want to take away your desire to compete, but Sany is a pain in the ass."

"Take away my desire to compete? What I want is to move up soon and destroy that idiot!"

###

"Course walking Beginners." announced the speakers.

Off we went to walk the course.

I was already used to walking a course. I no longer felt nervous. There were only four competitions until that day, but at that point I had already realized that if I wanted to do well, I had to do it calmly, using every available second and thinking about all the possibilities that could happen when running Arrow.

Sany, what an imbecile! Idiot! What kind of champion is that? Treating new competitors that way?

"Walking finished, please leave the track!" announced the speakers.

###

I was the eleventh to enter the track. I went back to prepare myself and Arrow. But I wasn't okay. Sany had managed to get inside my head and Leo knew it.

"Pay attention!" Said Leo. "I want you to forget what he told you."

"I already forgot!"

"No!" Leo said holding my shoulders. "You didn't forget! I can see it in your face, in your body. Relax! Forget it! Think about your run! Focus on Arrow!"

I lowered my head and pretended to comply. But it was still there. Stupid, idiot! A certain anger had settled inside my body. I felt chills when I thought about what I had heard. "I don't see much future for you guys". Shut up, you son of a bitch! You'll see when I get to the Masters.

On the pre-track while waiting for my turn, Amadeus and Augustus started their run. They had a great run. Perfect jumps, precise contact zones and a fast slalom. End of the run and immediately the result appeared on the screen: FIRST PLACE!

Now I had to beat my rival, knowing that I needed no penalties to be able to move up.

Three teams were in front of me. Butterflies in my stomach.

"Next team, Marcus and Arrow!" announced the speakers.

The same old walk, from the gate to the starting point! About ten meters of walking, a moment of silence where there is no turning back.

I put Arrow at the starting point behind the first jump. "STAY!" I gave the command.

As usual, I start to walk away and look at Arrow. Those giant brown eyes bulged even more. Her mouth opened and the drool began to descend. Attack position. Ready!

In those three seconds, a quick thought crossed my mind: "Beginners course, easy! Master's category here I come". Arrogant? Yes! But in competitive life, confidence and arrogance go hand in hand. To have confidence sometimes you have to be a little bit arrogant.

"OK!" I released Arrow!

Here she comes! Two steps and goodbye jump number 1. I started running ahead of her, as usual. Two, three, four. A Frame, perfect!

"TUNNEL!" I screamed!

Without blinking, there was Arrow, into the tunnel.

"Weaves!" I pointed at the slalom.

A perfect slalom entry! I could hear the screams from the stands. Four more obstacles and master's here we come! But then something happened. One second, exactly one second of distraction.

I found myself thinking how amazing it would be going to master's after just four competitions at Beginners.

"Damn it!"

I didn't give the command for one of the jumps. Arrow lost reference, looking for the closest jump, and jumping the wrong one! ELIMINATION!

For the next five seconds I tried to figure out what happened, I could hear the reaction of disappointment that came from the stands. Like when a soccer player loses a penalty kick, or a goal face to face with the goalkeeper. I was eliminated!

It took me a few seconds to process.

"Team eliminated, please leave the Arena" announced the speakers.

My first elimination. What a horrible feeling, what a pit in my stomach mixed with shame. What would I tell Leo? My God! I let him down! He will be so disappointed in me. I let Arrow down!

Arrow didn't understand what had happened. How did the game she likes so much ended up without a reward? No party? No tug of war with the leash? I looked at her and bent down to give her a hug. Tail wagging, she didn't quite know what had happened, but she was happy just to be there. I could see it in her eyes. I hated myself at that moment.

I walked out of the arena and Leo was there waiting for me.

"Sorry, man! Sorry! Totally my fault.", I said feeling the worst possible way.

Leo, a very experienced handler and teacher, and having been through this countless times, just said:

"Man, this will happen a lot in your life! Relax!"

We started walking towards our tent when Amadeus appeared in front of me. I was ready to tell him to go to hell if he said some joke.

"I'm sorry Marquito. Your run was excellent. Sorry! Congratulations anyway. You will be in the master's very soon."

I froze. He was very sincere. No teasing, no jokes. He was going to compete in the master's category now, and yet, he came and congratulated me on my run.

"Thank you, Amadeus. Really. It means a lot coming from you. Good luck at the Masters."

Amadeus would no longer compete against me. After his incredible first place brought on by my elimination, he had gained his access to the Masters. For me, not yet.

Amadeus walked away, and we went back to our tent to start packing up.

Back to training. Back next month for another competition.

4

THE CRIMES

June 2004, the day my mom and I met my dad's lawyer. Walter Silva was his name. I had never heard that my father had a lawyer. To me he was just the man who did his taxes every year.

My mother was confused. She really didn't know what was going on. My father was already being loaded into the police car. There were five police cars in front of my house, which attracted the attention of all the neighbors, making the scene even more shameful.

My father was taken into custody from inside our home on a normal Tuesday, while we ate breakfast as we did every day. The next few days of my life would change everything.

It was in the days that followed, where my real anger emerged and showed me how much my family and I had been cheated by my father. Not just me and my brother, but also my mother.

I have always believed that our family was a normal family, not wealthy. We weren't poor and I knew that, but I was sure as hell that we were not rich.

My father used to work a lot. Hours and hours a week. But the heavy workload had brought good results. We had our own house, a nice car, but we were never rich.

Both my brother and I were fluent in English, as we had started school very early in the United States. Our English was even better than my parents'. But they had not let the Portuguese language die in our house. Throughout our childhood we still spoke, wrote and practiced both languages, English and Portuguese.

Even though we lived close to Disney and Universal Studios theme parks, going to those places was not common for us. My dad always told us that those parks were too expensive and there was no way to buy tickets for everyone frequently. I remember that the last time we went to a Disney park was on my 15th birthday, and that was my present, a day at Disney.

Orlando's tourist area was almost off-limits to us. My dad always told us that the restaurants on International Drive were too expensive, and we couldn't afford it. The only exception was the Brazilian locations. My dad loved going to a Brazilian bakery and a Brazilian steakhouse on International Drive. It wasn't the cheapest places, but it was an exception to our budget.

We always got presents at Christmas and on our birthdays, but never anything too expensive. My first PlayStation, I had to buy with money from my first job at age 14 delivering mail for a family friend's office.

It was a big surprise four days after they took my father from our house, arrested, that my mother and I were in front of Mr. Walter Silva, and learned why he was arrested.

"I just want to understand why he was arrested." said my mother.

We were sitting in front of Mr. Walter, who was delicately trying to explain the situation.

"Miriam." Mr. Walter said. "How much do you know about your husband?"

"I don't understand what you mean by that."

My mother had not been able to sleep well since the day of his arrest.

"I mean, about your husband's business." Mr. Walter continued. "Bank accounts, transactions, savings accounts, real estate..."

"Properties??" she was surprised. "We don't have real estate, just the house we live in, and I don't take care of the finances. Renato always took care of that."

Silence. I could see that the lawyer was trying to handle the situation very gently.

"Miriam, Renato was arrested for embezzlement, tax evasion and tax fraud. Also, crimes against public health."

"I do not understand!"

I often felt sorry for my mother. My father was always a very authoritarian kind of guy, and, in his mind, women had to stay at home taking care of the house and children. My mother had never finished her studies, honestly, she was not the most educated or smart person in some respects. Financial and political topics were not her strong suit.

"If I ask you today what the balance in your husband's checking account is, and how much there is in your husband's savings account, would you know the answer to that?" asked the lawyer.

After thinking a while, and shaking a little, my mother replied.

"I don't know. Considering we have the fund for the boys' studies I would say maybe 40 to 50 thousand dollars?"

Mr. Walter stretched his arm with bank statements, handling them to my mother who held them and began to read it carefully.

It didn't take long for her eyes to widen and her face to change color from the traditional pink to pale white.

"This can't be right!" said my mother.

I couldn't resist I grabbed the papers, looking for the number that was there scaring my mother. That also left me terrified. In the lower right corner was the checking plus savings accounts balance in my father's name with a total of about 7 million dollars.

"Seven million?" I thought silently, but with my nerves frayed as my whole body screamed.

"Seven million?" my mother repeated looking at the lawyer.

"Yes!" answered the lawyer. "And there's more."

"More???" finally I broke my silence and spoke for the first time.

"Son, your father still has sixteen properties spread across Florida. Including an apartment near Miami Beach, worth 1.5 million dollars."

My mother was silent. My head was spinning for a moment. I thought it was impossible for my mother not to know anything about it. Really? Married for over twenty years and she knew absolutely nothing?

"Mom! Did you know about this?"

My mom just ignored me. I could see in her expression that she wasn't even listening to me anymore. Her thoughts were far away, probably wondering where it all started.

"Walter!", with a calm voice my mother spoke. "Could you please explain to me how someone manages to save so much money being the manager of a neighborhood pharmacy? My husband does not own a CVS or Walgreens. It's a pharmacy in the neighborhood."

"Miriam, Renato is being accused of counterfeiting medications, reselling expired medications, preparing weight-loss formulas without authorization, and selling psychotropic medications without prescriptions."

My mom and I could never have imagined that my dad was doing those things. He was for us the example of a hard-working man who woke up very early every day to open the pharmacy, he could never do something like that.

"One of the women he sold fake medication died in an emergency room 48 hours later. That's when the police started investigating your husband. It took eight months of investigation, all recorded on video. Including Renato trying to sell over-the-counter medications, and psychotropics to undercover police officers."

It was the coup de grâce in my relationship with my father. There was no longer a relationship where trust, admiration and respect once prevailed.

###

My father's trial was in October 2004. Just four months after that meeting with his lawyer, we were in the court room. My mom, my brother and I, watching my dad walk into that room with a judge ready to pass sentence right in front of us.

To try to cut down on the sentencing time, my father decided to plead guilty in front of the judge. Certainly, he was guilty, and fighting for months in court where for sure he would lose, ending with a sentence of 32 years in prison for the sum of crimes committed, he decided just to plead guilty and make a deal.

Admitting guilt to the judge ended up resulting in three years for tax evasion, two years for counterfeiting drugs, and another six years for wrongful death against the woman who died. Eleven years in jail, eleven years with the possibility of parole in five for good behavior. That was the sentence the judge imposed not only on my father, but on our entire family.

5

THE NEXT LEVEL

In August 2006 we went to Palmetto.

Palmetto is a small town near Tampa, on the west coast of the state of Florida, near Sarasota and Bradenton. It is a little farther from my home in Orlando, but often used for Dog Agility competitions.

The City's Fairground was not fully air-conditioned. Covered, but with an accessible area on the sides that let the scorching August heat come in from all sides.

Still, it was a good area to compete. Plenty of room to walk the dogs, huge parking lot, bleachers, crating area, and the red clay surface was quite reasonable to run with the dogs. The surface was a little harder than in Arcadia but excellent.

Since the elimination in Arcadia four weeks prior, and with us not making it to the Masters, it was still hard to swallow what had happened. But I knew inside myself that moving up to the master's would be a matter of time. If it wasn't that month, it would be the next one. But the loss was still hard to swallow.

Amadeus was not in the Beginners anymore. It would be his debut with Augustus at the Masters.

Every training session I realized how much Leo was working on my psychological problems. At that time, our training session was much more chatting about runs, travel, and walking courses, than Arrow on track. He definitely knew I had lost myself in Arcadia the previous month.

###

The walking timer kept going down but I was not too worried about the course. Leo was training me with much more difficult courses daily, and looking at that course it just seemed like a waste of time.

"So, all good?" asked Leo.

"Those straight-line courses are much simpler than the ones we do in Plant City."

"I know. But even so, stay focused. Pay attention to details and remember to try to be smart about every move Arrow can make."

"I know, I know! Everything is under control!"

Leo was always around during my walking course.

###

Arrow out of the crate. Quick stop for pee and we went to the pre-track line. Walking towards the arena was when Sany showed up in front of me.

"Marquito!" Sany greeted with open arms.

"Hey, Sany." I replied quickly trying to dodge him to go down to the pre-track.

"Is today the day? Going to Masters? I will be there watching.", laughed Sany.

"Let's see. We hope so, right?"

I was still trying to dodge him, but he was following me.

"Yes! Yes! We hope so. Just be careful there on that jump twelve. A lot of people are being eliminated there. Don't make the same mistake, huh?", Sany was being very annoying at that point.

"Excuse me, man! I need to go to the pre-track."

I passed on Sany's side, kind of pushing him away leaving him behind. I turned my back and walked to the pre-track.

###

"Next team Marcus & Arrow on track!" announced the speakers.

We entered the arena and walked hurriedly, as usual, to the starting point.

"Stay!" I commanded Arrow.

I started to walk away, Arrow waiting. I walked behind jump number 2 and looked at Arrow. How I loved that dog! Bulging eyes, open mouth drooling, attack position.

"OK!" I called her.

As usual there she came, swallowing the first jump with a physical strength that felt like a lion or wolf in search of a prey.

Jumps 1, 2 and 3 done in seconds. Dog walk ahead!

"UP!" I screamed! "Go! Go! Go!"

Arrow crossed the length of the dog walk at an absurd speed, making an amazing running contact and pulling gasps from the stands.

Two more jumps! We were on fire! Seesaw ahead and Arrow climbed that obstacle with maximum speed. BANG!!! The seesaw exploded on the ground!

At that point, I no longer needed to verbally command Arrow. A small sign with my hand was enough. And off she went climbing the A Frame with a huge desire for more speed forcing me to speed up to cross in front of her, on the way out of the next obstacle, already pointing to the last three!

A FRAME

16,17 and 18! My God! DONE! I looked at the results screen and a giant number number 1 appeared in front of our name! FIRST! No penalties! One and a half seconds faster than the second place.

Well, it had happened! We were in the Masters. We were going to compete from now on against the best of the best. I was ready! That's what I wanted!

For sure the best was yet to come.

6

BEST FRIENDS

The weeks that followed my father's arrest were challenging.

The same month of his trial, October 2004, the Attorney General blocked all our financial resources, and we had no way to pay the bills.

My mother, who never had to have a job because of my father and his authoritarianism, had to look for a job now. But in her fifty's and with no work experience of any kind, it wasn't easy. She finally got a job at a grocery store close to home as a cashier. The pay was terrible, but she worked as much overtime as possible to bring in money to pay the bills. She was working 65 to 75 hours a week, and still taking care of the house.

My brother was working as an assistant at a law firm in Orlando, earning minimum wage. Before everything happened, all the money he used to make he could just spend as he pleased. Video games, bicycle parts, hanging out with friends. But now, he had to help with the bills at home.

As for me, I had lost my job at the kennel where I was

working. Coincidence or not, two weeks after my father's arrest, the place where I was working just fired me. Cutting cost, they said. I thought it was too much of a coincidence, firing me exactly two weeks after the news of my father's arrest popping up in the media.

That's when Rafi and his father, Mr. Monterey, saved me.

Rafi was my best friend. We had a lot in common. We were the same age, both immigrants. Rafi had arrived in the United States at the age of 10, brought from Puerto Rico by his parents in 1993 who were looking for a better life in Uncle Sam's land.

I had arrived in the United States also at the age of 10, brought by my family from Brazil in 1993. Like Rafi's family, mine was looking for a better life in the United States.

We became best friends at school in 1997 at 14 years old, when he defended me from older kids bullying me because of my accent. I remember the day he put himself between that kid and me, four years older, and much bigger. We became friends instantly.

Rafi helped me improve my English. Taught me to pronounce words better. We were just two friends with weird accents. We learned how to joke about it and have a lot of fun with it.

His family had purchased a ranch in Plant City, a town near Tampa. It wasn't a huge farm, but a decent sized ranch. They had horses, cows, pigs, chickens, and Mr. Monterey was also breeding Border Collies for herding.

Rafi and I spent a good part of our teenage years there, and I gradually learned how to take care of the animals.

Obviously, my favorites were the Border Collies. All it would take was a new litter born and I would spend my whole day there. I learned how to take care of the puppies, feed them, and even do shots.

One day I answered an ad for a job at a kennel, and they hired me right away due to all my experience handling litters on the ranch.

In 1997 when we were 14 years old, a tragedy struck Rafi's family. His mother, Ms. Monterey, lost the fight to cancer and died at an early age. It was a terrible time for them. I tried to help as much as possible, staying as close as I could. Several times I saw them crying in the corners of the property. It was heartbreaking.

I remember asking my dad if I could sleep on the ranch with them for a few days. That's how I ended up helping on the property. Milking the cows, brushing the horses, mowing the lawn, and taking care of the other animals.

I was practically living with them for almost a month. Rafi and Mr. Monterey became my second family.

The day I lost my job at the kennel, just two weeks after my father was arrested, I went straight to Rafi's ranch.

I was feeling terrible and I didn't want to give more bad news to my mother who hadn't even recovered from what had happened to my father.

"Hey, brother! What happened?", Rafi asked.

We were sitting on the fence watching the horses.

"They fired me at the kennel, man!"

"What? Why?", Rafi asked.

"I honestly don't know. They said cutting costs. I don't

know if I believe that. It must be because of what happened with my dad."

"Damn it, man! I am really sorry!"

"It's all right! I'll get another job. No big deal."

"Hey kids!" shouted Mr. Monterey from the door. "Lunch!"

We went in for lunch. It was normal for me to have lunch at Rafi's house, or for him to have lunch at our house. We were practically one big family.

We sat down at the table and started eating the meal that Mr. Monterey had cooked.

"How are things at home, Marquito?" Mr. Monterey asked.

I shook my head back and forth. He knew things weren't going so well.

"And your mother, how is she doing?"

"She's been working a lot. But she is sad. You know."

Silence at the table.

"Dad, you said something about hiring some help here at the ranch, right?" Rafi asked.

"Rafi, shut up!" I said.

"Yes, I did. Why are you asking?"

I stared at Rafi. I didn't want him to say anything about me losing my job.

"Marquito. He needs a job!" Rafi said.

"Rafi!" I yelled at him!

Mr. Monterey looked at me, surprised.

"What happened to your job, Marquito?"

I took a deep breath.

"They fired me."

"Why?"

"Cutting cost, they said."

"Bullshit!" Mr. Monterey replied angrily. "Of course, it was not cutting costs. What a bunch of idiots."

Mr. Monterey took another bite of his food, chewing quickly and swallowing. He looked at me for a few seconds.

"So, when can you start?" he asked.

"What?"

"When can you start?" he asked again.

"Really?"

"Of course! Do you think I'm going to let you go without a job? Can you start tomorrow? I have horses to brush, hay to stack, cows to milk, eight three-week-old puppies to take care of..."

"Tomorrow!" I interrupted! "I can start tomorrow."

We all smile.

7

THE FIRST BATTLE

September 2006, Jacksonville Florida would be the place where I would compete for the first time in the formidable Master category. Well, not that formidable. Up until now, all the competitions I've been in were local ones. Sany was the biggest competitor in the State of Florida at that time, and it was clear and obvious that because of his experience, especially internationally, he was the big star of local events. But looking at other places around the country we could get a different idea about Dog Agility.

In Charlotte, Amy Arnold had already been national champion in 2004. She was the most victorious competitor in the East Coast. In San Francisco, Lisa Potoviski had already been world champion, as well as Pan-American champion, and national champion twice in 2002 and 2005, the most important handler in the West Coast, and most victorious in the country.

Not to mention Mario Lorenzo from Chicago, Caitlyn Parneki from Denver, Joe Burnett from Charleston, and

Natasha Zucker from San Diego. Extremely competitive handles across the country.

Sany was cheered on by many in Florida but was still a few steps behind handlers like Amy and Lisa. He only had one National League title in 2003.

When I started training Arrow, and getting her ready to compete, I remember watching broadcasts on ESPN or Fox Sports from the National League rounds, seeing all those competitors with their amazing dogs in arenas crowded with fans.

I remember the year before staying up until 3:30 in the morning to watch the World Agility Championship and see the national team, composed of Mario Lorenzo, Amy Arnold, Lisa Potovski and Sany Bastos. Mario had been eliminated in the Quarter-finals, Amy Arnold in the semi-finals and Lisa and Sany made it to the finals, where Lisa won the world title. Sany did not complete his final course and was eliminated early in his run.

Sany, even though he couldn't finish his run in the finals, was still largely received in Florida. He was congratulated by the city mayor who publicly called him "Son of Florida", and gave him a medal in a gold frame with a picture of his dog, Maximus.

"We are proud to see one of Florida's children defending our country's colors so eagerly and proudly." I think those were the words the mayor used. I remember watching, and also feeling proud of him.

It was common to see people approaching Sany to take a selfie, chat or just to say hi. Knowing now the size of ego Sany carried, it was easy to understand why he felt so good about all that attention.

###

It was 6 a.m. and my phone alarm woke me up. I wasn't at home, I was in a hotel. Jacksonville wasn't that close to my house and so I had to pay for a hotel.

Dog Agility can often become an expensive sport if you travel constantly to compete. Gas, hotel, food, entry fees, registration, all out of pocket. After all, I didn't have sponsors like Sany who was sponsored by the Top Dog team, one of the most important Agility teams in the country. Not me. I had to pay out of pocket and hope that maybe one day some company would look at me and decide to sponsor me.

I jumped out of bed, showered quickly and straightened things up to go to the arena which was ten minutes from my hotel. My hotel was crap, and I knew that, but at least it was close to the arena, and it was what I could afford.

The site used for the Dog Agility competitions in Jacksonville was located about twenty minutes from downtown. The local Fairgrounds were one of the most spectacular in the entire country. Large agricultural events took place there, including auctions of cattle and machinery. Sand surface, much softer than Palmetto and Arcadia, large parking area with room for motorhomes, one restaurant, two snack bars, huge area for crating, an area for training with some obstacles, and space in the stands for 2,000 people.

The National Agility League used to have competitions there. Without a doubt, the most fantastic place I had ever competed.

Car parked, backpack on my back and Arrow on her leash. We entered the Fairgrounds around 9:15 am. That time we did not have to arrive so early. After all, we were no longer in the Beginners category, which was always the first of the day around 8 a.m.

Long walk to our tent and I could already see the beginners competitors doing their runs with their dogs amidst applause and cheers coming from the stands.

Leo was already under our tent.

"Good morning!" I greeted.

"Okay, Marquito! Let's go to work! I already have a copy of the course here."

Leo handed me a copy of the course and I immediately began to study.

BOOM! My mind just exploded! No doubt this was what I had prepared for. It was what I wanted! The most complex course I had ever seen in a competition. Side slalom entry with a tunnel facing the same way, which would certainly be tempting for a dog to go over the wrong obstacle. Nothing straight! The only straight line on the track was a sequence of two jumps after the dog walk followed by a back side jump, which is nothing more than a jump where the dog needs to go around the back and approach the back side of the jump. Lots of traps with tunnels to make the dogs confused.

Forty-two teams in the master's category that weekend. Among them, of course, Sany, Amadeus and myself. The course was already set up and the competitors were waiting outside the track to start to walk the course. Amadeus approached and started talking.

"It's great to see you here, Marquito! This place suits you better."

I smiled.

"Thanks. Good luck to you today.", I really said from my heart.

Amadeus was a really nice guy. That older, almost fatherly man knew what he was doing and did not need to prove anything to anyone. I had a strange feeling at that moment that he was rooting for me more than for himself.

Sany was about four meters from me. I was expecting him to come over at any moment and try to tease me or even say a joke. But no, surprisingly he didn't. Sany was serious, focused, frowning and looking concentrated. Maybe this was the Sany competitor, or maybe he was concerned about something.

"Masters category opened for walking!" announced the speakers.

Sany was right in front of me, and while all the other handlers planned the same handling through a part of the course that involved three jumps and a tunnel, Sany was doing it differently. Is Sany crazy? Nobody was doing that, and it really seemed insane to take such a high risk doing an unnecessary move. I didn't see the need for all of that, but it stuck in my head. Was he bluffing?

The walking course bluff was simple. While you walk the course in what looks the obvious way, you pretend to be doing a riskier type of handling, when in reality you don't intend to do it. This is just for other handlers to try the same strategy and end up being eliminated opening the path for your victory.

"Masters walking course ended!" announced the speakers. Everyone started to head out of the track.

"Did you see Sany's walking?" I asked Leo in a deep voice.

"I saw!" Leo replied.

"I doubt he will do that handing between jumps 6 and 8. It can't be."

"Coming from him, anything is possible, but I think it is a bluff," said Leo.

"It doesn't matter." Leo continued. "You did your walking; you have your plan. Stick with your plan."

My first run at the Masters, and I was one of the first ones to get in, the sixth to be precise. Amadeus was the 22nd to enter, and Sany 40th to enter.

Being one of the first ones isn't the best of scenarios. The advantage is we didn't have to wait too long. As soon as the walking comes to an end, I just needed to go straight to Arrow, take her for a quick pee, and get in line for the pre-track. The big disadvantage is that being one of the first ones I couldn't observe other competitors before me, and see where most people were making mistakes. In other words, the first ones in were just test dummies.

"On track Marcus & Arrow" announced the speakers.

That was the moment! Finally competing against the best. Well, at least the best in Florida. The goal was really on trying to beat Sany. Of course, there were other good handlers on the track, but no one could stand up to Sany Bastos.

We went through the gate and walked to the starting point. Arrow, as usual, bouncy, tail wagging and ecstatic just to know she would run and have fun. I put her in the starting point!

"STAY!" I commanded.

Should I try that handling Sany did while walking the course? Or stick to what I had planned? Was Sany bluffing? Will his handling be faster than mine? I couldn't think about it anymore. I decided to follow my initial plan and make that course as quickly as possible.

"OK!" I released Arrow!

As always, crazy, focused and wonderfully beautiful there was my partner, completing the first two jumps in just under three seconds. Side entrance slalom, hard entry, ninety degrees from the left to the right coming from a speedy 2-jump straight. But for Arrow, Slalom's entry was never a problem. Her body just turned over completely, with drool flying all over the place as she was running through.

We approached the 6-7-8 sequence that Sany had walked differently. I followed my plan, and everything was perfect. Arrow didn't lose focus and didn't even threaten to enter the wrong tunnel when she passed through that dangerous part of the course.

Dog walk, perfect! A Frame, fast, flying over the board and, with a running contact that would make most competitors jealous. A few more jumps and...DONE! We finished without penalties!

Time: 39:52 and the number 1 appeared giant on the screen.

Of course I was happy to see our name in first position on the screen, but at that moment it meant absolutely nothing.

There were still plenty of other competitors to enter, including Amadeus and Sany.

Leo was waiting for me at the exit of the track.

"Good! Fast, focused and accurate!", Leo said with a hand on my back.

I didn't say anything, I was still catching my breath.

We walked back to our tent where I quickly put Arrow in her crate to get some water and rest. I quickly ran back to the side of the track to watch the next competitors.

One by one the competitors entered the course but nobody seemed to have the pace to beat my time. My 39:52 was proving to be pretty fast because no one could make it to the 39's.

40:22 was the fastest time after mine.

Amadeus and Augustus entered the arena and did a great job closing in 40:01, finishing in second place and setting the closest time to mine.

It was Sany's time. That iconic smile that he always used to show around the arena seemed to have disappeared. Brows furrowed, eyes fixed on the course, Sany would start his run.

"He is nervous!" Leo said.

I was quiet.

"Worried body language" continued Leo.

I remained quiet. Leo's eyes were on the track to see what Sany would do. Was he bluffing or not? Would his handling be different?

Sany released his dog, Maximus, a beautiful black and white Border Collie that looked like a tank with his physical strength.

One by one, Sany and Maximus were passing the obstacles. Fast! Incredibly fast! Sany was definitely trying to prove something.

He approached the 5-6-7-8 sequence, and no, he did not do a different handling. Bluffing! Sany handled Maximus like all other handlers, using the same strategy. I knew Leo wanted to tell me something, but we were so focused on watching Sany running that the silence remained.

"It will be close, very close!" Leo said.

Sany was at the end of his run and our time was very close. Last obstacles and...

39:45 seconds. The desired number 1 appeared on the screen after Sany finished his run and a smile reappeared on his face. 0.07 seconds faster than me.

Sany first, I was second! But it wasn't over yet. The second course was yet to come.

###

Leo and I walked back to our tent in silence. We both looked like we were still processing. Sany won the first leg, but there was still a second one, and the final combined result.

"That was close!" a voice came from behind us, it was Taylor.

"It was!" I replied a little awkwardly.

Taylor raised her arm with a tupperware full of cookies trying to "sweeten up" the atmosphere a little bit.

"Cookies?" she offered.

It was enough to make us smile, and happily accept the offer.

"Okay, your run was great." said Leo. "Seriously, it was

incredibly good, but we need to find something extra. Sany is not a fool; he knows how to get the results and that's what he did."

"Man, I gave it my all!" I replied with a slightly disappointed tone.

"0.07 seconds is nothing!" Leo was trying to bring me back. "It's practically a draw."

"I know, but it's his name in first, even if it's by a thousandth of a second."

###

For the second course Sany would be the last to get on track, and I would be the second to last.

Walking course opened. The course was challenging but nothing crazy. It was not a beginner run, and a lot of those other handlers would get eliminated, but I knew it was possible to do it. I knew I could beat Sany. And now I had to win and take the difference between us, 0.07 seconds.

Amadeus, Sany, and myself were among the last ones to go in the track for our runs. So, we were at the grandstands watching the other competitors before us. Amadeus sat two rows below Leo and I, Sany was higher up in the last row above us.

As much as I was feeling the pressure, for the first time, I also felt fantastic. How cool was that? Being there competing against those guys?

"Good luck!" Leo said. "Focus! Relax and do what you've been trained to do."

I nodded and went away.

Arrow out the crate, pause for a pee and we walked to the pre-track!

Amadeus started his run, and what a run Amadeus did! My God! To each obstacle, to each inversion, to each command, Augustus was responding flawlessly, and Amadeus finished his run in first place. Time: 28:32. The crowd came to a roar and Amadeus raised his right arm in celebration of what he had done.

His run was so incredible that none of the other three competitors who entered the course after him managed to beat his time. He was first in the combined result with just Sany and I waiting to get in.

"Marcus & Arrow on track" announced the speakers.

It was time. At that moment, I felt a surge of energy that came from I don't know where. I was sure I couldn't lose. I had my plan and knew everything I had to do. I was already predicting Arrow's moves and how she would handle all the obstacles.

I put Arrow on the initial mark.

"STAY!" I commanded.

I walked away, walking steady, confident. I think I even cracked a smile. Sure, I would win that thing. It was my moment. Winning my first master's run!

"OK!" I released Arrow.

1-2-3 obstacles, perfect! Slalom, perfect! Tunnel and...

My legs froze! Absolute silence on the stands!

I SENT ARROW TO THE WRONG OBSTACLE!

Me! I did! One second of distraction, one moment of arrogance, and all was lost! I completely lost my attention on her for about three seconds in the middle of the course. I didn't know what to do, didn't know how to hide my face. How embarrassing! What did I do?

"Please leave the track!" announced the speakers.

The walk of shame! Leaving the course crestfallen with Arrow by my side.

Leo was waiting for me outside and not a word was said. We just walked together towards our tent in silence.

In the distance, I could hear the crowd screaming at Sany's run. We weren't watching his run, but from the noise it was no doubt he had won again.

8

THE NATIONAL LEAGUE

The National League was the biggest Dog Agility Championship in the United States. The best competitors in the country were there. And it wasn't easy to get a spot.

There were only twenty spots available, divided into 10 teams with 2 competitors each.

The biggest companies in the pet industry competed against each other to determine who had the best Dog Agility team in the country.

Those companies invested heavily in competitions because the financial return was huge. ESPN and FOX Sports rotated the broadcasts depending on the month and location of the event.

Winning a round of the National League provided immense visibility for the companies, bringing brand exposure and the image of healthy dogs and healthy people competing around the country, taking the company's brand with them. For that reason, big companies pushed more money into the competition, making it even more coveted.

For the competitors, the level of pressure and stress was

immense. Being part of one of those teams was a dream come true but also a tremendous responsibility. The companies were constantly pushing its competitors for results.

Of course, team members had many benefits. Paid travel across the country, luxury RVs with every possible comfort, all competition costs paid full, plus a fixed salary, and marketing opportunities.

Sany Bastos was a member of the Top Dog Team, and was always appearing in marketing campaigns with his dog, Maximus.

Amy Arnold who had already been league champion once was part of the Real Canine Team, and she was always on the internet selling branded products, and filling her pocket with lots of money with the advertising campaigns. She also had a high paycheck on top of that.

The National League was divided in ten rounds, one per month. The competition started in February and ended in November in 10 different locations.

1. Miami
2. Atlanta
3. Austin
4. Las Vegas
5. Los Angeles
6. Chicago
7. Nashville
8. Charlotte
9. Boston
10. New York

The rules were quite simple to understand. Two days. Saturday and Sunday. Competitors arrived at the sites on Thursday. On Friday, there was a training session where competitors were allowed to enter the arena and run through some obstacles to adapt the dog to the surface.

On Saturday, two Qualifiers were held where all competitors would run two different courses. The top 10 would qualify for a semi-final on Sunday morning.

On Sunday, one semi-final. And only the TOP 5 would qualify for a final course.

The TOP 5 scored as follows.

1. 25 pts
2. 18 pts
3. 15 pts
4. 12pts
5. 10 pts

At the end of the 10 rounds in November, we would know who would be the national champion.

In recent years, since I started training Arrow with Leo, I always followed the rounds of the National League on TV. I had never had the opportunity to see a competition live in an arena, because the only round that took place in Florida was in Miami, and I didn't have the money to pay for a trip. I couldn't even afford the ticket. But on TV I'd always get hooked seeing those competitors doing amazing things with their dogs.

I always rooted for Sany, the only competitor from Florida.

To make it clear, since my first personal contact with him, things have changed a bit and I was no longer a big fan, to put it nicely.

Competitors could run in the National League, and at the same time in local competitions. It was always a matter of what the contract with the team would allow you to do. I've never heard of a team not allowing one of its competitors to participate in a local trial, because competing in other trials would keep their dogs in shape for the next rounds of the National League. Sany was always competing in local trials across Florida among the other "normal people".

Things were not going too well for Sany the year of 2006 in the National League. Only 6th in the overall standings and with his teammate in 3rd place more than 20 points ahead of him, his team, the Top Dog Agility Sports Team, were already putting Sany under pressure for better results. His national title in 2003, and the qualification for the World Championship final, had given Sany a certain guarantee within the team so far, but rumors were that TOP DOG was looking for a replacement for Sany.

Amy Arnold was rocking that year. With seven rounds completed and a 32-point lead over second-place Lisa Potoviski, Amy seems to be heading for a second national title with Real Canine Dog Agility Sports Team. The same number of titles that Lisa Potoviski had.

Lisa Potoviski, the greatest champion in American Dog Agility history with one world championship title and two National League titles, wasn't even able to keep up with Amy that year.

The fight between Amy and Lisa was old, and well known. It got personal when Lisa start dating Amy's ex-boyfriend. But honestly, I was never interested in the gossip of the Dog Agility world. What interested me were the fights inside the arena.

To be part of that world and to get a place in the National League was not simple. Everyone knew that team's scouts were always traveling around the country at local competitions looking for new talent to be hired. It was not hard to see them. All you had to do was look through the stands and see someone with a tablet in hands, filming several competitors and taking notes. You could be sure; they were one of those scouts.

I won't deny it, I always dreamed of being on one of those teams, but at that moment I didn't even pay much attention to whether one of those scouts were in the stands of one of the competitions I was in. When I was competing, I was competing, and I didn't keep looking around.

9

UNEXPECTED THINGS CAN HAPPEN

In the following month, October 2006, we went to Punta Gorda, south Florida, for another local competition.

Punta Gorda had one of the coziest and most comfortable places to do agility in Florida. Big championships didn't happen there because the arena was too small, and the crating area didn't support big competitions either. The place still didn't have stands, which limited the public to watch the competitions. But otherwise, the place was super comfortable. Indoor with air conditioning, perfect artificial grass, nice people and an atmosphere almost of brotherhood.

Daniel and Daniele owned the place. I called them Dan & Dan. Some of the coolest people I had ever met in Agility. They used to make everyone feel at home there, buying pizza for the competitors, drinks, key lime pies and fried chicken. It was like going to a weekend barbecue at a friend's house.

Sany was out for the rest of the year. After Jacksonville, he posted on his social media accounts that he would be focused on the National league until the end of the year. So, I would not compete against Sany anymore, which I thought was a bummer. I needed somebody big to compete against.

From that moment on, only Amadeus and I seemed like competitors in the master's category.

All other competitors, without exception, suffered in the category and the elimination rate was soaring.

It was there in Punta Gorda that I won my first competition in the Masters category with Amadeus in second. I knew I should have celebrated a lot that day, but I also knew that victory didn't mean much. I wasn't proving anything by winning that competition, and the feeling of victory was diminished. With all due respect to Amadeus, he wasn't a good reference for me to know if Arrow was fast enough to compete against the Agility's "big fish", and with Sany not competing in local competitions, it was a little difficult to know.

###

In November 2006 it happened again. We went to Ocala, not far from Orlando for another local competition.

Quite different from the trial in Punta Gorda, in Ocala the arena was outdoor and on natural grass. The place was very spacious and wooded, with lots of parking spaces. Competitors would open the car doors and trunks to use the cars as crating area for the dogs.

The grass surface was not good. A lot of holes and gaps made the runs dangerous. It was easy to step into a hole and sprain an ankle or a knee.

Even committing two penalties in one of our runs, dropping two bars, we still managed to win that competition. The uneven and unstable ground made things difficult for Arrow.

There was nothing she could do, knocking bars was something normal under those circumstances. Just being able to keep ourselves standing was a victory.

Winning there it had an even less impact for me. Not even Amadeus was there, and the other competitors were far behind us, not offering a big challenge for Arrow at that point.

Leo could see that I wasn't happy, even though I had won. He told me I should celebrate every victory no matter how small, but deep down we both knew that if the focus was on improving our performance, I had to look for better trials against better competitors.

###

At the end of November 2006, Leo and I watched on TV when Amy won the National League in an incredible performance in New York. The last round of the National League always took place at Madison Square Garden, televised by ESPN with a crowded arena.

Sany had a bad result and finished in 7th place in the overall standings, a bad thing for him. His teammate finished the season in a great 3rd position behind only Amy and Lisa. Rumors grew even stronger that Sany would not remain on the TOP DOG team in the National League, and Florida could run out of representatives for next year's season.

###

December 2006 and the last local competition of the year would be in Winter Park, very close to Orlando. I used to call it, "playing at home", because it really was the closest competition to my place.

The competition at Winter Park used to be a big party.

With the National League over, competitors used to come to Florida to escape the cold in the North. It was very common to see Amy in Florida at the end of the year. She had a lot of friends around here and used to go to South Florida's New Year's Eve parties. And with Amy winning the National League that year, many local competitors had sent their entries to participate in Winter Park. With luck take a selfie, and watch the National Champion competing with her spectacular dog named X.

I was looking forward to it. If Amy were coming to compete in the local competition at Winter Park, it would mean that I would be competing against her in the master's category for the first time. I could not imagine myself competing against the national champion. It would be great!

If Sany were there too, it would be really cool to participate, competing against Sany and Amy, two National League competitors.

###

We arrived early that day because I was excited. The competition in Winter Park took place in the city's public park next to a baseball and a football field. The venue did not have stands to allow a large audience, but because it was a public park no ticket was necessary to watch the competition. The area around the arena was crowded with people standing watching the dogs running.

After setting up things under our tent, and with Arrow properly settled in her crate, I went for a walk to check the place. That was when I saw Amy on the other side of the track. The current national champion was proudly wearing a

Real Canine Dog Agility Team jacket. But she wasn't experiencing much peace around her, there was already a reporter trying to interview her.

I walked around the track towards her but honestly, I had no idea what to say to her if I managed to get close. Actually, talking to her would be difficult. As soon as I approached her there were about fifteen people around, waiting for Amy to finish her interview and ask for a selfie. Not even my cellphone was with me at that time.

"And how are you enjoying your vacation here in Florida?" asked the reporter.

"I love Florida!" Amy replied smiling. "The people here are open-minded, warm, friendly, and the weather here is much more comfortable too."

"And we'll see you on track today with X?" asked the reporter.

"No, no! I'm in Florida to rest and visit some friends. I have a lot of friends around here!"

What??? Amy will not compete??? No! No! No! Why? What kind of bullshit is that about resting? UGHHH!

"Thank you very much, Amy!" said the reporter.

Amy thanked her and turned to meet the surrounding fans who were already waiting to take a selfie.

I walked back feeling half disappointed and half angry. After all, how important would it be to compete against Amy? I would have the perfect opportunity to check how much slower or faster I could be, comparing myself to the current national champion. Damn it, Amy!

###

"I have news." said Leo when I returned to our tent.

"I think I already know what the news is." I replied disappointed.

"Amy is not competing."

"I know!"

"And there's more" Leo said.

"What?" I was annoyed.

"Sany didn't come either."

"What? Sany is not participating in the competition at Winter Park?", I asked even more disappointed.

"He's not on the running list."

I just stayed quiet.

"Marquito, I want you to do something for me." Leo sat beside me. "Is very important."

I looked at him without answering.

"I want you to get on that track today and do the best run of your life. I want you to use all the moves we trained before. I want you to be the best in there, not by a small margin, I want you crushing everybody there."

"Why?"

"I know you're disappointed that Amy won't compete, and that Sany isn't here. Look around, there are sports reporters around the arena. Not to see you, of course, but use this opportunity. The National champion is watching the competition on site. Think about it for a few minutes."

Leo was right. I knew there wouldn't be any national-level competitors running against me that day, and that Amadeus was perhaps, the only one who could actually beat me on a lucky day. But the whole circus was there. The park was packed with visitors and at the other side of the track I could see Amy, watching the beginners running at that moment.

It wasn't the opportunity I wanted, but without a doubt it was a great opportunity.

###

My two runs were flawless. On the first course, the gap to the second place was so big that I thought there was an error on the electronic scoreboard. More than 3.5 seconds ahead of the second place, which had been Amadeus.

On the second course the gap was closer. Even so, the almost 1.5 seconds was huge. Arrow was consistent, focused, and fast. So fast! Passing through the dog walk and the A Frame drew applause from the crowd at the side of the track. Going through slalom was so raw and brutal that I thought Arrow was going to break some of the PVC poles of the obstacle.

My handling was the most aggressive I could use. Keeping myself ahead of Arrow and doing several blind crosses, inversions and other moves that no other competitor would risk doing.

In the final result, first place in both courses and first place in the overall result, which took us to the podium once again in a local competition. It was the third in a row.

"Good job, Marquito!"

It was the only thing Leo could say, and he honestly didn't need to say anything else. The smile on his face said a lot more than what he could put into words. Without a doubt, those were the best runs I had ever done.

###

Back to my tent, I remember when that voice came from behind me.

"Hello!"

I looked back and my heart stopped for a few seconds. It was Amy!

"Hello!" I reply still in shock.

With a smile on her face, she stretched her hand towards me.

"Nice to meet you, I'm Amy Arnold."

As if I didn't know who she was.

"Yes! Yes, I know!" I replied forgetting to let go of her hand.

"Can I have my hand back?" said Amy smiling.

I let go of her hand, completely embarrassed.

"I just stopped by to congratulate you. What a great dog you have, what's his name?"

"Her name is Arrow." I replied awkwardly, and at that moment I knew my face showed the stupidest expression anyone could make. "It's a girl!"

"And your name?"

"Marcus, but people call me Marquito!"

"Congratulations Marcus! I mean, Marquito!" said Amy still with a smile on her face.

"Thanks."

"Maybe we will see each other around, yeah?" She spoke.

She walked away still smiling, some people were already approaching her, probably for a few more selfies with the current national champion.

"Who knows, Amy!" I told myself. "Who knows?"

10

HOLIDAYS: NEW YEAR, NEW LIFE?

It was mid-December 2006, and the competitive year was over. No more official competitions until the following year, which made me feel a little depressed because since I started competing in Dog Agility I had definitely found a different meaning to my life.

Since 2004 we haven't celebrated the end-of-the-year holidays. Thanksgiving Day is an important day in the United States but my parents never celebrated because it was not a tradition in Brazil. So, Christmas was the big holiday for us. Celebrating, eating turkey, lots of food, exchanging presents, and putting together the Christmas tree. The year before there was no mood to celebrate anything.

In 2006, my mom wanted to celebrate. She wanted to exchange presents, roast a turkey, and try to make my brother and I to feel a little bit of joy. She was working her ass off as a cashier in a grocery store close to home, and I was working at the ranch in Plant City, trying to earn money to pay the bills at home. I just hoped something unexpected would happen and change the course of our life a little bit. I used to think about it all the time, especially on that Christmas Eve when I saw my mom cooking by herself to give us a decent Christmas dinner after working a 12-hour shift at the local grocery store.

My mother had lovingly prepared a huge turkey that the company gave to her, and it was delicious. There was also mashed potatoes, Christmas fruits, vegetables, and some Brazilian delicacies that she prepared, such as farofa and brigadeiro for dessert.

I could see the happiness on her face mix with exhaustion. After working a long shift at the grocery store she still spent the rest of Christmas Eve cooking for us. I could also see the sadness on her face. Even after everything my father had put her through, she was still strong in his defense, visiting him every month at the penitentiary.

"It's delicious, Mom!" I told her smiling.

Gently she lifted her head looking at me and touching my hand.

"Thanks." she said in a deep voice. "Glad you like it."

My brother was also finishing his meal.

"It is delicious, Mom." said my brother with his mouth full of food. "This is the best turkey I've ever had."

My mom smiled. And how good it was to see her smiling. She deserved it. I just wanted to help. Make more money, help her more so she wouldn't have to work so many hours a week.

She also bought us presents. After Christmas Eve dinner we dropped all the dishes in the sink, and walked over to the Christmas tree where she had two presents. One for me and one for my brother.

My brother quickly opened his present. Two years since

we had celebrated anything. Not even birthdays. My brother was euphoric when he found out that our mother had given him a new special sports seat for his bicycle. It wasn't the most expensive one, but it was the brand he wanted.

My brother Edward was passionate about bicycles. He had one of those special bikes made from an aluminum alloy, but it was old already. I didn't know anything about bicycles. The only bike I've ever owned in my life was bought at Walmart and it always worked just fine. But not my brother. He was into mountain bikes, trails, bike competitions and so on. Along with two friends, he was always crossing Orlando on his bicycle. From Downtown Orlando to Champions Gate near highway 429. They used to go everywhere. Even in Disney Springs and resort areas they used to ride. And that sport helped him a lot. It made him happy.

"Thank you, mom!" said my brother ecstatic with the gift.

When my mom gave me the present I felt bad because I hadn't bought her anything. It was completely awkward, but I didn't have a lot of money.

I opened my present and found that she had given me a Julius K9 harness, which was the harness I always wanted for Arrow. I was incredibly surprised she knew I wanted that harness. How did she know?

"I do not understand much of those competitions that you are doing with Arrow." she said. "But I know you want one of these, right?"

I was silent for a few seconds, then I ran to give her a big hug. Even Arrow, who was lying beside us, wanted to participate jumping over us.

"A mother always knows" That is what she always used to say.

After the presents we sat on the sofa, the three of us together. I mean, the four of us, because Arrow found a way to squeeze between us, and be part of that moment. On TV, Die Hard was being shown. That moment couldn't be more Christmas.

Although, it didn't last long because in less than ten minutes my mom was already sleeping on the couch. And there we stayed for the rest of Christmas Eve.

###

A few days later, I was at the ranch in Plant City. Mr. Monterey had asked me to take care of the property and the animals on New Year's Day, because he and Rafi were going on vacation to see family in Puerto Rico.

I honestly loved the ranch. I was beginning to see the kennel firing me from my old job as a good thing. Working in the ranch I had to take care of the dogs, feed the animals, and clean pee and poop. But there I had an incredible freedom, and I also could bring Arrow with me.

The work was harder than in the kennel. Not only did I have to take care of the dogs, but I also had to do all the hard work on the property. Mowing the lawn, feeding the horses, pigs, cleaning the stables and making sure that everything was working fine. I was not complaining. I was grateful to Mr. Monterey for giving me a job opportunity when the situation with my father exploded.

Afternoon of December 29th, I had just finished feeding the horses, and my cellphone vibrated. Someone was calling.

Unknown number. I used to receive countless calls from robots and organizations asking for donations at that time of year. I almost did not answer, but some force ordered me to answer that call.

"Hello?"

"Hello, good morning!" said a male voice on the other end of the line. "I would like to speak with Marcus Machado, please."

No doubts, another call asking for donations to an institution during the holidays.

"That is me!" I said.

"Marcus, I am glad I was able to reach you. My name is Rich Postas, and I am the Manager of the Planet Canine Dog Agility Team. Have you heard of it?"

HOLY MOLLY! My heart stopped for a second. Rich Postas??? Being a steadfast fan of the National League I knew that Rich Postas was the Manager of the Planet Canine Team in the National League.

"Hello? Marcus?"

"Yes! Yes! I'm here!"

Was this really happening or it was a prank from Leo? A National League team calling me?

"So, Marcus, I wanted to arrange a lunch with you on Friday the 2nd to chat."

"Sure!"

11

THE MEETING, THE OFFER, THE TEAM

Tuesday. January 2nd, 2007.

Leo and I were in front of the Brazlian Steakhouse in Orlando, the one my father always took us to. It was the first place that came to my mind when Rich Postas asked me which restaurant we could meet in Orlando.

I had fond memories of lunches and dinners together with my family at that place. Nothing better than going back to the same place to mark what could be the beginning of a new life for me, and maybe even for my family.

"Good afternoon!" Rich Postas said with a smile on his face.

"Good afternoon!" Leo and I answered at the same time.

We shake hands.

"Nice to meet you, Marquito!"

"The pleasure is all mine. Have a good trip?"

"Yes! Yes! You know how it is this time of year, don't you? Crazy airports all over the country, especially coming to Orlando with all these tourists."

"Yeah, the city gets a little crowded this time of year."

If you've never been to Orlando during the holidays, don't come. It seems that the whole world is here making the traffic dangerous, the restaurants crowded and people angry.

Rich, Leo and I entered the restaurant. It was around 1 pm and the restaurant was starting to fill up due to lunch time, but it wasn't difficult to find a good table to sit.

"Marquito, I think you already have an idea of the reason why I'm here today, don't you?"

"I hope it's about what I am thinking." I replied a little awkwardly.

"I would like to talk to you about a project that Planet Canine has in mind."

The waiter arrived with the drinks. Brazilian beer for everybody.

Rich immediately took a sip of the beer.

"Hmm!" Rich exclaimed. "Smooth, refreshing, this beer."

Nobody answered. Leo and I were more interested in knowing about the project.

"Anyway!" Rich continued. "Planet Canine at this moment has only one competitor confirmed for the next season of the National League. And we are looking for one more."

Just one competitor for next season? I thought. This meant that one of the team's competitors had been dismissed. But who? Until last season, the Planet Canine Dog Agility Sports Team consisted of Mario Lorenzo from Chicago and Joe Burnett from Charleston. Mario had been in the last world championship but was eliminated in the quarterfinals in Finland. Who would have been dismissed?

"Really?" I played dumb trying to get the information. "But who is off the team?

"That is information I can't give to you." Rich replied.

Until that moment I was thinking it was impossible that either Mario or Joe could stay out of the National League. They were amazing handlers, with experience and good dogs.

"Picanha?" one of the waiters passed by offering a typical Brazilian cut of meat.

"Yes, yes! Please!", Rich replied, certainly enjoying the gastronomic experience much more than Leo and I.

After chewing and swallowing a piece of meat, and washing everything down with another sip of his Brazilian beer, Rich continued:

"Anyway, the fact is that we are looking for a new member for the team, and for that reason I had to come to Orlando to talk to you personally and ask you some questions."

Another sip of the beer.

"How did you find out about him?" Leo asked trying to be part of the conversation.

Rich gave a small smile.

"We know how to do our homework, Leo. And besides that, we had a recommendation that came from another, competitor, let's say."

"Another competitor?" I asked.

"Maminha?" another waiter offering another cut of Brazilian meat.

More chewing until Rich could finish another bite of meat, more Brazilian beer. Rich was in heaven among all those waiters bringing giant pieces of meat on giant skewers.

"Wow! This food is really delicious!", Rich said. "You Brazilians know how to make a good barbecue, huh?"

Rich cleared his throat. He probably could already feel the meat filling his belly.

"Yes." Rich continued. "Another competitor, but I can't tell you who."

My mind was spinning for a few seconds wondering who could have been the competitor that mentioned my name at Planet Canine, one of the best teams to compete in the National League.

Leo, approached my ear and whispered:

"Amy!"

Of course! It could only have been Amy! Who else? She was in Winter Park a few weeks before and came to see me after that competition. It could only have been her. The only other competitor currently in the National League was Sany, and I highly doubt Sany would be the guy who would recommend me for Planet Canine. Rumor was said he was almost out of the Top Dog team. He would never recommend me to Planet Canine, never!

"Chicken heart?" another waiter and Rich was not saying no to anything!

More beer, more chewing.

"Being very direct, Marquito!" Rich continued "We want you on the Planet Canine team for the new season this year. And I'm here to make you an official offer."

As Rich continued to fill himself with Brazilian food in front of us, I felt a shiver down my spine from the back of my neck to the tips of my toes. I looked at Leo beside me who had no words, just a smirk and a subtle positive nod. He did not need to say anything else.

"Picanha with garlic?" another waiter, more meat, and more chewing.

Still with his mouth full, Rich continued:

"Standard contract for first year. Only one year of contract with the possibility of renewal at the end of the season, depending on your performance. Registration and entries fees paid in full, air and land transportation paid, travel insurance, food, support staff and this amount (Rich showed me a piece a paper with a number), per round deposited into your account, five days before each round, except the first one, that is paid when you sign the contract."

I felt a pang in my stomach along with another chill and my hands began to sweat.

I knew the amount was small compared to other competitors, but that would help my family tremendously.

"Pork and cheese?" the next waiter, and more food.

Rich took a deep breath looking at those succulent pieces of pork embraced with cheese. Probably already feeling like he couldn't take anymore.

"Why not?" Rich said looking at the waiter and accepting the offer.

I looked at Leo for a second, kind of asking for his opinion without saying a word. But I didn't really need to ask anything, the answer was already on his face. It was time.

"I think we have an agreement, Mr. Postas!" I extended my hand, which was promptly shaken by his hand, still greasy with all the food that he had eaten. I didn't even care.

###

My mother and brother still didn't know about the news. Until that point, I hadn't signed my contract yet. One of the most important things was not to let the news get out until everything was signed.

It was early in January, and the word spread that Sany Bastos had renewed with Team Top Dog for another year. Lisa Potovski, Amy Arnold, and Caitlyn Parneki had also renewed their contracts, but I still didn't know who my teammate would be.

In mid-January, about one month before the National League season started, we headed to St Louis to the Planet Canine's headquarters to sign the contract, and be welcomed to the new team. All paid by the team, of course. Rich asked me to take Arrow to be introduced to the crew, and also because they wanted to take some pictures of us.

I was so ecstatic about being part of a National League team that I didn't even think much about flying. For me, it was nice. Many passengers asked me about Arrow and wanted to pet her. Arrow has always been an extremely well-socialized and well-trained dog and has never had problems in noisy, stressful environments or with crowds. She took her first flight very well.

Arriving in St Louis a car was already waiting for us. Leo, Arrow, and I, were picked up by a giant Suburban with a private driver and taken straight to the company headquarters.

Rich was there to greet us. As soon as we entered the lobby, he appeared with open arms:

"Marquito! Leo! Welcome to St Louis!"

"Thanks!"

"Have a good trip? Was there a lot of traffic?"

"No, no. Everything was great. Thanks.", I answered.

After quickly petting Arrow's head, we followed Rich into the headquarters.

"You won't believe it!" Rich continued. "But after that lunch in Orlando I found a Brazilian restaurant here in St Louis that is absolutely amazing. We should go there later."

Rich was definitely addicted to Brazilian barbecue. Well, Brazilian food, especially barbecue, is without a doubt the best kind of food in the world.

We got into the elevator with a very talkative Rich, explaining about the origins of the Planet Canine brand, and how much the company invested in the pet world every year.

I wasn't even paying attention. We went up to the top floor and there we passed through a series of fancy offices until we reached a room where a short woman looking in her thirties, and a man in his late 60s were waiting for us.

"Marquito, Leo. This is Paula Hosenhein and Kurt Audian."

We did not know who those people were, but we quickly and promptly greeted them. Rich didn't take long to introduce us.

"Dr. Kurt Audian is the Director of Planet Canine Dog Sports. He is responsible for the entire area of canine sports development in North America. He is, also, the person who pays your salary."

Rich smiled, making the situation as relaxed as possible.

"Marcus or Marquito?" Dr. Audian approached. "I've

heard a lot about you. I'm sure you'll do very well around here."

How did he hear a lot about me? I've never even left Florida. How could a big fish from a big company like that have heard anything about me? Anyway, I just followed the conversation.

"Thank you very much Dr Audian. I hope I can live up to the expectations. And you can call me Marcus or Marquito, either is ok!"

"Marquito, you will. I have no doubts." Dr. Audian replied smiling.

Rich continued with the introductions.

"And this is Paula Hosenhein. She is one of our PR, and the person who will take care of everything for you. She will be the one booking hotels, air tickets, and helping with anything else you could possibly need."

"What is a PR?" I asked.

Everyone laughed, except Leo and me.

"Anyway, the contract is ready. Just like the copy we sent to your email.", continued Rich.

He pulled out a folder from his desk with a copy of the contract that I quickly signed. I even made a joke to try to break the ice.

"Does Arrow also need to sign? She can put her paw on it if you want."

A few fake laughs. The contract was signed and from that moment, I was part of the Planet Canine Dog Agility Team for the National League.

"Marquito." Rich went on. "Please follow Paula. She will

take over from here. I have some meetings but maybe later we can go to that Brazilian restaurant?"

"Sure!" I answered.

We followed Paula to the elevator and went down a few floors. Without a lot of time to waste, Paula handed me some bags of Planet Canine products which included folders, flyers, and most importantly, the team's clothes. It wasn't the uniforms we would compete with, but there were pants, shorts, T-shirts and jackets with the Planet Canine logo and Marquito & Arrow embroidery. Very cool!

"Welcome to the team!" a loud and powerful voice echoed in the back of the room.

We turned to see who owned that voice, and to my surprise there was Mario Lorenzo.

Paula did the honors:

"Marquito, this is Mario Lorenzo. He will be your teammate this season."

I knew it! I was sure Planet Canine wouldn't waste a talent like Mario Lorenzo's. Lorenzo was a much more experienced competitor than me. He had been with the team for six years and won the national championship in 2001. A big fish! But some said he was already dwindling because his dog, Rex, was almost nine years old, which could mean a decline in performance.

"Mario Lorenzo." I repeated "What an honor!"

Mario approached and quickly greeted us.

"Pleasure Marquito, welcome to the team!"

Mario was smiling and seemed to be excited to meet me.

"I've heard a lot about you!" said Mario holding and shaking my hand.

"Good stuff, I hope." I answered.

"Only good things, only good things! Look, don't let these vultures steal your soul, huh? A few months and if you are not careful, your soul will be sucked into this universe you are entering."

Mario chuckled.

Now it was time to tell my family and get ready for the National League first round!

12

MIAMI, FLORIDA
ROUND 1 NATIONAL LEAGUE
FEBRUARY 2007

My first official competition for the National League. A lot of things had happened in the last three weeks since I signed my contract in St Louis.

A week before my first official competition in Miami, Paula called me with all the information and guidelines.

"Hey Marquito, how are you?" Paula on the phone.

"Everything's good!"

"Nervous for your first official competition in the National League?"

"I'm ready!" I replied eagerly. "Can't wait"

"That's good. Anyway, you won't be flying to Miami. We're sending a car that will take you there. Normally we do not pay for flights when the competition is in the same state as the competitor, ok?"

"Yes, sure! No problem!", I answered.

"Once there, you will have an RV ready for you near the

arena. The RV will be loaded with everything you need for four days, including food, drinks and Wi-Fi.

"Perfect!"

"And one more thing. As we talked about before, the company does not pay your trainer's costs. If you want your coach to accompany you, he must pay for everything himself, including accommodation, transport and food."

That I also already knew. All National League competitors had their own private trainers. But they were not under contract with the companies, so they did not get the same benefits. That is why the day we were flying back from St Louis; I promised Leo that I would pay his costs for all the competitions. The money they were paying me was enough to help Leo, and bring him with me to every trial. I would pay for Leo's transportation, food, and lodging out of my own pocket. It was the least I could do for him.

With a different vision, not only of the sport, but also of how to prepare a dog, Leo believed in being 100% positive in training. Even if a dog takes longer to learn, the long-term result would be much more effective. And he was right. Arrow arrived in the Beginners category much more prepared than any other dog and that story we already know.

So my gratitude to Leo was enormous, and I would do everything I could to repay him.

###

It was Thursday morning and a giant black Suburban pulled up in front of the house. I was already waiting at the door with my backpack and Arrow on the leash.

A strong, tall, rotund man came down to help me with all

my stuff. A few minutes and I was in the backseat with my seatbelt buckled and Arrow in her crate in the back of the giant SUV.

My mother came to the car window to wish me luck.

"Good luck!" she told me with her hand touching my forehead. "And no matter what happens, have fun."

I turned over and gave her a kiss on the cheek.

"Thank you, mom!"

As the car pulled away from our house towards the turnpike heading south to Miami, I remembered the day after we got back from St Louis, the moment I told my mom what was going on.

Arriving home on Monday after work and my mother was waiting for me. She was holding her cellphone, pointing to a picture where I was wearing the Planet Canine Team uniform.

"What is this?"

"I was waiting until today to tell you."

"You went to St Louis without telling me? Did you lie to me, Marquito?"

That weekend I had told my mom that I was going to spend the weekend at the beach in South Florida, with friends.

"Mom, I didn't want to tell you anything that wasn't confirmed yet."

"This is your time to explain!" she replied with her hands on her hips.

My mother was never that kind of control freak person. In 2007 I was already 24 years old so, responsible for my own actions. But that wasn't the problem. Since my father's arrest, one of the things my mother had demanded from us was never, never, never lie. No matter what it was about, no matter how difficult it might seem to explain, we would never lie to each other again. And the fact that I went to St Louis, and told her I had gone somewhere else, would break that pact.

"I'm sorry, Mom!" I told her, embarrassed.

"Marcus, I know how much you want this. It may seem like sometimes that I don't understand, or that I don't know what's going on. But I know what is making you happy. I know how much time you spend with your dog and how much it makes you smile. If it makes you happy, I will always be on your side."

My mom knew how to break me. She understood me like no one else. I just remember hugging her tight and being grateful. All my first paycheck I had given to my mother, except of course the costs for Leo's trip and, I'll confess, something for myself. But the rest, I gave so she could pay some bills.

###

As soon as we entered the Turnpike pointing south and descending to Miami, the driver started a conversation with me:

"Hey, my friend! My name is Kevin. Pleasure to meet you."

"Hey Kevin! Marcus. My friends call me Marquito. Nice to meet you, too!"

"I know, I know! I saw your name there on Planet Canine's team. Congratulations! I have been working for the company for 12 years. Great company, they always helped me a lot."

"Cool! Always as a driver?"

"Yes, yes. I've been driving for the company since they started participating in the National League. I've driven a lot of competitors on that seat back there."

"Are you from Florida, my friend?"

The conversation was going very well, it was easy to talk to Kevin.

"Yes, I am from the Valrico area, Tampa. Do you know it?"

"Yes, I train in Plant City, very close."

"I know Plant City. Good strawberries over there."

"True." I laughed.

"Have you ever been to Miami?"

Silence for a few seconds. I felt a little embarrassed to say that I had never gone to Miami, living so close in Orlando.

"No, no! I've never had the opportunity."

"Listen, if you need anything in town just let me know, ok? I know Miami well."

"Oh, thank you very much!"

Kevin and I had been talking throughout the trip, which was a good thing. For a few hours I forgot about the competition and just relaxed with Kevin's jokes. During the conversation I discovered a little bit more about Kevin. Married, father of three, Iraq war veteran. Had lost one side of his hearing in the war. Started working at Planet Canine as a driver. What a nice person!

The three-and-a-half-hour trip passed quickly because of Kevin's conversation, and we arrived in the South Beach area late on Thursday afternoon. In the distance, you could see the arena on the beach. In front of us was the RV parking lot with all the teams' Rv's.

As soon as Kevin parked the car, Paula and Rich were there waiting for me. Leo would arrive the next day.

"Good afternoon!" both Paula and Rich welcomed me.

"Good afternoon!"

"Have a good trip?" asked Paula.

"Yes, exceptionally good. Kevin is a really nice guy."

"Yeah, he's the best. Please follow me and I'll take you to your RV.", Paula said already walking away.

Walking through the RV parking lot I started to feel a little bit of the pressure of being there. I looked around for the other competitors, but everything seemed calm. I saw the RV from Top Dog with internal lights on, and wondered if Sany was already there. Maybe so, maybe not yet. To my right, I saw the Paw Dog Team RV as one of the doors opened and none other than Lisa Potovski came out bringing her dog Fire to a pee stop.

Lisa Potovski, the biggest National Agility winner.

"Stop staring!" Paula said smiling. "You will see these people for the rest of the year."

Rich smiled too.

A few more steps and I saw the Real Canine Dog Agility Team RV with internal lights on, and I knew Amy was there preparing for the next day. I really wanted to knock on the door to thank her for what she had done for me. It could only have been her who recommended me for the spot at Planet Canine.

"We're here!" said Paula.

In front of me, a beautiful RV with the words Planet Canine Dog Agility Team on the side.

"This is your RV, here's the key. There's food, drinks and everything else you'll need for the next three days. If you need anything else just call me."

"Thank you, Paula."

"Mario's RV is right next to yours, but he hasn't arrived yet. And one more thing. You are free to go out and walk around the town. This is not a prison. But my recommendation, go rest, eat well, sleep well. The company is investing a lot in you."

We were free to go around town, but hardly anyone would do that. Everyone there took the competitions very seriously.

"Maybe after the competition on Sunday we could go to a Brazilian steakhouse, huh?" said Rich.

"Sure, Rich." I replied smiling. "Why not?"

Inside the RV I couldn't be more comfortable. I opened the fridge and there was absolutely everything. Much more food than I could eat in three days. Yogurt, fruit, cheese, ham, various types of drinks including beer and wine. In the cabinets, bread, chips, and even pasta, if I wanted to cook or use the stove. A nice comfy bed for me and a super comfy floor bed for Arrow.

It was time to rest. The show would start the next day.

###

FRIDAY

I got up around 6:30 am. Which was the time I normally woke up every day.

At 8 am we would have a briefing with the competition organizers, and at 10 am a training for handlers and dogs.

I started to get a real idea of the world I was in. In the same room waiting for the league director to start the briefing were all the competitors. I was quite shy and sat down in the last row, behind everybody.

Mario sat beside me.

"Good day!" said Mario holding a mug of coffee and looking hungover.

"Good morning! How are you?"

"You know Miami, don't you?"

Mario threw me a weird giggle and I honestly had no idea what he was talking about.

Sany walked into the room and stared at me for three seconds. It felt more like three minutes than three seconds.

"Look at that!" Sany said loudly with everyone listening. "A Brazilian in the group. This place has seen better folks."

Some of the other competitors laughed, including Mario.

Lisa Potovski entered the room and sat in the front row. She didn't greet anyone.

"Bitch!" Mario whispered beside me.

"What?"

"Nobody likes her!" said Mario.

"Why? What did she do?"

"Marquito, are you kidding that you don't know what she did to Amy?"

Of course, he was mentioning the fact that Lisa had dated Amy's boyfriend and caused a real circus among the competitors. Rumor has it that things were so ugly that at one round of the League in Boston, Amy grabbed Lisa by the neck and a raw fight broke out. But you never know the real story. After all, Lisa had recently married Amy's now ex-boyfriend and the two lived happily in San Francisco. In fact, they really had fallen in love. Those kinds of things happen in life.

"Marquito!"

A voice echoed from the other side of the room. It was Amy.

"Good morning, guys!" Amy greeted everyone.

Everybody responded. The current league champion was courteous to all the other competitors. In fact, in the previous season when they reached the last round and only Amy and Lisa had chances for the title, all the other competitors were rooting for Amy.

"Hey Amy!" I greeted. "All good?"

"Everything's good!" she replied smiling. "Have a good trip? Wait, you don't live far from here, do you?"

"No, no. I live in Orlando. I came by car."

"OK! Anyway, welcome! If you need anything just ask."

I have never looked at Amy that way before, but I started to see a very attractive woman there. Big smile, light brown eyes, hair tied back in a ponytail behind her team cap, and always treating me nicely. No doubt the national champion had caught my attention in another way.

"Good morning, everybody!" a tall man with gray hair and an unfriendly face entered the room. It was Steve Cornsmith, director of the National League.

Steve was the big shot in the league. He was responsible for organizing the entire event, selecting the judges, and also for assisting the competitors in case of any complaints.

After about twenty minutes of briefing where Steve made clear the rules and punishments for those who didn't follow them, he introduced me as the "New League Member," followed by a bland joke from Sany.

###

Time for training and to check the track's surface.

The arena in Miami had been built on the beach in South Beach, a perfect place to attract the public. Every day hundreds of thousands of tourists flock to South Beach on Ocean Drive for fun and entertainment. In addition, the month of February was handpicked to host the National League round due to the perfect weather. It was neither cold nor hot that time of year, and it hardly ever rained.

It was when I stepped into the arena for the first time that I got concerned about the surface. After meeting Leo that weekend, he also had the same concerns as me.

The soft white sand of South Beach could be extremely attractive for a resting day but, for dogs running in a competition it was a nightmare. Asking a dog to jump on such a soft surface could not only cause injuries but the risk of knocking bars and taking penalties was extremely high.

"Man, I'm really worried about that surface." I told Leo.

"I know. Today, don't worry about making contact obstacles during training. Make Arrow jump as many times as you can. Do multiple jump sequences. If she drops any bar, go back, put the bar back in place, and make her jump again. You will have to adapt her to this sand."

Leo was right, Arrow had never trained on such a soft surface. And I wasn't the only one with that same concern. Three meters away from us, Sany was also talking to his trainer about the surface. Lisa was crouched down squeezing the sand with her hands, and Amy tapping her foot heavily on the floor, testing the softness.

The soft sand problem in Miami was nothing new. Every year the competitors complained and there were already rumors that the Florida round would be moved to another city, but there was a lot of money in Miami, and the sponsors could not miss a round there.

There wasn't much to do, and we had to try to adjust quickly and prepare well for the two Qualifiers on Saturday. After all, I didn't want to be knocked out on day one of my league debut.

###
SATURDAY

Friday's practice was not so bad. Arrow knocked down three bars on the first training session, which would be a total disaster if it happened during the competition, but it gave us the chance to test the soft surface.

I knew that if I pushed her too much, making Arrow too "crazy", she would probably get penalties, dropping bars in that soft sand. The struggle I saw from dogs trying to go through the obstacles was immensely due to the little grip that the surface provided. How do you find speed and precision on such an unstable surface?

###
QUALIFIER 1

In the first Qualifer I was the 13th to enter the track. Not bad considering there were only twenty teams on the National League. In the first round of the season the Qualifers starting order was defined by drawing, and I ended up getting lucky, because all the great handlers would enter the course before me. Lisa, Amy, Sany, and Mario would run in front of me, and I could watch them and see how they would do.

Amy simply did a brilliant run in the first Qualifier. It was clear that she wasn't pushing X to his fullest to avoid any slips that could eventually lead to a penalty. But Amy found the perfect balance and showed why she was the current National Champion. A time of 38.45 gave Amy and X first place.

Lisa was hunting Amy and couldn't even afford to think about losing another national title to her rival, the way it happened the year before. Lisa came to the course and also managed a nice run with a time of 38.52, right behind Amy.

Both Sany and Mario had a poor performance in the first Qualifier. Mario was eliminated while Sany finished his run with two penalties. They were placed 17th and 12th respectively, and would have to try all or nothing in the second Qualifer or they would not make it to Sunday's semi-finals.

During my turn, with a plan in my head and knowing that I couldn't push Arrow too much due to the soft surface, I tried to control myself using a more conservative handling to not commit faults. We managed to make it to the end but lost a lot of time using the conservative handling, finishing in sixth place at the end of Qualifer 1. Not bad, but we still needed to improve to guarantee a spot in the Semi-Finals.

###

QUALIFIER 2

At the end of the first Qualifier, I went to Leo who was outside the track to get some advice.

The arena was crowded. Hundreds of people in the stands

shouting the name of their favorite handlers. Because we were in Florida, the whole crowd was with Sany. Posters, banners and shirts saying Sany & Maximus were the absolute majority with the fans. As the judge built the course for the next qualifier, the loud music cheered everyone who sang and shouted. Promoters tossed out T-shirts with cannons to the excited crowd.

The noise was so loud that it was difficult to talk to Leo on the side of the track.

"I need more!" I yelled next to him. "It's still not good!"

"Why are you holding?" Leo shouted back.

"Holding?"

"Yes! Holding! I've never seen you so cautious. Run your course course! Do your normal handling!"

"I'm worried that she'll knock bars."

"If she knocks any bar, so what? You are so cautious in there that she's confused with your handling. She wants to run and you're not letting her! Just run your course!"

Leo was right. One of the things we've always worked with Arrow since she was a puppy was her DRIVE, her willingness to run. Arrow was always rewarded for giving everything on track, and the way I was handling she was never going to reach her full potential.

Mario and Sany also needed to improve their results or they would be out of the Semis. Mario entered first, and it was clear that in the first Qualifier he was also holding Rex due to the soft surface. But now, with nothing to lose, Mario pushed his handling getting an astonishing run with a time of 38.56 taking them to the temporary first place.

Sany entered two teams after Mario and also went all-or-nothing finishing without penalties and a time of 37.42, gaining more than one second on Mario and taking the first position. The crowd in the stands went crazy.

It was clear that in the first Qualifier all the handlers were holding back. As Leo always used to tell me, one of the big problems with Dog Agility handlers is that most of them don't run in competition the same way they do in training. Usually in training the dog is already used to the track, the handler is more comfortable, and there are not hundreds of people looking at you, in addition to the TV pointing cameras at you all the time.

Just a few handlers can put all these aspects aside and enter the course to run their dogs the same way they do in training.

My turn! Forget the noise, forget the crowd! Even though Sany got all the attention that day from being home, I could see the crowd supporting me when the speakers announced "Marcus & Arrow from Orlando Florida". After all, I was at home too! There were two Floridians now in the League.

Change of strategy, full power now, aggressive handling! I let Arrow give it everything this time! Sand spreading everywhere! Open mouth, bulging eyes! Here comes my partner!

We finished our course with no penalties and a time of 36.84. I felt the crowd screaming and cheering when the number one appeared next to our name! There were now two Floridians in the top of the table!

Lisa got on track later and wasn't so lucky. She slipped on the sand, fell, got up, but lost time. Even so, she ended up behind Sany in third position.

Amy came after. The last one to go on track on Saturday. It was impossible to get Amy out of the semi-final. An incredibly good run from the Charlotte handler, but with a time of 36.82 she was just an amazing 0.02 seconds in front of me. She was leading the pack, but I was close.

At the end of the Qualifiers, Amy came in first, I was second, Sany in third, and Mario dragging in 8th place.

Now it was time to wait for the semi-finals the next day.

###

SUNDAY
SEMI-FINALS

On Saturday night, surprisingly a storm passed through Miami which helped with the situation of the track. With the sand wet and firmer there was no doubt that the dogs would feel confident to run, and the runs would be faster.

"It was pretty close yesterday, huh?" Amy approached me early in the morning when I arrived at the arena.

"Hey! It was, yes! I don't even know how I did it!"

"Oh, don't be humble. Your dog is one of the best here. Trust me!"

Laughs from both sides. We looked at each other and once again I felt something different for that woman. Not only was she by far, the best handler among us all, but she had something special. I could feel that.

"Well, good luck today!" said Amy already leaving.

"You, too!"

Semi-final, now things started to get complicated. There were ten teams and only five will make it to the final.

After the great second place on Saturday, I was already

starting to hear cheers from the fans. No flags or shirts, but I could already hear some "LET'S GO, MARQUITO" coming from outside, which I though was pretty cool.

I was definitely much more comfortable and ready to try out for the finals. But things weren't going too well for Mario. I could see him talking to Paula and Rich, and clearly things were a little heated. Mario gesticulating, and Paula with a result sheet in hand. Rich was trying to calm everybody down.

Mario was the second one to enter the track for the semis, and things couldn't have gone worse. With an elimination he threw away his chances of going to the finals.

I remember Mario sitting in his chair after coming back from the track right next to me with an unfriendly face.

"Nice try, man! Really nice try!", I said.

Without even answering me he gathered his things and headed for his RV. He didn't stay to the end of the day.

Lisa flying with Fire, destroying the clock with a time of 38.59 putting more than one second on the second place and practically guaranteeing a spot for the finals.

Sany entered the track under a platoon of fans pushing him, shouting his name, and cheering on the most famous Dog Agility handler in the State. But Sany ran into trouble in his run when Maximus dropped one of the bars. He finished third with two more handlers left to enter the track. Amy and me.

It was my turn! The moment I hit the track it was clear how much the surface had improved after the rain in the middle of the night. Knowing that, there was only one thing

I had to do, beat the clock. With Lisa hitting such a low time I had to beat that time no matter what.

It was the first time the fans really supported me. People had already understood that there was another handler from Florida on the track, and with a chance of going to the finals.

"Stay!" I commanded Arrow.

I walked away from Arrow while the crowd, for a few seconds, remained silent.

"OK!" I released her, and the crowd was with us, screaming and pushing us with extreme motivation!

That was the time to give it everything! We would either qualify for the final or go home. There was no middle ground. Aggressive handling with me always ahead of Arrow seeking maximum speed. Seesaw, BANG! on the ground, and sand flying everywhere! Jump, jump, tunnel! Arrow dove into the tunnel causing the obstacle to stretch out. Jump sequence, dog walk and slalom.

"UP!" I commanded Arrow towards the dog walk.

Fast and accurate as always, Arrow swallowed the dog walk and in less than two seconds was already entering the slalom! Two more jumps and DONE!

I looked at the electronic scoreboard: 38:32. First place! YES! We beat Lisa Potoviski's time! The crowd went crazy when the result popped up on the screen instantly! We were in first!

Still out of breath and after giving Arrow a hug, I left the track and looked at Leo outside applauding and sending me a thumbs up with a big smile on his face.

Amy was the last to enter the track in the semi-finals, and

her run had already started. It was clear that she would try to beat my time.

Amy just needed to finish in the TOP 5 to qualify, but no Dog Agility handler like to finish behind anyone else. Also, she knew that letting me win the semi-finals would ignite the Floridian crowd against her. But even though she tried hard, she couldn't do it. With a time of 38:49 she finished in second position. Yes, it happened! We won the semi-finals and now it was time to go to the finals!

FINALISTS

1. Marcus & Arrow
2. Amy & X
3. Lisa & Fire
4. Joe & Jungle
5. Sany & Maximus

###

"Marquito!" Amy approached me. "What a great run! Congratulations! I tried to beat your time, but it was impossible."

"Amy, thank you very much! A little bit of luck I think!"

"No luck! Your dog is very well trained and you are a natural! Very good! But now I'm going to play hard, ok?"

We both smiled and Amy walked away.

"Dude, what a show! Great run!", Leo said.

As Leo couldn't go on the track I was talking to him on the side behind a fence, next to the stands. Many people were shouting my name and supporting me!

"Now is the time, Leo! I think I can do it! I think it's possible! Have you thought about winning my debut competition?"

"Calm down! Remember what happened in Jacksonville. Don't let things get to your head. Do your job. You are at home, with the fans at your side! Calm down and focus!"

###

FINAL

Everything ready! Five handlers. Who would win the round in Miami and start the League at the front? Sany was the first on track! Tricky course with many traps including a terrible tunnel under the dog walk giving the dog an easy wrong path.

Tunneling under a contact obstacle was one of the oldest tricks from a judge to eliminate somebody. With the tunnel under the dog walk pointing in the same direction, it was common for a dog to get confused and be eliminated entering the tunnel when it should go up the dog walk.

Sany on track! Crazed crowd! Sany! Sany! Sany! And what a run Sany made! That Sany who won the National League a few years ago, that Sany who qualified for the World Championship final. What an incredible dog Maximus is! Fast, focused! With an absurd time of 29.42 without penalties, Sany was running to win.

Joe Burnett didn't take long to finish his participation in the final. Falling into the judge's trap with his dog Jungle entering the wrong tunnel, it was the end for him.

Lisa was next. She was a great handler, and her dog Fire was spectacular, but Lisa had a reputation for not having a good psyche. With the fans booing, the team didn't take long to be eliminated. She was out, and now one of the three, Sany, Amy, or I, were going to win the round.

Amy on track and practically giving Lisa a middle finger with a run worthy of one of the best, not only in the country, but in the world. She beat Sany's time: 29.21, taking first place with Sany in second.

Our turn! Not just our first official National League run, but our first final! The last team on track after finishing the semi-finals in first place.

"On track Marcus & Arrow!" announced the speakers taking the crown now very audibly screaming my name.

Florida had never had two competitors in a National League final, and that was only the first round of the season. Could I ever qualify more times? Would I have a chance to compete for the title?

"OK!" I released Arrow.

Screams and horns coming from the crowd as I run. I tried to use all the aggressive handling I could, to try to beat Amy's time.

Jumps, 1-2-3. Perfect! Fast, fast! A Frame with running and perfect contact zones. Slalom entry, from far I gave the command to Arrow who without blinking "dove" into the obstacle causing applause from the stands! Straight, fast, and perfect tunnel. Arrow was pure speed!

We approached the dangerous part of the track with the tunnel under the dog walk. "I need to be careful not to let her slip to the right..."

An "OHHHH" came from the stands followed by an

almost deadly silence! Arrow entered the wrong tunnel. We were out! I dropped to my knees as I tried to understand what I had done wrong. I felt a pain in my chest as if someone had stuck a hot knife into my heart.

Longest five seconds of my life followed by cheering from the crowd, probably trying to cheer me up at that moment.

"Team eliminated! Please leave the track!", announced the speakers.

The walk of shame. Coming off the track after being eliminated in the final with a real chance of winning for the first time, and in my debut competition.

RESULTS ROUND 1 MIAMI

1. Amy & X
2. Sany & Maximus
3. Lisa & Fire
4. Marcus & Arrow
5. Joe & Jungle

RANKING AFTER ROUND 1 MIAMI

1. Amy & X: 25 pts
2. Sany & Maximus: 18 pts
3. Lisa & Fire: 15 pts
4. Marcus & Arrow: 12 pts
5. Joe & Jungle: 10 pts

13

ATLANTA, GEORGIA
ROUND 2 NATIONAL LEAGUE
MARCH 2007

The effects of the result in Miami were felt in the following weeks. On one hand, the psychological fact of having to swallow one of the biggest disappointments I had ever faced in my life. On the other, the positive repercussion that came with the good performance in the first round of the National League.

In my training sessions the week after Miami, my mind was not in the right place. I was incapable of concentrating, to focusing, and Leo realized that my motivation was not in the right place.

Out of eight exercises that Leo had prepared for our training session, I had only managed to do two of them correctly. Leo stopped training after fifteen minutes.

"Man, I know what you must be feeling, but we need to put this aside."

I was quiet.

"What happened to you on that weekend is part of

learning, Marquito. Everyone goes through that. And look what you achieved in your league debut."

"Man, I could have had my first victory in the League. And it would be at my debut! In my State! Can you believe that? I let it go!"

"Look. Honestly, you have two options here. Only two. You can sit there feeling sorry for yourself, not train your dog, and throw away that contract you signed with nine rounds left in the League. Because believe me, there are a bunch of other handlers looking for a contract like yours, and they would do anything to be in your shoes.

Leo was right. He continued speaking.

"Or you can put on your big-boy pants, get back to your training, prepare well for Atlanta, and make up for the lost time. Honestly, I'm not here to try to convince you of anything. It's your choice."

Leo walked away with firm steps towards the training area. I took a deep breath and walked back to our training. Now, to give 100%.

###

On Monday morning I was the highlight in an article published on the National League website, referring to me as the big standout of the first round. The article was saying that some people should pay attention to me for the rest of the season. On Monday night, I went with my mother to a grocery store and three people stopped us to ask for a selfie with me. They had seen me on the TV broadcast over the weekend, and congratulated me on the results.

Leo was right. Even though it was a result that hurt my

soul, it was a good debut. I was on the right path. Now it was time to go back to training and make things happen.

###

The second round of the National League was based in Atlanta, Georgia. It wasn't actually Atlanta, but Perry, about a 45-minute drive from Atlanta.

Perry was a small town in the Atlanta metropolitan area that had hosted some of the sporting events from the 1996 Olympic Games. It was at the Georgia National Fairgrounds & Agriculture Center that the Olympic equestrian competitions took place, and it was there that the second round of the National League took place every year.

###

Kevin parked the black Suburban in front of my house on Thursday, and I was ready. My mother was at home that day and had already hugged me for good luck before my departure.

The month before when I got home from Miami, late at night, my mother was waiting for me still awake. That night I arrived home tired and devastated by the defeat in the finals.

She was sitting on the sofa in the living room, it was past two o'clock in the morning.

"Mom? What are you doing awake?", I asked surprised.

"I had to wait to talk to you." she said in a sweet voice.

"I'm very tired, mom. Can't it wait until tomorrow?"

"No! It's gonna be quick."

I sat on the couch with Arrow at my feet and placed my heavy backpack beside me.

"I watched you on TV today." she said.

"Ugh!" I mumbled. "Things didn't go as well as I expected."

"Your brother and I were watching today, and we just wanted to let you know that we are proud of you. Congratulations on what you did. I always knew something else was out there for you."

"Thank you, mom!"

Silence for a few seconds.

"Now come here to kiss your mother and go to sleep!"

We both smiled and hugged. I gave her a big kiss and went to sleep.

###

I entered the black Suburban where Kevin was waiting for me, with a big smile.

"Marquito! Nice to see you again, my friend!"

"Nice to see you too, my friend! How are the kids?"

"Everything's good! My youngest after seeing you compete asked me for a Border Collie. Look at the problem you caused me."

We both laughed.

Kevin had also brought me back from Miami after the first round. Coming home that weekend had not been as happy as going to Miami. But Kevin made it clear to me that I should keep my chin up and move on. "ALWAYS FORWARD". That's what he said.

The conversation went on and on until our arrival at MCO, the Orlando Airport, where I left the Suburban with a smile from Kevin.

"Good luck in Atlanta, my friend!" Kevin said screaming through the car window.

I waved back.

In the airport, at the check-in area, I met with Leo. We were going on the same flight to Atlanta.

Smooth ride, no delays, short trip from Orlando to Atlanta, a little more than an hour. We arrived in Atlanta at Hartsfield-Jackson Airport, simply gigantic. Paula and Rich were already waiting for us.

Leaving Atlanta, we got into the biggest traffic jam I've ever seen in my life and the trip to Perry, which would normally take 45 minutes, lasted two and a half hours.

"Welcome to Atlanta!" Rich said with his goofy smile.

"Man, this traffic is worse than São Paulo." I said.

"Atlanta is a pain in the ass!" Paula said. She was driving. "Perhaps the worst traffic in the country. And you also arrived at a difficult time of the day. Right at rush hour."

Around eight o'clock at night we arrived in Perry. Leo was in a hotel five minutes from the sports complex while my RV was waiting for me beside the arena. Even in the dark of night, we could see the huge multi-sport complex next to us with the lights on. Several RVs where already parked around the arena with the interior lights on, and probably with the competitors resting for the next day. The only thing I wanted was to eat and sleep.

###

FRIDAY

On Friday, the same routine. Meeting with Steve Cornsmith at the morning briefing. All competitors there. Sany making yet another ridiculous joke at my presence with some laughing but most just ignoring. Mario sitting beside me, always frowning. It seemed like things weren't going well for him within the team, and now, with a teammate being labeled the first round standout, Mario would be feeling even more pressure with a teammate willing to win. I didn't even care, I wanted to find my place.

In the National League they say your first big rival is your teammate. Whoever manages to stand out over their teammate, ends up getting more attention from the team, more support and better contracts. I didn't know Mario that well, so I didn't know if he was really frowning from my presence there, or if he was just like that.

The briefing ended, and we went down for the first time to step inside the arena, and feel the surface. It was on Friday that handlers could train on the track and adapt the dogs to the surface.

I was impressed with the location. The giant arena provided a lot of space for the judge to build the courses. As a result, more area for dogs and handlers to develop speed. The arena could hold three thousand people, three times the capacity of the arena in Miami. I was imagining that place full of people! My God!

The track surface was what made me the happiest! Made of red clay and nothing fluffy, it was remarkably similar with the surfaces in Palmetto and Arcadia in Florida, places where I always did very well, and Arrow was also very adapted. Quite different from Miami where the dogs were suffering from the soft sand on the beach, in Perry the handlers could apply full speed because the surface would provide much more grip.

A few runs on the track with Arrow, a few jumps, running contact zones, and I felt great! It was exactly what I needed.

"Looks good, doesn't it?" Amy appeared beside me outside the track after I finished training.

"Definitely better than Miami."

"Oh, no doubt! I know you're from Florida Marquito, but the arena in Miami is horrible. Nobody likes to compete there."

"It's a challenge!"

"It's dangerous!" said Amy. "The day someone breaks a leg there, or a dog gets badly hurt on that unstable surface, maybe they'll do something about it."

Pause for a few seconds, then Amy continued.

"By the way, congratulations on the result in Miami. I know you must have felt awful but it was a great result!"

"Yeah, it was hard to swallow, but in the end, I think it was a positive experience."

I found myself staring into Amy's eyes. Those beautiful light brown eyes caught me off guard. Seriously, standing so close now, how beautiful was this woman.

"Hey! Are you okay? Earth calling Marquito!", Amy joked.

"Yes, yes! I'm just thinking about the course."

"It looks like the bulging eyes of Jabba the Hutt."

"Did you seriously just make a Star Wars reference?"

"If you got the reference, it's because you're also a fan, am I right?"

"Are you going to tell me you're a female Star Wars fan?"

Amy pulled out her necklace and showed me her pendant. A beautiful Millennium Falcon pendant.

"And what's the problem with being a woman and a Star Wars fan?" she asked me, smiling.

"No problem at all. But you better know, you are a rare human being!"

We both laughed! I couldn't hide it anymore; I was interested in that woman. Beautiful, nice, great smile, awesome handler and I think she was also interested.

After a silence that lasted a few seconds with us both staring at each other...

"Lisa on the track!" she said pointing with a nod from her head.

"I know you are not best friends."

"No. But I got over it. What happened, happened.", said Amy "Now I just want to beat her, no matter where we go."

###

SATURDAY

Saturday arrived and it was time for the Qualifiers! Arena opened to the public and completely packed. One Atlanta handler on track among twenty competitors. It was Polly Buchanan with her dog Panda, competing for the PETCOM team. Even though she wasn't one of the most successful handlers, that weekend she had full support from the fans who had brought banners, posters, T-shirts and screamed non-stop the names POLLY and PANDA in the stands. Panda was the only mix-breed dog in the League.

Our team had set up two chairs, so Mario and I could sit and wait for our time to hit the track. Mario, as always, had a sulky face, and had barely spoken to anyone since he arrived. Paula approached us.

"Mario let's go my friend! I know you can do it! There's a lot of talent there!"

"Blow me!" Mario replied to Paula.

Paula just touched her hair, very uncomfortable with the situation, and replied.

"That attitude will not get you anywhere, Mario! You know that!"

She walked away with strong steps.

"Bitch!" said Mario.

I didn't really know what to say to ease the tension at that moment.

"Are you okay, man?" I asked.

"Perfect! Another day in paradise."

Clearly things weren't looking good between the team and Mario. When Mario entered the track for the first Qualifier it wasn't so bad. In fact, it was nice! He managed an excellent run, raising applause from the stands and taking first place ahead of host Polly, with a time of 34:51 without penalties.

When he returned to his chair, his expression was just relief.

"Congratulations, man! Great run!", I said.

"Thanks!" Mario replied still catching his breath. "It was really good!"

It was my turn.

"On track Marcus & Arrow" announced the speakers.

Applause from the crowd! Even knowing that there was still the second Qualifier to try to pass to the Semi-Finals, I didn't want to waste the opportunity and decided to give it all in my first attempt. But things didn't work out very well. Trying to push for speed and using an aggressive handling, I made a mistake that led Arrow to drop a bar. A few seconds later, and another mistake taking Arrow to commit a REFUSAL in the slalom. Even with a good time of 33:42, over one second faster than Mario, I was behind both Mario and Polly.

Lisa, Sany, and Amy entered the track after, and balancing the handling very well they all finished their runs without penalties. Even though I was the fastest among all the handlers, the two penalties pushed me to 7th place at the end of the first Qualifier.

Leo came to talk to me.

"Not good! What did I do wrong?"

"You don't know?" Leo asked.

"Of course not! I wouldn't be asking!"

Leo pulled out his cellphone and showed me my run. What a horrible run, WHAT THE HELL was I doing? I needed to pay attention. Be aggressive, but always be careful when running. Follow the plan! Think about a plan! Have a plan!

In the second Qualifier fans were extremely excited about Polly's position, fifth overall at that moment. Something surprising for her who had never qualified for a final before. And Polly wanted to break that taboo because in the second qualifier she was even faster, and her dog Panda showing incredible precision. After an exceptional time of 29:33, Polly appeared on the screen in first place ahead of Mario, putting the stands on fire.

It was my turn! A complex course. But I knew I had to give it all to recover from my bad run in the first Qualifier. I did not want to go home early. Not qualifying for the semifinal. No way!

"On track Marcus & Arrow!" announced the speakers.

"STAY!" I commanded Arrow!

I walked away ten meters. "OK!" I released her!

Spreading the red turf everywhere and leaving her claw marks on the ground there came my partner. 1-2-3-4! Beautiful sequence with three jumps and a straight tunnel giving Arrow even more speed! Seesaw ahead...BANG! on the ground, perfect! Tunnel under A Frame, also perfect! We headed to the dog walk. "GO! GO! GO!" Arrow crossed the entire length of the obstacle with such speed that the dog walk almost left the ground. Another sequence of jumps and DONE! 27:57 against 29:33 from Polly, with the crowd going insane!

Still catching my breath, I looked at Leo outside. A shy smile with a positive nod of his head.

My time was so good that no one was able to be faster than Arrow and I in the second Qualifier. And with that, we qualified for the Sunday Semi-Finals along with Lisa, Sany, Amy, Polly, Mario and four other handlers. Time to rest!

###

SUNDAY

The day in Atlanta dawned half cloudy, different from the sun and blue sky of the first two days. The Qualifiers victory left me full of motivation for Sunday, and a feeling that things were going our way.

All morning Leo reminded what had happened in Miami. "Focus and don't get carried away" he had already repeated five or six times.

The competitors were tense that morning. Our times were close, and it would not be a surprise to see someone considered not a favorite like Polly or Mario winning the round.

Some people at the side of the track place me as one of the favorites to win, alongside Amy, Lisa, and Sany. But anything could happen.

The Semi-Finals course was quite complex. For the first time I would compete on a double tunnel course, when the judge places two tunnels side by side, one inside the other's circumference. One of the most stressful exercises, always causing a real headache for the handlers. And now, only five teams would qualify for the final.

Mario was the first to go in, and it was clear that he was pushing and giving everything he had. But Rex clearly did not have the same drive as a few years before. The poor 8-year-old Border Collie struggled. They finished with a time of 35.16, without penalties, but Mario's expression leaving the track already showed that he knew, that time was not enough to qualify for the finals.

Polly came two teams later to the crowd's delight, and it was clear how much of a difference the crowd was making that day. Panda, the only mutt in the entire National League was a very well-trained dog, and even having aerodynamic disadvantages when compared to Border Collies, she still managed to get an exceptional result. Polly finished her run without penalties and with a time of 33:42 taking the lead and making the arena almost collapse with so much noise coming from the stands.

Sany on the track! Another sensational run by Sany with

Maximus! He used the same handling as Polly, but had an advantage over her, a faster Border Collie, dropping the time to 33:12. Boos in the stands.

Lisa was next and had trouble on the track. She slipped and fell as she approached the entrance to the slalom. Her dog Fire, looked back at her, what would clearly have been a refusal and therefore a penalty for the team. But Lisa got up quickly and managed to finish the run, but with a higher time. 34:49.

Amy and I were the next ones.

Amy was serious. No small talk, no jokes that Sunday morning. And I totally understood. We were there to compete and win for our teams. That was the main goal. And Amy knew very well how to do it! What a spectacular semi-final run. If there is a word to describe it, I would use perfection! She finished her run without penalties and with a time of 32:56.

It was my turn! Let's go Semi-Finals!

I knew that if I wanted to win, I would have to show in the semi-finals that I had the ability to do it. Finishing first in the Qualifiers were important but winning the semis would send a message that I did not make it to the league for fun. I cannot even explain how I was so calm. My confidence was so high that Sunday in Perry, I just muted the noise coming from the stands. Nothing else mattered, it was just me and Arrow inside that track. The only thoughts that came to mind were me and Arrow training in Plant City, playing, having fun like a normal weekday after a day's work.

One by one we left the obstacles behind us until we passed

the last one. I came back to reality listening to the cheers and looking up at the electronic scoreboard where the 32:22 time appear next to the number 1. We won the Semi-Final!

FINALISTS

1. Marcus & Arrow: 32.22
2. Amy & X: 32.56
3. Sany & Maximus: 33:12
4. Polly & Panda: 33:42
5. Lisa & Fire: 34:49

###
FINAL

The final course was not simple. Sharp turns and jumps positioned at challenging angles. It would be an incredible challenge to cross that course without dropping a bar and getting a penalty.

We were walking the course and Lisa walked past me mumbling something like "stay on the outside, let him cross in front". She was memorizing her handling. It did not seem like a clever idea because letting the dog run ahead of you slows the dog and increases the risk of elimination. A dog looking back searching for the handler would end in missing the obstacle ahead. Was Lisa bluffing? Had she intentionally said that out loud next to me just so I would try the same?

It was not just Lisa doing that. Sany was walking the course and using the same strategy as Lisa. Two bluffing? Is that possible?

Amy clearly had another plan. She was walking differently,

like me, leaving the dog behind her. Who would be planning the best handling I did not know, but I would stick to my plan.

We would soon know who was correct because Lisa was the first one to hit the track. She puts her dog on the starting mark and began her run. Fire, a 6-year-old Border Collie who was extremely experienced and very responsive to Lisa's commands. They had already conquered the world together. But I was curious about Lisa's handling. Was she bluffing? No, she was not! Lisa's handling worked brilliantly, and the team finished the run in an incredible 29:56.

Polly came after and there is no need to mention the crowd's reaction in the stands. For the first time running in a final Polly was clearly ecstatic, and we can say even a little distracted from doing her job when she stepped onto the track waving to the people in the stands.

Dog Agility is a wonderful sport, but it can also be cruel. Start a run without paying attention to what you are doing and that is it, you are done! That is what happened to Polly, eliminated after six obstacles. Even so, it did not faze her. She waved back to the fans who got up to give her a standing ovation as she left the track after her quick participation on her first final.

Sany on track, and now I would really know if Lisa and Sany's plan was the best one because Sany had walked the course using Lisa's same handling. If it had already worked for Lisa, and would work well for Sany, it could mean that Amy and I chose the wrong handling.

My fears were correct when Sany proved my theory by

doing the same handling as Lisa, ending up close in time: 29:59.

At that moment I looked at Leo outside the track with a worried face, wondering from a distance if my decision was the worst option. Should I change my handling?

Leo, seeing my concern from a distance, waved at me: "NO! STICK TO YOUR PLAN." In other words, do not change your handling, do what you planned when you walked the course.

Amy hit the track and handled X differently than Lisa and Sany, using the same handling I was planning. Could she be faster than everybody? NO!!!! She finished her run in a time of 30:22, slower than Lisa and Sany.

I could not beat their time using Amy's handling. I looked back at Leo, even more concerned. Again, Leo waved: "Calm down! STICK TO YOUR PLAN!"

"On track Marcus & Arrow!" announced the speakers.

I hit the track now with my confidence shaken after seeing what had happened to the handlers before me. Decision time! Let's do our run. It does not matter what others have done!

I left Arrow at the starting mark and walked away! The crowd was silent for a second. Last team of the day on the track, again, like in Miami. I could not mess it up again, not again! I needed this.

"OK!" I released Arrow!

Once again, I turned off my radar from whatever was happening outside the track. I could no longer hear the crowd. If there were boos or shouts of motivation, I had no idea. It was just me and Arrow, like in Plant City.

One by one we were overcoming obstacles. Slalom: perfect! Seesaw: perfect! Fast and accurate jump sequences. I had no idea whether we were fast or slow. I just made the run the way I had planned before, following my plan no matter what happened.

Last Jump: DONE!

Screams from the stands! I crouched down to hug Arrow before looking at the monitor and seeing the result. Monitor? I did not need to look at the monitor because I looked straight ahead to see Leo in the background celebrating with a punch in the air. Our first National League victory! Yes! It did happen!

Leaving the track now with the first-place result on the screen, the first person who approached me was Amy. Without any shame, she hugged me very tightly and next to my ear she said:

"You deserve it! You deserve it! Many more will come!"

I did not have much time to talk to her, right after Leo came to greet me. Followed by Lisa who approached me for the first time.

"Congratulations! Great run!" Lisa said shaking my hand.

"Thanks."

Polly was the happiest person that day just because she got to the final. She also approached me.

"Congratulations, Marcus! Absolutely beautiful!" said Polly.

"Thanks!"

Sany did not come to greet me. But in the distance, he sent me a thumbs up with a nod. My first National League victory.

RESULTS ROUND 2 ATLANTA

1. Marcus & Arrow
2. Lisa & Fire
3. Sany & Maximus
4. Amy & X
5. Polly & Panda

RANKING AFTER ROUND 2 ATLANTA

1. Amy & X = 37 pts
2. Marcus & Arrow = 37 pts
3. Sany & Maximus = 33 pts
4. Lisa & Fire = 33 pts
5. Joe & Jungle = 10 pts
6. Polly & Panda = 10 pts

###

Later that day, back in my RV while cooking pasta for my celebration dinner still smiling to myself at what had happened, someone knocked on my door.

I walked to the door and looked out the small window, it was Amy.

Amy? At my RV in the middle of the night?

I opened the door quickly, more nervous than when I was competing in the finals that afternoon.

"Hey!" I greeted awkwardly.

"Good evening!" said Amy smiling.

Weird silence for a few seconds. Staring at each other until finally someone said something.

"Can I come in?" said Amy.

"Sure! Sure! Please!" I said, stepping back.

"Smells good! Cooking?"

"Yes. Spaghetti. My specialty. All you need is water and salt. And believe me, I mess up sometimes."

Smiles.

"Please, sit down!" I offered her a chair.

Amy sat.

"I won't be long; I just came to congratulate you on your victory today and to bring you this."

Amy reached into her pocket and pulled out an X-Wing pendant, one of the coolest aircrafts in the Star Wars universe.

"Oh, my God! You didn't have to do that! Thank you very much! It is very cool!"

"I found it with my other pendants, and I thought you would like it."

"Yes, I love it! Thanks."

Finally, a different hug. Not a congratulations hug or a hello hug. No, a strong one. I hug where I could feel her body for the first time. Long, long hug. We started to separate slowly, with our faces close to each other. I was sure I was going to kiss her. Yes! Now! I was going to kiss her.

Someone knocked on the door! We quickly pulled away from each other.

"Are you expecting somebody?" asked Amy.

"No, I am not."

I glanced quickly out the window. It was Paula, Rich, and someone else.

"Damn! It's the team people!" I said almost whispering.

"I don't want them to see me here." Amy whispered back.

"Why not?"

"I'm from another team! All right, distract them! I will step out from behind the RV."

"Really?" I said disappointed!

"Relax, we will have another chance!"

Amy kissed me on the cheek and went to hide in the back of the RV, in the bedroom. I went back to the door and opened it. It was Paula, Rich, and Planet Canine director Kurt Audian, who immediately opened his arms, stormed into the RV, and hugged me.

"Marquito! What an incredible result! Congratulations! I knew we were doing the right thing bringing you! You are a future champion! I'm sure! We need to celebrate."

"Mr. Audian. Thank you very much!" I replied after finally managing to free myself from his weird hug. "I really appreciate it but I'm already cooking."

"No, no, no! I insist! Today let's celebrate! We're going to a 5-star restaurant in Atlanta!"

"I told him you needed to rest Marcus." Paula said. "But he insisted."

"Yes, I insist. What are you doing here? Spaghetti! Turn it off!"

Kurt Audian turned off my stove.

"Let's celebrate in a lovely place!" he insisted again.

"I suggest Brazilian food. Churrasco!" said Rich.

There was no way I could escape from the situation. I had to accompany the bosses to dinner and Amy had to sneak out of the RV. The end of our conversation would have to wait for another day.

14

ARROW

Even before I start working for Mr. Monterey, even before all that had happened with my dad, I used to watch Dog Agility competitions on TV. National League and World Championships were events I didn't miss, even if it happened in the middle of the night. But to be competitive in a Dog Agility event, of course, you needed a good dog. And a good dog from a sport-specific breeder costs a fortune.

Usually Border Collies bred for herding do not have the best body condition and structural development for Dog Agility competitions. At least that's what the "experts" in the sport always said, but at the time I didn't even care.

###

November 2004, and already working for Mr. Monterey, I never denied that the area of the ranch I most enjoyed working was the kennel. Twice a year, Mr. Monterey used to have Border Collie litters. That year the puppy business was not going very well, and he was paying more attention to the other animals at the ranch such as pigs, cows and chickens, which were far more profitable. For that reason, Mr. Monterey decided that he would have only one litter that year, and then perhaps he would no longer breed Border Collies on the property anymore.

"Good morning, kids!", greeted Mr. Monterey bringing a package of dog food on his back.

"Hello Mr Monterey!", I replied.

I was watching him check all the puppies to see if they were okay.

"Are they ok?", I asked.

One by one, he checked the puppies, which were apparently quite healthy.

"Yes. All good! Good weight, they are eating well. Everything in order!"

"Any interested buyers?", I asked curious.

"Three interested families contacted me. But the puppy business is not good right now. People prefer those large breeders with champion lineages. Our kennel is small, and we are not famous. So, hard to compete."

He continued checking the puppies, one by one.

"That's why I don't think I'll breed anymore. A lot of work and the profit is minimal."

"Hmm!", I mumble.

Pause. I went into the kennel and started helping him check the puppies.

"How much are you asking for them?", I asked.

He turned to me, looking curious.

"Why, Marquito? Are you looking for a Border Collie?"

"I love Border Collies. You know, they're great for training and doing Dog Agility."

"True, they are great working dogs. But these here, I don't know if they are the best idea for agility."

"I think the trainer makes the dog. If you train from an early age, it's totally possible."

Mr. Monterey laughed.

"True that!", he replied. "There are some interested people coming today to see the puppies. They are still young. Wait a few weeks. If we don't sell them all, maybe we can work out a deal, ok?"

I continued working on the property, taking care of the puppies and other duties that were my responsibility.

Of all the puppies in the litter, there was one female who got along best with me. All black with only some parts of her head white. That female was different from the rest of the litter. Shy, she always hid or kept her head down in the corner of the kennel every time a family came to choose a puppy to buy. That behavior always meant that she was never chosen.

I never understood why, but with me she always behaved differently. Every day when I arrived at the property, she was the first one to come running to play with me, but if someone different arrived, there she goes, hiding in the corner of the kennel.

People looking for herding dogs to work with sheep always choose the craziest puppies from the litter. They need to be outgoing and not shy to become confident adult dogs for a good herding job.

Weeks passed, and one by one the puppies were all sold, except for her, who was left alone in the kennel.

I remember that normal working day she came running as usual to welcome me. Mr Monterey was there.

"Good Morning!", I greeted already playing with the little puppy, almost 9 weeks old now.

"Good morning."

Outside, Mr. Monterey watched me.

"Any buyers for her?", I asked.

"Not so far."

Silence for a few seconds.

"You know, it's good to see you two getting along well.", Mr. Monterey continued. "She is a timid puppy but it seems that with you she is different."

"I think she feels safe with me."

"I think that is a good thing, that she feels safe with you."

"Why?", I asked confused.

"Because she's leaving today, with you."

I felt an electric shock in my legs. Did he really say that? Leaving with me?

"I do not understand.", I said confused.

"She's yours, Marquito. I know you will take good care of her."

"Mr. Monterey, I don't know if I have all the money to pay you.", I replied worried.

"No money. She is yours. You can take her. It's a gift. You always help here on the property. It's an early birthday present."

"I don't know what to say. Thanks!"

"You don't need to say anything. Get a bag of food in the room and take her home. I need to wash this kennel."

Mr. Monterey waved his hand as if kicking me out of the kennel. I picked her up and walked away. It was the beginning of my relationship with Arrow.

15

AUSTIN, TEXAS
ROUND 3 NATIONAL LEAGUE
APRIL 2007

The weeks after Atlanta were absolutely crazy. Social media messages tagging me on countless posts from different people. In the grocery store or in the places I used to go, more normal people started stopping me and congratulating me. Even asking for a selfie. It was surreal. I kind of enjoyed it. Arrow also became famous. Wherever we used to go for a walk, people would stop us, ask to pet her or even take a selfie with her.

###

The round in Austin was held in an outdoor area, no roof over our heads, no air conditioning. Only two rounds out of ten happened outdoors, and Austin was one of them. The place chosen was an open space beside the Circuit of the Americas, a racetrack that hosted MotorSport events including Formula 1, which I've always loved.

No gigantic arenas or grandstands. The site was wide open, and the track was marked using yellow tape. The audience was spread out standing around the track, or on a small hill to the side, where it was possible to have an almost aerial and complete view of the track.

Even with a limited space for the public, which could not approach the yellow tape, people were still very close to the track, putting extra pressure on the competitors. The natural grass floor was very well maintained. No holes, unevenness or risk points for handlers and dogs. Everything looked perfect for another weekend.

We arrived early on Thursday. Our flight left at 6 am from Orlando and due to the time difference, we arrived in Austin in the morning.

As soon as I arrived in Austin, I was picked up by Paula and Rich. They were saying that the whole team was delighted with the result in Atlanta, and how great it would be to repeat in Austin. Pressure! It was cool. I had other thoughts on my mind besides the competition, and the most important one was about Amy. That "almost kiss" in Atlanta had been on my mind for the last month.

I was one of the first ones arriving. Only two other competitors were already there. Some teams hadn't even brought their RV's yet, and empty spaces at the parking lot were visible.

From my RV window I could see the Circuit of the Americas tower. Very cool to imagine that I was so close to the place where great F1 champions like Lewis Hamilton, Fernando Alonso and Rubens Barrichello had also been, it was like stepping on sacred ground.

###
FRIDAY

I woke up early on Friday and left the RV to take Arrow to the first pee of the morning. Several handlers were already doing the same, walking their dogs around the area. Amy saw me in the distance and waved smiling, I waved back. Sany was also outside and saw when the two of us waved to each other, letting out a small coy smile.

Later, we went to the briefing with Steve Cornsmith. I sat in my chair waiting for the briefing to start and unexpectedly Sany sat down next to me.

"Good morning!", said Sany.

"Good morning", I replied without much excitement.

"How are you, Marquito?"

"I'm great! How are you, Sany?"

"I could not be better. I have a feeling that I will have an exceptionally good weekend.", Sany replied smiling.

"Good for you. You haven't won anything yet, right? You really need a good one."

I confess, it was too much. I had only won my first round at the National League in my life, and Sany had already won several, including being champion once. Even though I didn't like him, I needed to respect him and that was really uncalled for. It just came out of my mouth. And of course, Sany was pissed off about what I said. I tried to apologize.

"Sorry, Sany! I did not mean to..."

"Okay, okay", Sany interrupted. "Little advice. Be careful with who you get involved with. You might think that with your incredible and enormous experience in the National League you already know everything about everyone, it might surprise you."

Sany got up from his chair and turned to say something else.

"And another thing. Having another handler sneaking out of your RV in the middle of the night, doesn't look good either."

Darn! He saw when Amy ran away from my RV in Atlanta. Of all the people who could have seen it, it had to be Sany? It was only logical that he would spread that news to everyone. Could this get me into trouble with the team? Or cause problems for Amy with her team?

CRAP! No, no! This is just another Sany strategy to emotionally destabilize me for the competition. Relax!

On the way out of the briefing I was still worried about Sany's attitude. I was walking hurriedly out of the room and back to my RV.

"Hey, Marquito!", a voice called me from behind. I turned around, it was Amy.

"Hey! Everything all right?"

"Sure. Have a good trip?"

So used to seeing her with a ponytail under that cap, that seeing her for the first time with her loose hair walking out of the briefing room left me even more in awe.

"Yes, I did. You?"

"Delayed connection in Chicago, arrived late, but here we are.", Amy replied smiling.

Silence and staring.

"Oh, about that spaghetti..."

"Oh, yes, we can try this weekend, of course!", I was uneasy and apprehensive.

"What's wrong, Marquito? You look weird."

"Do you think it's a good idea for us to see each other like this in our RVs? I don't know. I don't want to get either of us in trouble."

"Oh ok, I get it. If you don't want to there's no problem. I understand." Amy looked disappointed.

"No, no, I want to! Believe me, I do. Very much."

We both laugh.

"So, let's talk later, okay?", Amy smiled. "That spaghetti smelled great in Atlanta."

Amy winked and left, heading back to her RV.

###

The training went very well. The surface was like a nice carpet, it was so well prepared. Organizers used the same grass we normally see on soccer fields. Soft without being fluffy or solid, perfect for dogs.

The judge was a bit of everyone's concern. Brought from AKC trials (American Kennel Club), he had the reputation of preparing very open courses, that means, courses with long straight lines and with few challenges or "traps" for the dogs.

AKC judges were famous for that. The courses prepared in local AKC tournaments were always formed with many straight lines, which provided a lot of speed for the dogs, but they were like beginner's courses, and nobody competing in the National League liked that kind of course.

The organizers occasionally justified bringing judges from other organizations to offer different challenges at different rounds, but that justification never worked, and the handlers always turned up their noses at courses prepared by AKC judges.

With two rounds completed, one won by Amy and one won by me, Lisa and Sany knew that to keep the situation still favorable for them a victory was necessary. Before the season started, everyone placed Amy, Lisa and Sany as favorites for the season title. But at that point, my name was already on the same list

Both Lisa and Sany seemed to have got the message. On track Friday for training and surface adaptation, the two were exercising bold handling skills and practicing exercises with long straights lines, already anticipating what could come for the weekend.

###
SATURDAY

I woke up early on Saturday and stuck my head outside checking the sky. The sun was not there. The cloudy sky and the possibility of rain could bring a different challenge to the weekend, especially as it would be an outdoor round.

Course being prepared for the first Qualifier of the day. Fans crowding around the track. It was nothing compared to the crazed crowd in Atlanta or the festive crowd in Miami. No house handlers, no handlers from Texas competing at the National League, and those who came to watch the competition were there more out of curiosity than to root for someone. Taking place right next to a busy highway near the Circuit of the Americas, Highway 130, also helped bring in public to the site, who parked their cars to see what was going on that weekend with all the dogs around.

The first Qualifier of the morning had already delivered what everybody was expecting. Long sequences with obstacles in straight lines, terribly similar to beginner courses in local tournaments.

From the first obstacle up to obstacle number 13, there were no changes in directions, back sides, or anything else that could be indicated or recognized as a turn. Jumps, straight line tunnels, dog walk, tire, A Frame and seesaw all in straight lines. After jump 13, a left reversal and another six obstacles aligned in another straight line. A course with just 19 obstacles, the minimum required by rule.

"Too lazy that judge!", Mario said sitting next to me while we waited to get on track.

"Dude, how is this allowed by the organization?", I asked.

"Everyone already knew this would happen. They do it on purpose.", Mario replied.

What followed was a freak show. A course with so many straight lines significantly increases the dogs speed, and when dogs increase the speed too much, there is less reaction time between obstacles resulting in bars being knocked down, contact zones not being touched and refusals.

Out of the first ten teams on the track, no one managed to finish the course without taking a penalty. It was only Mario who, with a naturally slower dog, managed to be the first to finish the course without penalties and thus the first position.

Sany came to the track and, of course, was doing his best to not give full speed to Maximus trying not to risk a penalty, but he left the track with two penalties anyway.

The same happened with Lisa who tried to balance her

dog's speed, naturally fast, with a much less aggressive handling, but was also the victim of two penalties.

Amy was so cautious handling X that, believe it or not, she was knocked out of the Qualifier after X couldn't slow down, touching the outer side of the tunnel before approaching the right obstacle. Elimination on the first Qualifier.

As for me, I also joined the list and finished my first Qualifier with three penalties. Two bars on the ground and one refusal.

Mario was the only one finishing the course without penalties. Half a second slower than the others, he still had taken the first position. Which had put a giant smile on his face.

After the horror show of the first Qualifier, I left the track area to meet Leo.

"What do I do?", I asked.

"You need to pay attention to your handling. I want you to do something. Don't run too far ahead of her."

Running ahead of Arrow was what gave us the best results since I started competing. Keeping Arrow behind me gave her a target to follow, me. Also, it pushed her to full speed as she chased me down the course.

"Leo, we never train like that. I don't even know how to position myself like that."

"We'll have to try. If you stay too far ahead of her, pushing speed, she won't be able to find the right pace to approach the next obstacle. All handlers are getting it wrong. Stay by her side. Keep the pace, but don't be aggressive in your moves."

###

In the second Qualifier, another nail-biting course. The

only thing the judge did was change the direction. What was once the last jump became the first, and what was once the first jump was now the last. The same course again, with two long straight lines, and a single inversion in the middle. But now in the opposite direction.

It seemed like every other handler had overheard my conversation with Leo, because that was exactly what everyone was doing. No aggressive handling, no running in front of the dog. Just running side by side, not allowing the dog to push for speed. Finishing the course without penalties it was clearly everybody's strategy.

Things changed completely when Amy, who had been knocked out in the first Qualifier, and needing to do well to qualify for the Semi-Final, completely ignored that recommendation and handled X in an extremely aggressive way, pushing him at full speed.

The other handlers, trying to figure out what Amy was doing, just watched, waiting for the inevitable elimination. But no! Amy was overcoming every obstacle with her dog brilliantly. With speed, aggressiveness and an absolutely unrivaled confidence, she finished the course without penalties and with an incredible two seconds ahead of all the other competitors who had entered the track up until that moment. Her handling was so insanely amazing that she drew applause from the other handlers.

Amy looked at Lisa as she exited the course.

"Beat that! I want to see it!"

"Damn!", I said after Amy's run.

Amy had created a problem for every other handler,

including myself. Anyone who wanted to qualify for the semifinal now would have to at least try to get close to her time. And that meant everybody would need to risk and handle aggressively at full speed, on a course easy to make mistakes.

With a few minutes for me to get in, I ran back to the side of the track to talk to Leo.

"Amy makes everybody's life hard now." I said.

"Not too many options now. Do you want to go to the semis? Get in there and risk everything because handling cautiously won't get you anywhere near that time."

As we talked, Sany entered the track and of course everyone had to risk everything now. And that's what he was doing, desperately running with Maximus, trying to beat Amy's time when BANG!, a bar on the ground! And BANG! another one.

I looked back at Leo:

"I have a bad feeling about that."

"Go there and do your best. What's the worst that can happen?"

"Being eliminated?"

"If that happens, we'll go home and take a break for the rest of the weekend."

Lisa also got on track, and it was all or nothing. But Amy seemed to have done the impossible, because Lisa also tried the same handling, unsuccessfully. Lisa was another handler with two penalties.

My turn. I entered the course, tense, like no other run before. The calm I'd had in Atlanta was gone in Austin.

"OK!", I released Arrow. As always drooling and digging her claws in the grass, beginning to chase me.

1-2-3-4 jumps, ok! Dog walk, fast, contact zone nailed it! Tunnel in front, all in a straight line, that was crazy! What a horrible course! I felt a twinge in my right thigh but my adrenaline level was so high I didn't care! I continued. Tunnel exit with slalom ahead.

"WEAVES!", I yelled to Arrow in vain!

She was so fast that she passed, running on the side of the slalom, REFUSAL! I had to call her back and continue.

I couldn't waste any more time. I had already taken a penalty and lost a lot of time! Let's go! Three more jumps and DONE!

My legs were throbbing from running. I looked at the screen and there was the number three side by side with our names! Yes, we got it! A spot in the Semi-Finals.

Walking off the track as Mario was preparing for his run, I ran into Amy.

"Good run!", greeted Amy.

"Jesus from heaven! ", I was trying to catch my breath. "How did you get a run like that?"

Amy came up to my face, and almost whispering...

"The best way to put pressure on other handlers if you enter the track first. Handling crazy without fear of losing. If you get it wrong, patience. But if it works..."

Amy was right. The pressure she had put on the other handlers after her run was brutal, and the possibility of being knocked out in the Qualifier after Amy's run, pushed the other handlers to go all or nothing.

Out of the corner of my eye I could see Mario finishing another run without penalties. Even with an absurdly high time he still qualified for the Semi-Finals.

Amy finished the Qualifiers in first, with Mario in second, I was fifth, Sany in seventh, and Lisa in ninth. A true mess.

Sunday would be intense, to say the least.

###

SUNDAY

At 2:30 in the morning I woke up with a loud bang and Arrow jumping on my bed to lay down on my side. I got up and looked out the small RV bedroom window. The night became clear with a strong flash of lightning followed by the sound of more thunder. It was raining. Not a little rain, but a storm that gently shook the RV.

It took me a while to realize. Wait! It's raining! My God, the grass!

###

The next day I got up around 7:00 in the morning. I left the RV to check outside. Of course, everything was wet and those who left things spread out in the RV outdoor area like sneakers, socks, backpacks, chairs, or clothes, now had to run to dry everything because the semifinals would start in a couple of hours.

The parking area was soaked, some areas with about two inches of water on the floor. It was easy to soak your feet on the way to the arena. But nothing could be compared to the track situation.

The perfect natural grass we had before had practically melted, and had turned into a treacherous field with some puddled areas and other areas where the grass seemed to have vanished.

There were no competitors that morning who weren't worried about what they needed to do in the next few minutes. Sany came to my side and I could almost hear his thoughts coming out of his head. Lisa was another one who, with her arms crossed, stared at the track, probably thinking about what she was going to do to try to run her dog under those circumstances.

I started walking away from the track when Amy approached.

"We can't compete.", Amy said in a serious tone.

"You sure?"

"It's dangerous, Marquito. Someone can fall and get hurt. And the dogs, considerable risk of injuring a leg or even the head colliding with an obstacle."

"Do you think they'll cancel?"

"I doubt it!", Amy replied quickly. "I'll talk to Steve, but I doubt it."

"Well, you are the current champion. If there's anyone they need to hear from, it's you."

In the distance we saw Lisa already talking to Steve, probably about the conditions of the track. Amy didn't say anything, just turned her back on me and walked towards them both. I followed. I had a feeling things weren't going to end well.

As soon as Amy approached Lisa and Steve, Lisa walked away. From a few steps behind, I heard when Amy started the conversation with Steve.

"Hey Steve!"

"Hey Amy!"

"I don't think it's possible to run, right? We can't take that risk."

"Well, you know that a cancellation only happens when 100% of the competitors are in agreement, don't you?"

"Yes, I know."

"So, I was talking to Lisa now and she is not in favor of us canceling the competition. From her perspective, we can continue."

"What?"

A look of fury showed in Amy's face. She turned her back on Steve and started walking with strong steps towards Lisa. I went after her.

"Amy!", I screamed. "Wait!"

It didn't do much good because Amy quickly made it to Lisa.

"Damn it, Lisa?", Amy was furious. "Did you tell Steve you want to compete under these conditions?"

"I just think the conditions aren't so bad.", Lisa replied in an air of superiority. "And after all, as canine sport professionals we have to know how to deal with bad weather conditions."

"Are you completely crazy?", Amy yelled. "Do you want to see someone get hurt here today?"

Amy put her finger in Lisa's face, and I had to get in between them.

"Amy, please! Don't do this!" I said.

"If you touch me, I'll open a formal complaint against you, asking the organization to punish you.", Lisa said.

"You Bitch! You only think about yourself! You have no respect for anybody.", Amy was fuming.

"Amy, please!", I was in the middle, trying to calm her down.

I grabbed Amy by her arms and gently started pushing her away from Lisa.

"Go to hell, Marquito!", Amy screamed at me. "I don't need anybody to protect me, or to tell me what to do."

I froze. I hadn't seen that side of Amy. I could see the vein in her neck throbbing with anger. Even spittle came out of the corner of her mouth. Breathing hard and panting. Wide eyes and flushed face.

After a few seconds Amy turned and started walking away.

"Trouble in paradise?", asked Sany approaching me.

"Get out of here, Sany!"

###

The competition was not going to be canceled, that was for sure.

With calmer spirits, we went to walk the semi-final course, or at least try to walk the semi-final course. Walking on that wet grass was hard. With puddles everywhere it felt more like quicksand than grass. The atmosphere among the competitors was not the best one. Everyone's expression was one of concern.

When the semi-finals started, it was another mess. Dogs slipping, bars flying across the ground, and even one of the dogs rolling down the A Frame, after slipping off the top of the obstacle. But no one mentioned anything about stopping the runs.

When Lisa came to do her run, it looked like she was caught in her own web. The person who didn't want the competition to be canceled came to the track and her poor dog Fire, was unable to stand while running the course. In every step, every attempt to jump, water flew in all directions and sometimes it was impossible to see Fire in the middle of so much water. With four penalties it wasn't easy to believe, but Lisa was out of the finals. She had to get off the track. It was the end for her.

Sany entered the track afterwards and handled Maximus very conservatively, almost walking instead of running to keep from falling. Little by little, even with a time well above what they could do, Sany managed to bring Maximus to the end with just one bar on the ground. He was qualified for the final.

I was the next one! It was a lottery. Trying to be aggressive at that moment would be death for sure. A conservative handling was necessary. The game was trying to survive.

"OK!", I released Arrow, waiting for me at the initial mark.

Arrow started running, scattering water everywhere and skating like a race car using bald tires in the middle of a storm. But there she came! 1-2-3 jumps! I took her in a very conservative way along the dog walk. Then, a sequence of tunnel with seesaw. Arrow skated into the tunnel entrance and fell inside the tunnel taking a much longer time to exit on the other side. Everything was fine until BANG! I slipped in a puddle and hit the ground. I tried to get up quickly to save my run and BANG! went down a second time. I could feel the mud on my neck and sliding into my shirt. I got up for the second time and Arrow had already committed a refusal. I managed to recover and finished my run without elimination, but one penalty. It was the best I could do.

Leaving the track, my clothes caked with mud. Mud running down my neck all over my body to my legs. I think it was enough to qualify to the finals.

Mario was already on the track, and it seems that day was his day, because Mario was very comfortable on the messy surface. With a dog with much less DRIVE and less explosion, he could lead Rex through the difficult and slippery surface with grace and skill. He was the only one who had finished the run in the semi-finals without penalties and in first place. I felt so happy for him.

The last handler to enter the track for the semi-finals was Amy. Visibly upset by the situation, Amy would have her worst performance in the last two years of competition. A run that would last just over fifteen seconds and five obstacles. X slipped and landed on the top of one of the jumps, destroying the sides of the jump and imploding the obstacle. Obstacle destruction according to the rules was equal to an elimination. Amy was out of the finals.

In the distance I saw Amy crestfallen and annoyed, leaving the track and walking away with X on leash. I thought about going to talk to her, but I knew it was best not to. Let her cool off.

FINALISTS
Mario & Rex

Sany & Maximus
Marcus & Arrow
Joe & Jungle
Polly & Panda
###
FINALS

It was time for the finals, and the drama wasn't over yet. A few minutes before we hit the track to compete in the finals, more rain came. Not a storm like the night before, a light but steady rain would keep the track treacherous.

The constant rain at least helped me to clean the remnants of mud that still clung to my body. Drenched handlers and dogs, drenched track with puddles and very slick areas. What would be the best handling to do? Fast and risky, or try to balance with a more conservative handling?

Of the five teams in the final, the slower dogs had the advantage, including Joe & Jungle, Polly & Panda and of course Mario & Rex. Sany and I were the two handlers with the fastest dogs. But speed at that moment didn't mean much.

Polly & Panda and Joe & Jungle hit the track respectively and no surprises. Slow but effective handling. Both ended with a penalty each, but no elimination.

As we watched Polly and Joe handling, Leo gave me some important instructions.

"You enter before Sany. If you risk pushing speed and it works, you will force Sany to do the same to try to win. But if it goes wrong, it will leave the way open for Sany to enter the track and only manage the handling to win the round."

"I know! What do you think I should do? Risky or not? Speed and risk or slow down to get to the end?"

Leo put a hand on my shoulder.

"This is a decision you need to make on your own."

Silence for a few seconds. I looked at Leo.

"I'll risk!"

"I wouldn't expect anything different from you.", Leo smiled.

I walked away from Leo. It was my turn.

I entered the wet track under the rain that I could feel in my eyes. Arrow, happy as always, was having fun with all that water. I put her on the initial mark and walked away.

"OK!", I yelled to Arrow!

Water everywhere, Arrow diving into a tunnel splashing water off the track onto a few brave fans who still lingered. Most fans had already left the arena a few hours before. Without a doubt it was the emptiest National League round in years. The contact obstacles were slippery, but I was determined to win this round. I couldn't lose to Sany who was outside watching my handling carefully. If I could push speed without penalties I would be forcing Sany to do the same if he wanted to beat me.

Arrow climbed up the A Frame, slipping on the sides, and descending on the opposite side forcing herself to not roll down. Three jumps in a row, water splashing. I slipped at a certain point in my run but kept my balance to keep from falling. Seesaw ahead, Arrow very quickly approached the obstacle. The approach was perfect, but she couldn't stop. She skidded down the length of the plank and landed on the other side of the obstacle before the seesaw touched the ground! NO! Penalty! We continued the run finishing with a great time but with a penalty.

I was disappointed! We were so good, almost perfect. I looked at Leo from a distance who gave me a thumbs up. It had been a good run.

Sany got on track! What a son of a bitch! Without being aggressive, without taking risks. He knew that the only thing he needed was to finish the run without committing penalties. And that's what he did, taking first place in the final.

Mario came last. Even with chances of winning the round, it was clear that Mario didn't have the speed to beat Sany & Maximus. They finished the run without penalties, handling the same way they did for the entire weekend but without beating Sany & Maximus' time, who won the round! Sany had won his first one in the year! Asshole!

RESULTS ROUND 3 AUSTIN

1. Sany & Maximus
2. Mario & Rex
3. Marcus & Arrow
4. Joe & Jungle
5. Polly & Panda

RANKING AFTER ROUND 3 AUSTIN

1. Sany & Maximus = 58 pts
2. Marcus & Arrow = 52 pts
3. Amy & X = 37 pts

4. Lisa & Fire = 33 pts
5. Joe & Jungle = 22 pts
6. Polly & Panda = 20 pts
7. Mario & Rex = 18 pts

###

Walking back to my RV, soaking wet, dirty, and tired, I saw Amy's RV being towed away in the distance and being prepared for removal. She was no longer there. She had probably gone right after the Semi-finals. Too bad, I wanted to talk to her.

16

LEO

December 2004, a few weeks after taking Arrow home as a puppy, I started searching the internet for places to train. Orlando has never been a good place for dog agility. There were no good places to train. The only training facility close to Orlando was in Mount Dora, but the inexperience of the trainers and the technique they used never impressed me.

At that time, and of course before I got to know Sany better, my dream was to train with him. But being so far away from Orlando and charging $150 per session, it was impossible for me.

I needed to find a place to train quickly, so I decided to start attending the nearby dog agility local competitions looking for trainers, and also to socialize Arrow in the environment.

Brooksville wasn't that far from my house, about 40 minutes driving, and it always hosted local competitions with lots of competitors. That weekend, Sonia Bates was organizing a local event there. I arrived around 10 am with the competition already underway. With little Arrow in my lap, I started walking among the competitors.

It is already known how a cute puppy in someone's lap draws attention from people around, and with Arrow it was no different. Wherever I went, everyone came to ask me about little Arrow. "How many months old?", "Which breeder is she from?", "Already training?", were the most common questions I heard from everyone who approached me.

That's when Kristen Halcey approached us.

Kristen Halcey was famous in Florida. Despite no longer being part of the National League circuit, and no longer among the most competitive handlers in the country, Kristen was part of a not-too-distant past when she was part of big teams, including a quick appearance in the National Team. For the past six years Kristen had dedicated herself to her own business, a dog training center for dog agility, dock diving, flyball and other sports. Her training center was located in Brandon, near Tampa.

"My God, what a cute puppy!" said Kristen approaching.

"Thanks!"

"Boy or girl?" Kristen asked smiling and seeming extremely interested.

"Girl, her name is Arrow."

Kristen smiled.

"Can I hold her?" she asked already stretching her arms to hold Arrow.

I never liked the idea of anyone else holding Arrow when she was a puppy, but I needed to socialize her, so I allowed it.

"She's really cute!" Kristen said with Arrow in her lap.

Two other people approached. I had no idea who they

were, but it was easy to guess they were two other handlers training with Kristen at her training center.

"My name is Kristen, by the way." Kristen stretched her arm and introduced herself as if I didn't know her.

"Marcus! Nice to meet you."

"So, are you already training with her?" Kristen asked.

"No, not yet. Just basic obedience. I'm looking for a place to train her for dog agility."

"Ah, we have a training center in Brandon. What are your goals for dog agility?"

"I would like to be competitive. One day compete in major championships."

The three of them let out a shy laugh, as if they despised what I had just said.

"Of course, of course! Big championships are a good goal. Which breeder did she come from?"

"She came from a herding farm in Plant City."

Even trying to cover up the reaction, it was clear that those three people were laughing inside about what I had just said.

"I don't want to destroy your dreams, but to be competitive in big championships you will need a dog from a better breeder." Kristen said half smiling. "She doesn't have the best conformation for a competitor, you know. Her paws don't have a good alignment, the back line…"

"Well…" I interrupted Kristen. "I'll get in touch with you for more information about training."

Gently I stretched out my arms taking Arrow back into my lap.

"Yes, of course! Google my name. It's easy to find."

"OK, thank you."

Kristen and the other two handlers walked away from me.

"Don't be concerned about what she told you." a voice echoed from beside me. I turned around, it was Leo. "These people do not understand what dog agility means. It should be for everyone."

"Truth. But I was not kidding about going to big championships."

Leo looked at me, interested in what I just said.

"My name is Leo!" he stretched out his arm to greet me. "Nice to meet you."

My story with Leo started that day. A couple weeks later I was training with him.

Leo never let my dream of competing in the National League fade. He was always very realistic with me. He always said that I would have to train twice as hard to one day, possibly, have a shot at the National League. He never lied to me saying that Arrow was the perfect dog. In fact, he always pointed out the natural aerodynamic problems in Arrow's body, a dog relatively smaller than an agility Border Collie. And for that reason he told me it would be difficult, but not impossible. It was a matter of being persistent and consistent in training.

Any other coach would have acted like Kristen or even Sany, but Leo never let me down. And that's why I respected him so much.

17

LAS VEGAS, NEVADA
ROUND 4 NATIONAL LEAGUE
MAY 2007

With three rounds already behind us, the season arrived at an extremely defining moment, the rounds on the West Coast. The majority of agility competitors in the country were on the East Coast, and for that reason most of the competitions took place on the right side of the country. But there was one key factor that made the West Coast events so important, Lisa Potovski.

Originally from San Francisco, she was the biggest dog agility winner in the country, including a world championship title. But not just that, she drew crowds to the rounds in Las Vegas and Los Angeles.

With only fourth place in the table until that moment, Lisa knew that the West Coast rounds would be a crucial point in her quest for yet another national title. It was either win or win to get back to the East Coast with a chance to fight.

No need to say much about the feelings of local fans for Amy. Her main opponent won the National League in the previous season by beating Lisa in the last round in New York. So, Amy would be public enemy number 1 in the next two rounds. Incredibly, after her elimination in Austin, Amy remained third in the overall standings.

Sany led the National League after three rounds with his best season since his title in 2003. I was second, and being the rookie in the pack I was curious to see how the West Coast crowd would welcome the Florida competitors.

###

Our arrival in Las Vegas was super nice. Actually, boarding in Orlando was a little tricky when some people recognized us and wanted to hug and play with Arrow. I had to walk away because even though Arrow was well socialized, the situation was clearly bothering her a little bit.

One of the coolest parts of our trip was arriving at McCarran airport to see a huge illustration in the arrivals area advertising the 4th Round of the National Dog Agility League, taking over an entire wall. Of course, with a photo of Lisa & Fire. It was so cool!

Riding from the airport with Paula, Rich, and Leo, we passed the famous strip beside the giant casinos. Paula was giving me instructions.

"The RV is already waiting. Usual routine with a briefing tomorrow morning."

"First time in Vegas?" asked Rich.

"Yeah. This place is amazing.", I replied. I was really awestruck by all those casinos.

"Welcome to the city of sin, my friend!" said Rich.

"Yes, but let's try not to commit any sin and focus on

the competition." Paula interrupted. "Marquito, the team is incredibly happy with your second position in the standings so far. A victory on the West Coast would be sensational. Did you know the team has never had a win on the West Coast?"

Of course, the pressure.

"No, I didn't know. Let's see what we can do about that."

Leo looked at me with a small smile.

We arrived at the competition location in the late afternoon. The round would take place in an area right across the street from Mandalay Bay Casino and the Luxor Casino, where music concerts normally happened. A covered arena with grandstands all around, where about a thousand people could sit.

###

FRIDAY

It was a sunny Friday morning and there was no forecast for rain in the Nevada desert. I was happy to be in the desert after the Austin flood.

We arrived at the briefing that morning. It was the first time I saw Lisa saying "GOOD MORNING" to everyone when she walked into the room. For sure, she was more comfortable competing on the West Coast.

Sany also entered, excited. "FOLLOW THE LEADER!" he yelled to all, making a clear allusion to his leadership in the championship. Few laughed, most ignored him. Amy also arrived at the briefing room. She was serious and looked at me for a few seconds out of the corner of her eye, sitting down about ten feet from me. Mario was by my side.

"Hey man! I'll tell you something. I don't want to intrude

on your personal life, but be careful with what you do, right bro?"

"What are you talking about?"

"I'm just saying. Sany has been saying that he saw Amy sneaking out of your RV in Atlanta. It doesn't look good for you, you know? It's your first season, you don't want to get involved in that Mexican soap opera, you feel me?"

Sany, that idiot! Apparently, he had already told everyone. And if the competitors already knew, then likely the teams did too.

"Relax, bro! Nothing happened. We are just friends." I answered.

"Sure. And I am the president of the United States."

###

With the briefing finished, we went down to the track for training and adaptation with the dogs.

The arena in Las Vegas was very well organized. With a shade sail over the track and providing cover for all competitors and fans. It minimized the heat on that weekend. The track had an artificial grass surface. It wasn't the first time we were going to compete on artificial turf, but we didn't have a lot of experience on that kind of surface. The artificial grass was one of the surfaces most accepted by competitors for giving good grip in addition to providing speed.

Arrow quickly adapted to the surface. We did a thirty-minute training and everything went wonderfully. The grip was flawless, and Arrow could do her jumps with precision. But that was also true for the other competitors who would probably use a very aggressive handling having a surface with such good grip.

Amy was around all day, but didn't come to talk to me at all. After her outburst in Austin I'd rather stay away and let things roll. The focus was on the competition.

###

That Friday night I was cooking my traditional spaghetti in my RV when someone knocked on the door. I looked out the small window. It was Amy outside.

"Hey!" I opened the door.

"Hey, Marquito. Can I come in?"

"Sure."

Amy walked in and I closed the door.

"Spaghetti, huh?" she looked at the stove.

"Yep! My specialty. Everything okay?"

"Yeah, fine. I just decided to stop by to apologize to you. I didn't want to treat you that way in Austin."

"It's ok. I get it."

"You didn't deserve to be treated like that. I lost myself for a moment."

"I confess, it was a side of you that I didn't know." I said smiling. "You scared the heck out of me."

Amy smiled back.

"Relax, I'll bark but I won't bite."

We both smiled.

"Want to stay for dinner?" I invited.

Amy thought for a moment.

"Is your first time in Vegas, right?" Amy asked.

"Yes, why?"

"I think I have a better idea."

Amy approached the stove and turned off the burner.

"Let's take a walk." she said with a naughty little smile.

"Seriously? It's the third time I've tried to cook my spaghetti, and somebody turned off the stove."

Amy grabbed me by the arm and I barely had time to get my wallet and cellphone. We left the RV, locked the door and started walking quickly out of the competition area. It was around 9 pm and hopefully no one saw us leaving the RV parking lot.

Being my first time in Vegas I honestly didn't know anything about the city, but Amy had been there countless times. We went to Fremont Street, a place with lots of bars, shows, and a lot of crazy people walking around.

The street was full of performers who dress up as celebrities and take pictures with tourists. Half-naked women, and lots of alcohol. The first stop was a bar where female dancers swayed their half-naked butts on counters in the middle of the street. There, we had our first drink.

We stopped for a bite to eat at The Heart Attack Grill, a restaurant where waitresses dressed as sexy nurses and would whip lashes at customers who couldn't eat all their sandwich. I had three or four lashes on my back. Amy had fun with that.

After a few hours there, and a little bit drunk from so many drinks, we went to the strip to walk through the casinos. We stopped at the Venetian, and tried our luck on the slot machines. We didn't win anything, but it was nice to find out that the drinks were free for anyone who was playing, so we stayed there for a while.

Half drunk, we left the Venetian and walked to the Bellagio to watch the famous water and light show at the Bellagio fountain.

Watching that show with Amy by my side I remembered all the shit my family had gone through for the past two or three years. How ironic is life, full of ups and downs. I was living the worst moment of my life and look at me now. In Vegas, competing in the most important dog agility league in the country, and with a beautiful woman by my side. Not just beautiful, but the current national champion.

I found myself staring at Amy forgetting about the light show in front of me. Amy noticed.

"Hey, the show is over there!" said Amy pointing in front of us.

I don't know if it was because I was drunk, but I couldn't wait any longer. I brought my body closer to Amy, leaned in, touched her hair and kissed her. She wrapped her arms around me and kissed me back. For a long time. I felt the same adrenaline as when competing in a final round. An electric shock in the back of my neck. What an amazing kiss.

###

SATURDAY

I woke up with a start! Jumping out of bed with a loud knock on my RV door. Amy also jumped out of bed. We had spent the night together in my RV.

More knocking on the RV's door.

"Marcus!" screamed Paula outside.

"OH NO!" said Amy! "It's 8:15!"

Eight was normally the time we were supposed to be at the arena. Qualifiers would start at 9 am that Saturday.

I got up quickly, still in my underwear and shirtless. Amy was only in her panties and a T-shirt. I quickly put on some shorts and ran to the RV door.

Paula once again knocked on the door, this time even stronger.

"Marcus! Are you there?"

I opened the door, quickly.

"Hey Paula!"

"What is happening? You are never late! Is everything all right?"

"Yes! Yes! I just overslept a little. But I am up already and..."

Amy walked by us, leaving the RV as if nothing had happened.

"Excuse me." said Amy gently leaving the RV and passing between Paula and me.

Paula said nothing. Her facial expression said a thousand words.

"If you'll excuse me." I said. "I need to take a shower quickly. Excuse me."

I gently closed the door with Paula standing outside stunned.

###

Qualifier time!

The moment I stepped inside that arena I knew that round would not be a normal one. With the bleachers completely full, it was impossible to see a single empty space in the middle of that crowd. Banners, flyers, T-shirts, and lots of screams clamoring for "LISA" "LISA" "LISA"

No doubt that this was Lisa's territory! A mass of people would be cheering Lisa down the track that weekend.

Handlers were starting their runs and it was impossible to hear anything coming from the middle of the track. The noise was so absurdly loud that not even the referee's whistle could be heard. Instructions over the speakers were also impossible to hear. The best thing to do to be able to follow the results was keeping an eye on the electronic monitor, in the corner of the track above the bleachers.

The course for the first Qualifier was not that complex. A fair level of difficulty but with few points of elimination risk. The good grip of the surface helped the dogs, and the handlers could use an extremely aggressive handling.

The first handlers came to the track and the only one who managed to calm the euphoria of the stands, was Polly. With her mix breed Panda, Polly managed a good run ending first at that moment. Polly was the most loved handler in the league, and it was easy to explain why. Handling the only mix breed among all the contestants it was like rooting for the underdog, it was like rooting for David against Goliath. Every time the little mix breed managed to beat a mighty Border Collie the crowd would go crazy. And Polly was starting to get good at taking out Border Collies.

Mario also hit the track. But with an extremely fast course old Rex stood no chance. At that point, he had already fallen below Polly & Panda.

Things went even crazier when Lisa first stepped onto the

track. Screams, applause... "LISA, LISA, LISA!" She waved back to the crowd. A crowd in your favor gives you incredible motivation on the track. I wondered if I would ever feel something like that.

Lisa knew how to enjoy the moment. Confident, precise, and exceptionally fast. She also knew how to put pressure on the other handlers, and she did. With a shocking low time of 26:58, she took first place, still with Amy, me, and Sany to get on track.

Right after Lisa, Amy went in. Once again, the stands started participating but this time with boos and shouts against Amy. The speakers even tried to calm things down.

"Please let's respect the competitors."

It did not do much good. Amy started her run under a lot of booing.

Some people might understand that as lack of respect, but I think that's part of the game. The fans are there to cheer. Do you think it would be any different in Charlotte? At Amy's home

Even under a lot of taunting, Amy managed to make an exceptionally good Qualifier. But she failed to beat Lisa's time, finishing the run in second place with a time of 27:32.

I was next. Boos, of course! What the fans wanted at that moment was to see Lisa winning, and anyone getting in the way would be a target. But as I walked with Arrow onto the track up to the starting spot, I confess that I was even happy with the booing. That meant people saw me as a threat to Lisa. So be it.

My first run of the day was good. During the run, Arrow

responded very well to my commands, and I could almost feel the grip under her paws. Perfect turns, consistent back side jumps and perfect contacts. Running to the last jump I was quite sure I could take the first position. We crossed the finish line, I was out of breath from running the fast track when I looked at the electronic scoreboard, a number 3 appeared next to our name. THIRD??? IS THAT RIGHT?? Time: 27:38. Just 0.06 seconds behind Amy. It had been as good as Amy's, but how had Lisa managed such a low time? Unbelievable.

Sany on track. The last handler in Qualifier 1. Boos! No surprises there. The current championship leader was expected to receive boos. Sany even blew kisses to the crowd on his way to the starting spot, further inciting the fire that was already high in the stands.

Sany flying! Tons of speed, perfect slalom, seesaw…BANG! on the ground! Sany was on fire! It was clear that he was going to fight for the first position. And DONE! Sany crossed the finish line and the number 4 appeared next to his name. WHAT??? REALLY??? Time: 27:43. Unbelievable 0.05 seconds behind me and 0.11 seconds behind Amy.

Lisa was so fast that nobody was able to beat her time in the first Qualifier, and needless to say drove the crowd crazy.

Pause between Qualifiers, it was time to put thoughts in place for the second Qualifier.

I walked to Leo beside the track. By then, the crowd had calmed down a bit, but the loud music still made conversation difficult.

"It was a good run. I don't know why my time was so high." I said to Leo.

"Your time wasn't high. You, Amy and Sany are on the same page. There is no difference between you three. Lisa is flying. She knows she needs to win here. Losing here means the end of the championship for her."

"Have you ever seen something like that before?" I asked, pointing with my head to the crowd.

"The rounds here are always like that. You will see in Charlotte. The crowd goes crazy rooting for Amy too."

"Handlers, course opened for walking Qualifier 2" announced the speakers.

"Talk to you later!" I said to Leo.

"Good luck!"

I walked away from Leo and went onto the track to walk the course.

The course for the second Qualifier was a little more complex. A speedy section with three reversals of direction followed by a well locked sector with a dangerous trap involving two tunnels aligned with the entrance to the slalom. It was quite easy to make a mistake and let the dog dive into the tunnel instead of entering the slalom, ending up eliminated.

It did not take long for the first victim of the trap set by the judge. The first was Polly, who to the fans' disappointment ended up going home early after allowing Panda to enter the wrong tunnel.

Mario was close to elimination in the same spot. But with a scream that echoed throughout the noisy arena, "REX!" and because he had a slower dog, he still managed to get away with it, qualifying for the semifinals.

Joe Burnett had a good run; with a good pace he secured a

spot for the semi-finals. But the question was, will any of the favorites be out of Semis?

Sany entered the track and at that moment the smile had disappeared along with the kisses for the crowd. He was serious now. He wanted a spot in the semi-finals. He entered the track focused, serious, without jokes and managed a beautiful run without penalties and taking the first provisional position with a time of 28:11.

I was next! No boos! The crowd was not even paying much attention to me. Fast course, Arrow flying, precise, not even aware of the trap set by the judge. Perfect turn, pointing to the slalom and not even for a second looking at the tunnel to the side. Time: 27:58. Temporary first place, faster than Sany.

Amy and Lisa were the next ones to get on track. Things were going to get insane again. As Amy stepped onto the track and started walking towards the starting spot, boos! Insane Boos! But Amy did not get carried away. She put X at the starting position, walked away and started her run. And what a run! The first part was perfect, with X digging his nails into the artificial grass and taking pieces of plastic off the ground. I could see Amy's expression. Brows furrowed, focused on what needed to be done. They approached the judge's trap and...

"X!!!" screamed Amy.

The entire arena was silent for a second when X turned to the wrong tunnel, but Amy was able to save the run with a "OHHHHHH" coming from the stands. She finished her run without penalties just losing time. 28:08, placing herself behind me but ahead of Sany.

Lisa on track with the entire world beside her. That was

the feeling. With "LISA, LISA!" coming from the stands, she had full support from the crowd. And she did not disappoint them. Fast, precise, and with Fire flying under her handling, Lisa destroyed the clock making 27:10, running almost one second faster than me.

Qualifiers finished and all favorites classified for Sunday's Semi-Finals. In order, Lisa, myself, Amy, and Sany. Joe Burnet and Mario were also among the TOP 10 for semi-finals.

###

Saturday night, and all competitors had retired to their respective RV's. Well, not everyone, because in my RV I was not alone. Amy was with me finally enjoying my traditional spaghetti.

"Hmm" she tried to speak with her mouth full. "This is good!"

"You're kidding me, right?" I answered.

"No, I am serious! It is very good."

We both laughed.

"I really enjoyed last night." I said.

"Yes, me too. I just don't remember everything."

More laughs.

"I think we had a few too many cocktails" she said.

"Your fault, taking me to the dark side." I replied smiling.

"But I think the best parts I remember well."

"Me too."

I approached her, and even though my mouth was a little smeared with sauce, I kissed her.

"What do you think about the finals tomorrow?" I asked.

"I don't know. Lisa is not easy to beat around here. If I

had to choose between winning or seeing her lose, I would probably choose to see her lose."

"Really? Where does all this hate come from?"

Amy looked at me out of the corner of her eye.

"Okay, okay! Dumb question, I know!"

"You know, Marquito. You know the story."

"Sensitive topic, or want to talk about it?"

"Meh, I don't even care anymore." Amy replied.

"If you don't care anymore, why do you get so annoyed when we talk about it?"

Amy remained quiet for a second.

"How was your relationship with him before everything happened?"

"Crap!" Amy replied quickly.

"Then why not see the situation as a relief? At least the guy got out of your life. If everything was already bad, right?"

"That's not the point, Marquito!"

"What is the point?"

"Humiliation. Do you know how humiliating it is to have to compete against a person who everyone knows was sleeping with your boyfriend? How people look at you? Knowing they are judging you?"

"And do you care about what other people think?"

"It's hard not to care when people dig deep into your personal life. This is personal, it should be personal, not brought into your professional environment. People do not have the right to judge you for that. People don't even know the full story to judge."

My phone beside me vibrated loudly. I took it and checked quickly.

"Everything all right?" Amy asked.

"Yeah. It's just my mom sending me good luck and asking about helping her at the grocery store when I get back."

"Mr. Marcus, do you still live with your mother?" Amy laughed out loud.

I felt a little embarrassed to confirm that.

"Speaking of humiliation, huh?" I said.

Amy continued to laugh. I tried to explain myself.

"My family had problems a couple of years ago. Anyway, finances were not good, my father..."

"Marquito." Amy interrupted me putting her hand on the back of my neck. "I know about your father. There's no reason to feel ashamed."

Silence for a few seconds.

"I'll make you a promise. Give me about three months and you can visit me at my own place in Orlando. Deal?"

"Deal!"

Another Kiss. We finished our dinner, put the dishes in the sink, and went to bed.

###

SUNDAY

Sunday morning, we managed to wake up at the right time. Amy, me, Arrow, and X spent the night together in my RV.

Early morning and the arena were already on fire. Completely packed with the crowd cheering, White Stripes on the speakers.

The semi-final course surprisingly was not that complicated, but it had a trap that handlers would have to be careful about. With two tunnels under the A Frame, the approach to the obstacle could get hidden depending on the angle the dog was coming from, and it would cause eliminations, for sure.

The first handlers began to enter the track and the first victims began to appear. Mario & Rex were the first ones. Clearly inattentive, Mario paid no attention to Rex's direction and the dog ended up inside the wrong tunnel. Elimination!

Mario returned to his chair, next to mine. But it looked like he was not too disappointed with the result.

"Sorry, man!" I said to him.

"It's all right. At least I'm going home early." Mario replied.

Natasha Zucker from San Diego, a handler who for some time had not been able to do well in the league, decided to appear for the West Coast fans, and with a brilliant handling put her name in first place temporarily.

Sany entered the track for his participation in the semifinals looking for a place in the finals. Maximus was extremely comfortable on that surface. The artificial grass was the same surface Sany used to train Maximus at his training center, and it was clear that they were both wonderfully confident. Perfect contact zones, precise jumps, and tight curves. Sany approached the judge's trap and for a second was careless! It was visible when Maximus looked down the tunnel and committed to the wrong obstacle, but Sany screamed "MAX!", and Maximus dodged the wrong obstacle. With his tail Maximus touched the tunnel, clearly an elimination, everyone saw, except the judge who did not stop Sany's run, and did not eliminate him. It was so clear that the crowd booed the non-elimination. Sany managed to finish his run in second position, behind Natasha Zucker.

Amy on the track! Boos! Lots of boos! Clearly Lisa's main rival would not get a warm reception again. But Amy did not blink. She did not let herself be affected by the fans, showing how a champion should behave, finished without penalties and with the temporary first position to the fans' disappointment.

I went on track right after Amy. Again, I was expecting more boos, but the crowd did not even pay attention to me, they were still thinking about Amy's exceptional run seconds before.

Arrow on the mark! "OK"! I released her.

Our Plant City training center had always been natural grass, but I saw that as an advantage. Arrow clearly had a much easier time finding grip on artificial turf than on natural grass and that was an advantage for us. We were fast and the trap the judge set did not bother Arrow who was trained always to look for the A FRAME after my command "UP", ignoring any other obstacles around us, including tunnels.

Even so, it was impossible to beat Amy's time. We finished less than two tenths of a second behind her.

To finish the semis, Lisa came on the track. To the delight of the crowd waving pom-poms with Lisa's name. Serious as ever, Lisa put Fire at the starting mark and began her run. I had never run with a crowd that size on my side before, so I could only imagine the motivation Lisa could feel and the vibe pushing her, because her run was perfect. More than perfect. Lisa put 1.5 seconds on Amy to close the semi-finals in first place.

FINALISTS

Lisa & Fire
Amy & X
Marcus & Arrow
Natasha & Sparky
Sany & Maximus

###

As the judge prepared the final course, organizers tossed T-shirts and goodies to the cheering crowd, I looked at Amy in the background, crouched on the ground petting X. A moment between handler and dog that I did not want to interrupt. It was time to concentrate on the final.

The final course was difficult. The judge had left the "best" for last because there were multiple potential points for elimination in that course. Difficult angles that would make the dog's reaction time extremely important.

When a judge approaches the jumps using the minimum distance allowed between obstacles, about four meters, it makes the dog's reaction time shorter. The dog has less room to get out of one obstacle and prepare for the next. Good reflexes would be important.

Sany was the first to enter the track for the finals. People could say anything about Sany's behavior, but nobody could say a thing about his quality as a handler, especially on such complex courses. He managed to get some applause from the opposing fans with a clean and precise handling. The time had not been so good, Sany had to help Maximus through a complex sequence of jumps and slalom, wasting a bit of time. But they had finished without penalties.

Natasha & Sparky came to the track for their first season finals, and unlike Sany & Maximus they did not show as much skill. The team ended up eliminated around obstacle eleven and had to leave the track.

We were next. We entered the track amidst a few cheers from the crowd. I already knew that what the public was really waiting for was the battle that would come later between Lisa and Amy.

Arrow on the initial mark. I walked away from her.

"OK!" I released her.

From a distance I could see her claws digging into the artificial grass and bits of material flying backwards. All Power! Maximum power! 1-2-3-4, the first sequence was fast with OOHHHHHs coming from the crowd. Arrow dove into the first tunnel with so much strength that the sandbags behind the obstacle moved away. Seesaw, BANG! on the ground. Complex jump sequences were never a problem for Arrow who was ok running in small spaces, so she easily passed those challenges prepared by the judge. Last jump and... DONE! Provisional first place with Amy and Lisa yet to get on track.

Amy on track. Do I need to say? Boos! Shouts! Amy placed X at the starting mark and walked away. "LET'S RESPECT THE COMPETITORS" but nothing said would quiet the crowd for even a second. Amy was unfazed. She started her run and like a true champion passed each obstacle, silencing the crowd. With perfect contact zones, extremely fast slalom, and X drooling around the track, she finished her run beating my time without penalties and taking the temporary first position. Quiet in the crowd with some applause in the background.

Last handler, Lisa. Under shouts of motivation and mantras of "Lisa, Lisa, Lisa" the world champion and two-time national champion was able to do the impossible, knocking down Amy's time and winning under a crazed crowd. Lisa had won the round in Las Vegas. The championship was open and with six rounds to go, it was still impossible to predict who would be the champion of the season.

RESULTS ROUND 4 LAS VEGAS

1. Lisa & Fire
2. Amy & X
3. Marcus & Arrow
4. Sany & Maximus
5. Natasha & Sparky

RANKING AFTER ROUND 4 LAS VEGAS

1. Sany & Maximus = 70 pts
2. Marcus & Arrow = 67 pts
3. Lisa & Fire = 58 pts
4. Amy & X = 55 pts
5. Joe & Jungle = 22 pts
6. Polly & Panda = 20 pts
7. Mario & Rex = 18 pts
8. Natasha & Sparky = 10 pts

18

BIRTHDAY

June 2007 I was back in Orlando after facing the craziest crowd I had ever seen in a dog agility competition. Las Vegas was just the most outrageous place.

I took a few days to stay at home with my family.

Things had changed a lot at my house. The money I was bringing in from competitions had changed our lives. We still had some difficulties but my mother no longer had to work so many hours in the grocery store.

That month was my brother's birthday and my mother and I had prepared a party for him. Nothing super fancy but we managed to call some friends and have a barbecue at home. My mother had baked a cake, and everything went very well.

Lots of laughs, people having a lot of fun and of course making my brother feel embarrassed with everyone singing "Happy Birthday To You", while wearing little pointed hats.

That night after everyone left, I decided to give my present to my brother. I went to the garage and brought out a giant gift-wrapped box that I had hidden all day.

"For you, Ed! Happy Birthday!", I said dragging the giant box into the living room.

"Marquito, knowing you the way I do, I think this is just a giant box and inside there's only a little package." Ed said.

"There's only one way to find out."

My mother came into the living room and sat on the sofa. Arrow was there too. But after so many people at the house all day, she just wanted to lie in her little bed on the floor.

My brother started to unwrap the giant box.

"What the hell?" he said.

He continued to open the box faster and faster, stopping suddenly and taking two steps back staring it for a few seconds.

"What's wrong? Did I get it right?", I asked smiling.

It was the coveted aluminum alloy bike he'd always wanted. I never understood anything about bikes but I knew that one was the one he really wanted.

His face went from a normal color to pale white and back to pink.

"I do not know what to say!"

"No need to say anything."

Edward hugged me tightly.

"It's ok! It's ok! If you don't like it, I'll take it back."

"Thanks man! Thank you very much!", he spoke.

My mom was sitting to the side, smiling. She got up and went back to the kitchen.

"Let me go help because there's a lot to clean after this party."

"I'm not going to build this thing." I said pointing to the box. "You take care of that!"

"Leave it to me." said my brother.

I left the living room and followed my mother into the kitchen.

"Hey mom! Can I talk to you?"

My mom was at the sink putting dishes and pans into the dishwasher.

"Sure!" she answered. "What's up?"

"I was thinking. I don't know. I was thinking..."

"What is going on? Just say it!"

"I was thinking about looking for a place for myself. You know...a place that's just mine, my first house..."

After I started speaking, I realized I was telling my mom I was going to leave the house. My mother had already lost her husband, to jail almost three years before, and now her son would leave? What was I doing?

"But mom, I just want you to know that I'll continue helping here at home..."

My mom stopped what she was doing and walked towards me, looking me in the eyes. My God, what did I do? I didn't want to hurt her. Slowly she approached me, placed her hands on the sides of my face and kissed me on the forehead.

"Nothing makes me happier than seeing you leaving the nest and creating your own life. If you need any help in your new home you can count on me."

I didn't know what to say. I just hugged her. And there we hugged for a long time while I listened to the noises coming from the living room, where my brother was starting the process of assembling his new bike.

###

In Plant City, at the training center, I was sitting in one of the chairs in the office waiting to start our training. On my cellphone I read the latest article on the National League website about the championship.

Leo entered the office.

"Hey Leo! Look what they wrote on the League's website yesterday."

Holding my cellphone, I started reading the article.

"The National League this year started with a highly competitive level. While everyone was expecting another isolated fight between Amy Arnold and Lisa Potoviski, last season champion and runner-up, both competitors only find themselves in third and fourth position for now. Sany Bastos seems to have been reborn this year, maintaining the championship lead…blah, blah, blah. But the big highlight is the newcomer Marcus Machado who in just his first season is the current second place, and maybe, in the running for the national title. With four rounds completed so far, we have four different winners, the highest level of competition ever seen in the league's history."

I looked at Leo who sat in his chair listening.

"How cool is that?" I looked at Leo smiling.

Leo had his head down and was frowning.

"What's up?" I asked.

"Marquito, I need to talk to you about something."

Leo looked worried.

"What's up, man? You are scaring me."

"You know I don't get involved in your personal life. That is your problem. My job here is to try my best to prepare you for the League. But I need to talk to you about this thing between you and Amy."

I took a deep breath.

"Okay. What's the problem?"

"Do you really think getting involved with her is a good idea?"

"And why wouldn't it be? She's cool, we have fun, she's beautiful, smart..."

"She's a competitor!" Leo interrupted, rising his tone of voice.

"And?"

"She's a competitor, Marquito! She will do everything she can to win the title. Even running over you, even destroying you if necessary. You are going to get hurt!"

Leo, continued.

"What do you think will happen if the championship continues as it is, and you both go to the last round fighting for the title? Do you think she will play easy because she's sleeping with you? What do you think will happen when the company that pays you, thinks, even if is not true, that you might be going easy on her to help her?"

"I would never do that."

"Explain that to the company that pays you! You are sleeping with the enemy. There's zero possibility of that kind of relationship working. It's a time bomb. And it will explode sooner or later in your face. Believe me."

Silence for a few seconds.

"You have the biggest opportunity of your life. You have a nice company paying you to compete in the most desired championship in the country. There's a line of people waiting for a spot like yours. Do you really want to lose everything? Do you really want to take that risk?"

"I don't see why you are concerned. I don't see anything like that happening.", I replied.

Yes, Leo had raised an important point. The company could misunderstand everything. A simple suspicion that I could be helping Amy in some way, and that would be the end of me.

"I really hope!" Leo said. "Let's practice."

19

LOS ANGELES, CALIFORNIA
ROUND 5 NATIONAL LEAGUE
JUNE 2007

We were approaching mid-season. Another stop on the West Coast, in Lisa's territory. The fifth round would take place at the Los Angeles Convention Center, right next to the Staples Center. Beautiful place and very well organized. Due to the madness and lack of physical space for RVs within the city of Los Angeles, the teams placed their competitors inside a hotel near the arena. The chosen one was the Hotel Figueroa, about two blocks from the Convention Center.

Competitors were spread over two floors of the hotel, along with organizers, judges, and team representatives. The entire hotel was practically taken over by people who were working on the event.

From LAX to the hotel, approximately 16 miles, it took us almost an hour due to the horrible traffic in the city. Leo couldn't stay in the same hotel because technically, reservations were only made for those working in the competition. The coaches were at a hotel across the street.

Paula walked me into the hotel after we parked the car at the valet. We entered the elevator and walked to room 338 where she opened the door and Arrow and I entered.

"OK!" Paula said. "There's food in the fridge, microwave, and a small kitchen. You can have dinner and lunch at the hotel, which is already covered."

"Thank you, Paula."

"You're welcome."

I was already closing the door but clearly she wanted to say something else because she just stayed there holding the door.

"Marcus, I need to talk to you for a second."

"OK."

"It's kind of known by everyone that you and Amy are seeing each other, if we can put it that way."

"Oh no!". I thought. "Here we go".

"I just wanted you to know that the company does not interfere in the personal affairs of its competitors. We are only concerned about a possible conflict of interest. Do you understand me?"

"Yes, I understand. I just want you to know that nothing will affect my performance."

"It's good to hear that. I think this is a good opportunity for you to prove to us how professional you can be. OK?"

"OK, I understand."

"Good. I'll let you rest now. See you tomorrow."

Paula turned away and closed the door behind her.

###

FRIDAY

We arrived at the arena Friday morning for the briefing.

Once again Sany entered the room overflowing with arrogance. "FOLLOW THE LEADER!" he said, again, as had happened in Las Vegas. Lisa also entered the room. "GOOD MORNING!". Lisa was much more comfortable after her big win in Vegas, her first of the season.

Mario as usual sat beside me.

"Good flight?" asked Mario.

"Yes, flight was good, but this time difference is killing me." I said.

Amy entered the room. She looked at me and shot me a wink. I smiled back.

"You know you're sleeping with the enemy, don't you?" asked Mario.

"You know what, you're the second person to say that to me."

"Brother, watch out!"

###

Later that day on the track for surface adaptation and training, things looked promising. The same surface we had seen in Las Vegas. Artificial grass, perfect alignment, nothing too fluffy, nothing too hard.

Around the track, grandstands obviously empty. I wondered if we would have the madness and Lisa fan club back.

Training with Arrow was excellent. The surface was perfect and the grip exceptionally good. No doubt that there would be a lot of speed from the dogs that were already comfortable with the grip on that track. We did not know yet if the courses would encourage the speed that all handlers were expecting at that moment.

###

Back at the hotel, and after several text messages between us during the day, Amy arrived at my room with a bottle of wine in one hand and a packet of spaghetti in the other. X was with her.

"It's time for me to show you how to make spaghetti." she said smiling.

We both laugh.

Later that night, eating our traditional "competition dish", we chatted at the table.

"You know, I need to tell you something." I said.

"What?"

"I'm a little worried about people talking about us."

"Why?" Amy asked.

I took a deep breath.

"Well, my team PR came to talk to me, and it seems they are not happy. Something about conflict of interest."

"Marquito, I'll tell you something. The only way to not allow them to use anything against you is to delivery good results. You are the current second place in the championship, and have already won your first round in your rookie year. With those kinds of results, they won't be worried about who is sleeping in your bed. Deliver results and that's it."

"I know, but that means beating you."

I looked Amy from the bottom up as she chewed another mouthful of spaghetti.

"You can try." She said smiling.

I smiled back.

"But not in Charlotte!" she said pointing her finger at

me. "If you beat me in my house, I'll kill you while you're sleeping."

Laughs.

###

SATURDAY

The arena was packed! More craziness and screams of "LISA LISA LISA!". We were definitely still in Lisa's territory. The Los Angeles round marked the end of the first half of the season, and Lisa knew she needed to win at home to stay alive.

In fact, the fight was so close that Amy, in third place, also knew she had to win to stay in the season. Sany was the leader and was enjoying holding that position. But me? Why just dream of a second victory in my rookie year, why not dream about fighting for the title.

Loud music from the speakers. Hip Hop in Los Angeles style had people dancing in the stands.

"Ladies and gentlemen, welcome to Round 4 of the National Dog Agility League!", announced the speakers.

A huge screen at the top would show the results in real time with images of the competitors, their city, and scores.

Even with the fans not in our favor, it was impossible not to be excited by the energy coming from the stands. What a party!

"Pretty cool, huh?" Sany approached me on the side of the track.

"Yeah, pretty cool."

The walking course was open, and all competitors entered to check what the judge had prepared for the first Qualifier of the day. But it wasn't a good first impression.

The course for the first Qualifier was horrible, and that opinion was not just mine but unanimous among all competitors. Short spaces between obstacles and nothing flow.

A course called "flow" is a course that offers challenges with low-speed points and tricky exercises with substantial risk of elimination, however, it gives fluidity so that the dogs can run, develop speed and recover between obstacles to prepare for what comes next. And the first Qualifier had nothing like that. The judge had used minimal spacing between all obstacles and there was no straight or flowing lines along the entire course. Even with the surface offering a good grip for the dogs, we certainly wouldn't see a lot of speed. Also, no doubt we would see a lot of bars on the ground.

It was easy to see the worry on faces at that moment. Lisa, even though she looked calm, knew that kind of course didn't help her at all. But she was not alone. All handlers with faster dogs would suffer a lot. Including Sany, Amy, and myself.

"My kind of course." Said Mario passing by my side.

Completely understandable why Mario was happy. With an 8-year-old dog who was slower, a course like that would balance things a little bit in his favor.

When the first handler hit the track, everyone's fear was justified. Of the first five on the track, none managed to finish without receiving at least one penalty. Three of them had knocked down bars. The dogs were struggling to make the turns and suffering with the short spaces between obstacles.

It was only with Mario on the track that the first no penalty run took place. Applause from the crowd that made Mario leave the track with a smile plastered on his face.

Polly was another one who finished her run without penalties, beating Mario's time to the delight of the fans who always enjoyed watching the little mix breed on the track.

Caitlyn Parnecki from Denver was the first on the track with a truly fast dog, and proved to everyone that it was possible to win on that course being fast. Caitlyn's dog, Target, was famous for being in movies and TV shows. Even though they were not a competitive team it seemed ironic to see them doing so well in Los Angeles, the land of the film studios.

It was time for the top four to hit the track. Following the current ranking order would enter Amy, Lisa, myself, and Sany.

"On track Amy & X!" announced the speakers.

I was expecting huge boos like in Vegas, but no. Amy took to the track with 90% of the crowd quiet and some applause in the background.

"No booing?" I said in a low voice.

"The people here are a little more polite" said Mario beside me.

"Seriously?"

"Las Vegas and Charlotte, you will see."

Amy started her run under a quiet crowd and her strategy was clear: CONTROL! She was not pushing X at full speed, but balancing her handling, finishing her run in first place with no penalties.

Lisa on track. Screams echoing in the arena. "Lisa, Lisa, Lisa" screamed the crowd. More cheering. Lisa entered the track and repeated Amy's strategy, balancing her handling masterfully and finishing her run 0.3 seconds faster than her rival.

My turn. With the two more experienced competitors balancing the handling and using a much less aggressive approach, I decided I would try something more aggressive to jump ahead in the Qualifiers. I pushed Arrow for speed! But the lack of space between obstacles did not help us. A noise sounded in the arena as Arrow tripped over one of the jumps, dropping the bar. When I didn't think it could get any worse, another wrong jump and a bar on the ground. We ended our run with two penalties.

I left the track and went straight to the side where Leo was waiting.

"What was that?" asked Leo annoyed.

"I decided to be a little more aggressive, you know! I wanted to finish ahead."

Leo was irritated.

"Did you really decide to risk that way in the first Qualifier on a course like this? Do you want to stay out of the semis? This run was just to guarantee a place for tomorrow."

In the distance we saw Sany finishing his run, also using a non-risky handling. I felt like an idiot.

"We have to take it easy now." said Leo. "We have one more round to qualify for tomorrow."

"I know."

"Use your head, Marquito! Qualifier 1, easy! Let's see what kind of course that judge will prepare for Qualifier 2."

Leo was right. What did I have to prove by winning

Qualifier 1 on a horrible course like this? At the end of the first qualifier we were eighth. Lisa, Amy, and Sany led the pack.

In Qualifier 2 the course was better. Still with short spaces between obstacles, but not as bad as the first.

The big problem was the angle of entry to the dog walk. Turning 90 degrees from the jump before the dog walk, it was easy for a dog to climb the obstacle with a bad approach angle, which made that point of the track dangerous.

Everybody complained. Sany, Amy, Lisa, Mario and even Polly and Caitlyn were worried. A little meeting between handlers was established as we walked the course at that point between the jump and the dog walk.

The judge ignored the complaints and things would go south at any moment.

A few minutes before hitting the track, with the music blaring and the crowd cheering as T-shirts were tossed by organizers, handlers were brainstorming ways to get past that dangerous spot.

"Someone is going to get hurt!" said Amy.

"I don't know what some judges are thinking." Mario replied.

Sany was on the side too, but quiet. Fixed looking at that point on the track, it was clear that he was thinking about how to get through it without any major risks.

The Qualifier 2 started. The first dogs suffered with the track prepared by the judge. Several dogs climbed the dog walk at a completely wrong angle, causing frightening moments of dogs slipping from the highest part of the obstacle. Many dogs approached at such a wrong angle that they completely ignored the obstacle, backing away, not climbing, and being penalized with refusals.

Several times "OHHHHHs" came from the crowd gasping as the dogs almost fell from the top of the dog walk. But for us competitors, we knew that something wasn't right, and it was dangerous.

That's when our biggest fear came true. Mario & Rex were on track. Rex made an enormous effort not to refuse the dog walk and climbed the obstacle completely twisted. He tried to balance but fell. Mario attempted to grab his partner in mid-air, but it was not possible. Rex fell from the highest point of the dog walk, head down, crashing violently into the ground.

A terrifying silence hung over the arena. The competitors outside knew that such an accident could severely hurt a dog, and we were also apprehensive.

In the middle of the track, Mario bent down and picked up Rex on his lap who was apparently fine. He put him back on the ground and after a few shakes of his head Rex walked away normally as if nothing had happened, to everyone's relief.

Even from a distance, we could see the judge asking Mario if Rex was okay. Mario just stared at the judge and put a finger on his face. "Someone's going to get hurt around here and it's going to be your fault," Mario later told me he'd told the judge.

With a standing ovation, Mario & Rex walked off the track, eliminated, but Rex was fine.

"Is he ok?" I asked quickly as Mario passed us.

"Yes." Mario replied breathlessly.

From then on, handlers began to lead the dogs more

cautiously, using extreme care when passing through that treacherous point on the track. And the judge did nothing to change the course, exposing other dogs to the same danger.

I got on track knowing I would have to do well. After my horrible first Qualifier I knew there was a huge risk of being out of the Semi Finals. But at the same time, we needed to be careful on that perilous course.

"STAY!" I put Arrow in the initial mark.

I moved about five meters away and released her. The good grip of the track made Arrow use full strength and seek full speed. The track wasn't as tight as the first qualifier so I was able to let her go and let her run without major worries, allowing her to use her natural fluidity. Arriving close to the risky point of the track I had an idea on how to deal with the bad entry angle. I was running two obstacles in front of Arrow and when I approached the jump I turned to her and with both hands extended I gave the command "STAY". Arrow, not understanding anything probably thought: " What the heck is this guy doing, asking me to stay in the middle of my run?". Immediately and violently Arrow slowed down, skidding on the artificial turf. It was enough to reduce her speed and help me to angle her to the dog walk! PERFECT! IT WORKED! We finished the course without penalties and with the best time.

Our unique handling caused applause from the stands and opened the eyes of the other handlers who followed.

Polly did a similar thing with Panda, which also worked. Caitlyn copied the same move. Worked.

In the TOP 3 Sany didn't even try to hide copying my move

using the STAY command. It also worked. Amy came after and almost "parked" X in the middle of the track before the dangerous point with a command "DOWN". And Lisa also copied the move but using the "WAIT" command. Everyone had passed to the semi finals. With Lisa almost unbeatable in first, Amy in second, I was third, and Sany fourth. Followed further by Polly and Caitlyn. Mario was out of the semis once more.

###

Earlier that evening, Amy and I were having dinner in my hotel room. Amy was quiet.

"Is everything all right?" I asked.

"Yeah. Just thinking about the runs tomorrow. I need to beat Lisa. If she wins here, things will get complicated."

"Calm down, it's round five. It's only halfway through the season."

Silence, Amy didn't respond. I persisted.

"You don't need to be worried. I will be the one winning tomorrow." I joked trying to get a laugh from Amy.

Amy looked up and answered after a long silence.

"Will you be mad at me if I sleep in my room tonight?" She asked.

"Oh, no. Of course not. Are you feeling, ok? Anything I can do?"

"No, I just need to focus for tomorrow."

Amy got up and grabbed the dishes taking them to the sink of the small kitchen in the hotel room. She called X and leashed him.

"I'll see you tomorrow, okay?"

"Are you sure everything's okay?" I asked again.

Amy walked towards me and gave me a kiss.

"Everything is fine."

Then she walked to the door and left.

###

SUNDAY

Beautiful sunny morning outside the arena. Tons of excitement from the crowded. Music, people singing and dancing in the stands.

The most important news was a memo released at seven in the morning, stating that the judge was replaced due to personal problems. Bullshit! After a dog nearly breaking its neck during the Qualifers, it was clear the reason for the judge's replacement.

The new judge, brought in the last minute, was the same one that had judged the round in Las Vegas. And that made all the handlers very happy. A track with good grip associated with a judge who likes to set up courses with more space and more flowing, there was no doubt that Sunday's show was going to be much more interesting than Saturday's.

###

SEMI-FINALS

Probably trying to change the competitors' spirits, the new judge prepared a course for the semi-final with a lot of straight lines. A lot of running is what could be expected.

The fastest dogs had a shocking advantage on courses like this. That meant serious problems for slower dogs like Panda. There was no way to compete against the mighty Border Collies on such an open course. The difference in speed was unimaginable. While dogs like X, Fire, Maximus, and Arrow ended their run in the 25 seconds, Panda was behind more than two seconds, running at 27 seconds.

At the end of the semi-finals, Lisa was unbeatable amid a beautiful party coming from the stands. Amy and I were head to head in second and third, followed by Sany and Caitlyn, qualifying for finals for the first time that year.

FINALISTS

1. Lisa & Fire
2. Amy & X
3. Marcus & Arrow
4. Sany & Maximus
5. Caitlyn & Target

###
FINAL

Speed was the word to describe what the judge had prepared in the final course. But the challenges were there. The straights lines were followed by jumps with difficult angles, and with two tunnels close to each other creating a trap for the dogs. An easy course to get an elimination. Two side-by-side tunnels followed by a 180 degree slalom entry, forcing the dogs to use good flexibility to enter correctly and not commit refusals.

Caitlyn was the first one on the track and did a good job even though she was penalized with a refusal when trying to help Target exactly at that difficult Slalom's entry.

Sany came after. The current championship leader decided

to wave to the public while entering the track and it was not well received. Lisa's massive crowd in Los Angeles understood that Sany was mocking them, and heavy boos followed. Sany smirked as he walked to the starting mark with Maximus. Nobody questions the speed and how well trained Maximus is. But Sany would once again pay for his arrogance. He hesitated to give the command to Maximus who dove into the wrong tunnel. Sany was out, eliminated.

The crowd cheered and Sany had to take the walk of shame, stopping his run, and walking out with Maximus. He got out and walked straight to the exit of the arena, head down.

We were next! We had won in Atlanta and it was time for a second victory. When I entered, I was neither booed nor cheered by the crowd. Just got some shy applause from afar. Arrow on the starting mark. I lifted my arm and placed her under the command "STAY". I walked away. "OK!" I released Arrow!

What a beautiful thing to see! Digging her claws into the ground and throwing herself forward, Arrow easily overcame the first three jumps angling gracefully to the seesaw that exploded on the ground. More obstacles, 5-6-7-8. A Frame, perfect with Arrow taking her body off the ground for several seconds and flying over the board. Dog walk, perfect, fast enough to make the obstacle sway as if an earthquake shook everything around it. Sequence of tunnels ahead, dangerous point, I had to be careful. I looked out of the corner of my eye and noticed that Arrow had started to swerve and head for the wrong tunnel. "ARROW!!!". My scream thundered in the arena and brought a "OOHHHHH" out of the crowd. I was saved from certain elimination but lost a little bit of time. Last obstacles!

"I am going to win, for sure" I whispered to myself.

My second victory! It had to be now! BANG!!! I couldn't believe what had happened. Arrow touched the bar on the last jump and knocked it down! At the last jump, NO! I fell to my knees. A penalty. The fans realized how good that run was. They stood up and gave me a standing ovation. What a run! It was perfect and that penalty at the last jump was like a hot knife inside my heart.

The crowd would not remain excited for long because Amy was next and what was expected happened. Boos! Lots of boos! The polite crowd was not there anymore.

Amy raised her head and began her run, pushing X as much as she could. It was obvious she wasn't saving anything. I knew how she wanted to beat Lisa in her house. Imagine the repercussions. It was visible. Amy used a different handling than mine, running behind the tunnels to avoid the risk of elimination. She finished her run but couldn't be faster than me. But with the penalty, we were behind, and Amy was first.

Lisa on the track. Last handler on track in the finals. Standing cheering "Lisa Lisa Lisa!" were the screams that didn't stop! She put Fire on the starting mark and started her run being motivated by around 1200 people in the stands. An exquisite sight to behold, I admit. Even with my heart broken, at that moment I was hoping Lisa would make a mistake. But no! Lisa was perfect and was faster than Amy, winning her second consecutive round of the season, after Las Vegas.

The crowd almost invaded the track. Lisa hugged Fire and

ran to the crowd in greeting. A beautiful scene, but there was no doubt that my heart was broken at that moment. Both Lisa and Amy weren't any faster than Arrow and me, but due to my penalty, that damn bar on the last jump, we'd ended up third. My second win was so close, but I let it escape.

RESULTS ROUND 5 LOS ANGELES

1. Lisa & Fire
2. Amy & X
3. Marcus & Arrow
4. Caitlyn & Target
5. Sany & Maximus

RANKING AFTER ROUND 5 LOS ANGELES

1. Lisa & Fire = 83 pts
2. Marcus & Arrow = 82 pts
3. Sany & Maximus = 80 pts
4. Amy & X = 73 pts
5. Joe & Jungle = 22 pts
6. Polly & Panda = 20 pts
7. Mario & Rex = 18 pts
8. Caitlyn & Target = 12 pts
9. Natasha & Sparky = 10 pts

###

I didn't even see Amy leave the arena, she had simply disappeared and gone back to the hotel.

Later that night, I decided to knock on Amy's bedroom door. She answered with a defeated expression on her face.

"Hey!" said Amy.

"Hey! Are you okay?", I asked.

"Meh, I've been better."

"You had an amazing run today." I was trying to encourage her.

"No, you did, Marquito. You should have been the winner today."

"Yeah, that last bar will give me nightmares for a few weeks. Damn bar!"

Amy laughed shyly, I continued.

"You know, there are still five rounds to go. Anything can happen."

"I'm ten points behind her. I'm only fourth place." said Amy discouraged.

"Ten points is nothing. You can make it up in one round."

"We will see! The next round is closer to my home. I hope I don't disappoint my fans."

"I'm sure you won't."

Silence for a few moments. I was still at her bedroom door.

"Do you want to come to my room and have dinner with me?" I asked.

"Sorry, Marquito. I need to rest. I need to think about a few things."

"I get it. I get it. So, have a good night and a good flight back home."

"Thanks. I am sorry."

"No reason to be sorry. I totally understand."

"OK. Bye!"
"Have a good night."
Amy gently closed the door, and I went back to my room.

20

NEW HOUSE

July 2007, two weeks after I came home from Los Angeles I couldn't wait to show my family my first home. Something just mine.

I opened the door so my mom and brother could enter. There was no furniture yet, and it needed cleaning, but I was extremely excited to show off my new place.

"Come in! Come in!" I said excited after opening the door inviting them to enter.

My first house was not luxurious, on the contrary. It was a small house on the outskirts of Clermont, south of Orlando. Living room, kitchen, one bathroom and one bedroom, with a fenced grassy yard.

"This is the living room." I kept showing them everything, excited. "Here on this wall will be where I will put the shelves for my medals and trophies."

Both my mother and my brother followed each other looking around.

The house wasn't that new, and I could rent something better, but I didn't want to get myself in trouble, after all,

I didn't even have a confirmed contract for the next season. What if the team decides not to renew my contract?

"This is the kitchen." I continued to show the house. "It has a fridge, microwave, dishwasher. It's a little old but it works fine."

I couldn't hide a small leak in the kitchen's ceiling that was quickly noticed by my mother. Even so, the two remained silent.

The rent fit my budget and I could continue helping my mom at her house. I continued walking through the kitchen towards the backyard. I opened the sliding glass door to the yard.

"And this is where Arrow will have fun!"

The backyard wasn't that big, but it was possible to put some jumps and even a A frame or a dog walk for some training during the week.

"I'll change that fence, put in a new one." I pointed to the backyard. "I'm even thinking about putting a grill here. You know, those ones with a coal side and a gas side? Invite friends here to get together."

No reaction from either of them. I was starting to get worried. Being the oldest son, this was the first time my mother had to deal with this situation. A son leaving home. And after everything that had happened to the family just over 3 years ago, I could only imagine what she was feeling. However, I wasn't that young anymore. In 2007 I was 24 years old, it was already past time to leave the nest and create a life of my own.

"And it's not that far from home, you know? Fifteen minutes driving and we are in Windermere."

Pause.

"So..." I said concerned.

My mother approached me getting very close. She stared at me for a few seconds and finally said something.

"Congratulations! Your first home is so much better than my first home years ago."

She gave me a strong hug. My brother also approached.

"If you think you're going to take the PlayStation, forget it."

We laughed.

"No, no. You can keep it. I'll go there from time to time for us to play."

"Oh, good!" my brother said relieved.

After the initial inspection, my mom walked me around the house and started helping me with a list of things we would need. New toilet seat, paper towel rack, new blinds on the windows and of course, a cleaning that would give us a good two days of hard work.

After a few minutes we decided to leave. But before that, my brother and mother had another matter to discuss with me:

"Hey Marquito. We need to talk to you." said my brother with a serious tone of voice.

"Ok. If is about the roof, don't worry, I'll fix it too. I know there's a leak there..."

"No! No!" interrupted my brother. "No, it's not that. It's about dad."

Long pause. My expression completely changed.

"What about him?" I asked.

"Marquito." my mother said. "You need to go to see him."

"Mom, this conversation again? We've talked about this before."

"Son, your father asks about you every time we visit him. He is your father. He made a mistake, and you haven't seen him in over three years."

"It is not my fault!" I replied. "He did those things, not me!"

"Marcus!" `my mother interrupted sternly! "Pay attention to your mother. I love you and your brother more than anything else in my life. You know that. So, I will ask you. Please, for me! Go visit your father. Please!"

I lowered my head for a few seconds. I did not want to. I didn't know what my reaction would be when I saw him again, especially in a place like that. Just thinking about it, I shivered.

"Did you know he's watching your competitions on TV?" said my brother.

"Serious? There is a TV there?"

"Of course, Marquito!" my mother said. "There's not a day we've talked to him, he doesn't mention you."

I took a deep breath.

"Okay. I'll next month!"

21

CHICAGO, ILLINOIS
ROUND 6 NATIONAL LEAGUE
JULY 2007

HEAT! I never thought I would feel that hot in Chicago. I was ok with the heat. I am from Brazil and living most of my life in Florida, hot weather was never a problem. But that year a hellish heat wave was sweeping across the country, and we were "lucky" to witness "the hottest day in Chicago in 42 years", as the news that morning said.

The round would take place at the Lake County Fairgrounds & Events, a well-equipped arena located about 45-minutes from downtown Chicago. Due to traffic, a little bit more than that. Once again it would take us twice as long to get across town from O'Hare airport.

During the flight I was checking my social media when a message posted by Mario caught my attention. Leo was at my side, and Arrow at my feet.

"Leo, have you seen Mario's post?"

"No, why?"

"Listen to this!" I started reading Mário's last post. "I

would like to communicate to all friends and fans that after this season I will be retiring from the National League. Rex and I really appreciate everyone's support. I feel it's time for us to retire. You'll still see us in local competitions out there, but our National League moment is over. I would like to invite everybody to a big party this weekend at my home in Chicago for the sixth round of the National League"

"It doesn't surprise me." said Leo.

"Really?"

"Yeah, man. His dog is almost nine years old. And he must be under incredible pressure from the team for results. In the league today you, Amy, Lisa, and Sany are the bosses. The other dogs have no way to catch up with you guys. And with a dog that is almost 9 years old, it's even harder to be competitive."

"I feel bad for him. Very nice guy. I hope he's all right."

###

On Thursday when Leo and I arrived in Chicago, before being driven to the Fairgrounds north of town, we went to a downtown restaurant for a meeting with the Planet Canine Team.

Surprisingly, or not, it was a Brazilian restaurant.

"Hey, welcome to Chicago!" Rich met us at the restaurant entrance as we got out of our car.

"Did you pick the restaurant, Rich?" I asked smiling.

"Of course!" Rich always replied with that goofy face. "I thought you would like it too!"

"Yes, of course! I never say no to Brazilian food."

We went in. Leo and I with Arrow on the leash. Seated and

already waiting for us were Paula and Kurt. As soon they saw us Kurt got up and came over to give me a hug!

"Marquito! How's our champion doing?"

"Good, very good! Thanks."

Kurt also greeted Leo, and pet Arrow's head.

We were eating for a few minutes, and after a lot of small talk the real talking started.

"So, Marquito!" Kurt changed the tone of the conversation. "First, I would like to say that we are very satisfied with your performance so far. I'll confess something, I didn't want to hire you. But these two here (pointing to Rich and Paula) convinced me, and I don't regret it."

Weird silence.

"Thanks?!" I replied a little awkwardly.

Kurt continued.

"You are the second placed in the championship so far and we believe that this time we have a real chance to be champions, right?"

I did not answer. Kurt continued.

"So here is the deal." Kurt was leaning in his chair. "You haven't had a victory in five rounds. We really want to see you winning again. Is there anything we can do to further improve our chances? Are you needing something? Any help at home that might help your performance?"

It was a really weird question.

"No, no. Everything is great. You saw that I didn't win in Los Angeles by bad luck, right? That last bar in the last obstacle…"

"Yes, yes, we did. That's why I'm asking. Does your training site need anything else? New obstacles?"

I looked at Leo beside me who remained silent.

"I appreciate it." I replied. "But we have everything we need."

"Right! Right! You know that Paula, here beside me, did some math about chances of being champion and I thought it was interesting to share it with you."

"This is a very even season." Paula began speaking. "And the only handler with two wins so far is Lisa. Whoever wins three rounds has a 76% chance of being champion."

I remained silent. The conversation was very strange. I just wanted to compete, I didn't want to know anything about stats or odds. There's only one statistic in my head, whoever win most rounds will be champion, and that's it. But Paula continued.

"Therefore, we need at least one more victory in the next two rounds. And don't let Lisa win anymore."

"I understand. Well, what I can promise is that I will do my best to win every round in the future.", I said.

"Excellent!" Kurt said with a punch on the table. "We need to start thinking about a contract extension for the next year, right? And we need results for that."

I gave a little smile. That little push for wins would become more common in the second half of the season. I was beginning to see that.

"Well, we'll be there this weekend, rooting for you." Kurt said.

"May I ask you a question?" I asked.

"Yes, of course!" Kurt responded effusively.

"I saw that Mario is leaving the team. In case you renew my contract for next year, who will be my teammate next season?"

Pause, silence. Kurt and Paula looked at each other. Rich dropped his fork and stopped chewing with his mouth full of Brazilian barbecue. Paula replied.

"Marquito, Mario's departure was by mutual agreement. He wasn't fired. As for the future team member, we are still evaluating. We have recommendations and we are looking into all possibilities."

Logically they wouldn't tell me. But I had to try to get some information out. You never know, they might talk. But no. I definitely didn't trust Kurt or Paula. They were typical professionals who were just doing their job. I knew that if I stopped delivering results, they would dump me very quickly. That's how the game works.

###

FRIDAY

I woke up early in my RV on Friday. We went to the briefing with Steve and all the handlers were already there when I arrived. I was the last one to enter the room.

Briefing done, we went down to check the track and to adapt to the surface with the dogs. On the way, Amy greeted me. Reserved, not much talk.

"Hey, how are you?"

"Fine and you? Did you have a good flight?", I asked.

"I drove."

"Seriously? 8, 9 hours driving?"

"About 10.", Amy replied. "It's a good time to think a little bit."

"Well, good luck over the weekend!"

"You, too."

We walked away from each other as we entered the arena. The arena in Chicago was the typical arena I was used to in Florida. Stands for about one thousand people, electronic scoreboard on the ceiling. But what made me happiest was the surface of the track.

Made of red, solid clay, it was pretty much the same used on tracks in Florida, like Arcadia and Palmetto. The same one Arrow was so used to.

Each handler had their own preference for the surface, because each handler trained on a different type. Sany for example always did very well on artificial turf because his training center in Florida was equipped with artificial turf. Our training center in Plant City was outdoors with natural grass so I was happy when the competition took place on natural grass. But both Sany and I were also very used to the clay, because most of the competitions in Florida took place on that kind of surface.

Mario and I went in together to do our training. Mario was clearly different but he was training Rex with the same motivation. In Chicago, his home, there was no doubt that in the next two days with an open arena to the public, people would fill those seats to cheer for Mario.

"Hey, man! Are you all right?", I asked.

"Perfect!" Mario replied breathless.

"Man, I just wanted to tell you that it was an immense pleasure to have you as a teammate."

"Brother, I'm not dying. Just taking a break", Mario replied smiling. "I've been living this life for six years. Since Rex was two years old. I am happy."

I could understand that. Six years of competition that got him one national league title in 2001. The last title the team had achieved. It was clear why the team was pressuring me for the title that year.

Arrow gave me a lot of confidence during training. Very comfortable with the surface, lots of speed, and good grip. Perfect jumps, good contact zones and, as always, a lot of motivation and desire to run.

###
SATURDAY

Arena packed! Once again it was impossible to see any empty seats in the stands. According to the National League website, the competitiveness and unpredictability of who would be champion that year, had increased the number of ticket sales, and the next rounds in Nashville and Charlotte were already sold out. In Charlotte it was easy to imagine why. With Amy fighting for the title, her home round would be crazy.

We entered the track to walk the first Qualifier. The course prepared by the judge was perfect and pleased all competitors. Merging high speed points with straight lines between jumps, and contact obstacles with traps placed at strategic points, the course would require a good level of skill from the handlers without risking the physical integrity of any dog.

The first handlers entered the track and several of them managed to finish their runs without penalties. Times varied a lot between handlers, yet more proof of a well-prepared course that allowed different types of handling from everyone.

Very cheerful crowd when Mario entered the track. That's when the stands trembled amidst applause and hearty cheers for the home competitor. Between shouts of "GO MARIO" and banners with the words "WE WILL MISS YOU", and "CHICAGO LOVES YOU", Mario gave the audience what they wanted, an exceptional run, without penalties and with the best time so far, surpassing Polly, Joe and Caitlyn. Time: 29:32.

It was really cool to see Mario running like that! There was no doubt that the home crowd pushed the handlers to another level. Mario and Lisa were proof of that. When he returned to his chair, beside me, visibly out of breath, he was ecstatic.

"Dude, what a run! What a run! I gave it all!", said Mario panting.

"Brother, your run was beautiful! Congrats!" I said.

"With a crowd like this pushing me, I just wanted to do my best! Only give the best!"

Mario's first place didn't take long to be overtaken. When Amy entered the track with a serious expression, staring at the track, and arranging her hair inside her cap, I knew something special was ahead. Lisa already with two round victories and with Amy only in 4th place, she knew she couldn't let Lisa win anymore, and she would need to have more victories to keep the championship fight going.

Amy put X at the starting mark and without pause started her run. With perfect curves and taking advantage of the good fluidity the course provided, Amy took X to temporary first place, a run without penalties and a time of 28:59.

The fans stood up and applauded Amy's beautiful performance. She celebrated in her own way, a punch in the air!

Sany on track. Sometimes I think that Sany doesn't take competitions very seriously, or he is simply an idiot, because there was Sany coming in once more waving to the crowd, and with a smile on his face, as if nothing there was important.

Sany started his run and after the first four obstacles we could see that something wasn't right. A childish mistake when approaching the slalom and Sany let Maximus escape, resulting in a refusal, one penalty. But the worst was yet to come when at the exit of one of the tunnels, Sany did not sign correctly the next obstacle and Maximus decided to choose on his own where to go, ending inside another tunnel. Wrong obstacle and elimination!

We were next! I can't explain why, but I entered that track full of confidence. That feeling happened every now and then, and it was usually a good sign that I was calm enough to do a good run. It happened in Atlanta when I won the round. But I had to be careful. I had the same feeling in Miami in the finals, when I got knocked out, and in Los Angeles when victory looked certain, but Arrow knocked the bar on the last jump. My God! Two rounds I could have won. I would be in a solid leadership of the League right now. So, I had to be careful. Lesson learned, I hope.

I put Arrow on the start mark. I walked away and... "OK" I released her!

Arrow, very familiar with the clay surface, showed intense confidence throughout our run. And when Arrow shows me confidence, I feel like I can keep pushing for speed. Everything worked out! Time 28:45, beating Amy's time and taking the lead!

Lisa was the last to hit the track in Qualifier 1. Unlike Amy and I, Lisa didn't look as confident as the previous two rounds, in Las Vegas and Los Angeles. Most likely because Fire couldn't find the same speed on that red clay surface. Fire was drifting on his turns, which I thought was pretty weird considering the track's grip was good. But it wasn't just Fire, Lisa was also not well balanced. The team managed to finish the course without penalties but with a slower time. Time: 29:14.

End of the first Qualifier and I was in first, with Amy in second, Lisa in third, and Mario in fourth place to the delight of the crowd. Sany was in bad shape after being eliminated in the 1st Qualifier. He would need to go all or nothing in the 2nd Qualifier or he would be out of the semis.

At the break, while the judge was preparing the course for the second qualifier, Mario was enjoying every second. He took Rex close to the crowd for pictures. He even threw sponsor's T-shirts and free dog food samples to the crowd. Without a doubt, a special day for him.

I approached Leo to talk about the first Qualifier.

"Good run, right?" I asked excited.

"Yes, yes, very good! But it worries me a lot when you push

that hard on the first Qualifier. Remember, the first Qualifier is more for adaptation. Remember what happened in Las Vegas? Let's not make the same mistake."

"I know, I know! But I am confident. Today is our day, today is our day!"

Leo's concern was valid. Getting an elimination in the first Qualifier, just like what happened with Sany, would force the handler to go all or nothing in Qualifier 2. I had been in that situation before. But on the other hand, a strong and fast run in the first Qualifier sends a strong message to the other competitors. "I AM HERE. WATCH OUT FOR ME".

We entered to walk the second Qualifier course, and things had changed a little bit. The judge had a more open course this time, with a few traps and demanding high speed. It could be Sany's salvation and Mario's downfall.

Sany went in ahead of everybody due to his elimination in the first Qualifier. Now, much more serious. Sany did a champion run to recover from the bad first qualifier and lift the crowd with a flawless performance. Time: 25:49.

None of the handlers who came after Sany could beat his time. In fact, Sany had fully recovered from the fiasco in the first Qualifier and had practically guaranteed a spot in the semis. That's when Mario got on the track!

Amidst the applause and cheers coming from a crazed standing crowd, Mario didn't hide that he still had something to show. I won't ever forget his expression running that day, trying to lead Rex on that open and fast course. Mario was unstoppable, by beating Sany's time and temporarily taking the lead in the second Qualifer. Time: 25:41.

Shouts of "Mario! Mario!" echoed through the arena.

Lisa came next and even with a lot of effort and using a different handling to find time on the course, she was visibly struggling to find the right pace in the arena in Chicago. With Lisa once again slipping and nearly hitting the ground, she managed to finish the course with a time of 26:18, behind Mario and Sany.

Amy was next, and there was no doubt that she was committed to winning the round. The serious expression hidden under the low cap, and the heavy steps on her way onto the track, sent the message that Amy wasn't there to play. She ran without penalties, which drew applause from the fans and some other competitors who were on the side of the track. Time: 25:29. Temporary first place.

She passed by us as she walked off the track without so much as a glance. Her expression said it all.

Our time! I went on track with Arrow, the last handler of the day. The first place in the Qualifier 1 had given me a lot of confidence. I was feeling good, relaxed, confident. But at the same time, I couldn't let that confidence get in the way. We started our run and Arrow was on one of her best days all year. Perfect on turns, with inversions so short I had to run even harder to catch up. It wasn't a question of being more conservative at the moment. Arrow was so fast that I just had to keep up with her. And what a sensational run! One of my best of the year. With a time of 25:19 we ended our participation on Saturday leading the two Qualifiers, and classified for the semi-finals alongside Amy, Mario, Sany, Lisa, plus Polly, Joe, Caitlyn and Natasha. Top ten of the day.

###

Outside the arena, as we were walking back to our respective RV's, I saw Amy in front of me.

"Hey, Amy!" I called for her.

She stopped and turned to me. I approached.

"Hey Marquito, congratulations on the Qualifiers today! Arrow is flying, huh?"

"Thanks. She is feeling great today."

Amy smiled.

"Do you want to have dinner with me tonight?" I asked.

"Sorry, Marquito. Today I really can't."

"Really?"

"Yeah, I have dinner with the team. You know, to discuss goals and even my contract for next year. I don't know if you know but my contract expires at the end of the season."

"Oh, yes, I know how it is. Had my lunch with the team on Thursday."

She smiled.

"That kind of meeting." said Amy.

"Yes. Okay. So, see you tomorrow?"

"Sure, see you tomorrow."

Amy turned her back on me quickly and walked back towards her RV.

###

SUNDAY

A quiet and peaceful night inside the RV. I hadn't gone anywhere. I stayed in my hideaway eating my spaghetti and thinking about how things with Amy were always so fickle. Sometimes everything was beautiful, sometimes everything was terrible. I wondered if things changed depending on her results. When she was doing well she treated me well, when she was doing bad she treated me badly. No, she is not like that. She was worried about the team meeting, I thought.

###

I arrived at the arena and the crowd was already there. Like the day before, completely full. The music from the speakers stirred the crowd that sang, danced, and jumped in the stands.

Mario was already there and more excited than ever. As a matter of fact, I had never seen Mario that excited before. Why was he so eager if he knew he wouldn't have a team to compete on next year? Well, maybe retirement and not coming back had taken a giant weight off his shoulders.

"Good morning!" I greeted. "Feeling excited today?"

"Haha! I am! Look at these guys!"

Mario waved to the people in the stands who immediately responded with shouts. I decided to participate and waved too.

"Today we will qualify for the final!" said Mario enthusiastically. "You will see!"

###

SEMI-FINALS

The semi-final course was quite different than Saturday's courses. Clearly the judge decided to complicate the handler's lives on Sunday, a little bit more. It was a flowing course, no doubt, but now a trap with a high risk of elimination at the entrance to the dog walk. The same exercise that had taken my victory in Miami earlier that year, a tunnel under the dog walk. With a tunnel side by side with the dog walk's entrance, it was easy for any dog to get distracted by two clear options to choose, entering the tunnel rather than climbing the dog walk, resulting in elimination.

During the walk, all handlers used the whole time thinking of ways to get through that spot with as little risk as possible. But it was a delicate part of the course, and each handler was going to have to show a high level of control not to let the dog "dive" into that tunnel.

Things did not start well. Right at the start of the semi-finals the first three handlers fell into the judge's trap. Natasha, Caitlyn, and Joe, all eliminated at the same point with their dogs entering the wrong tunnel and completely ignoring the correct way to go, the dog walk.

Polly managed to get past the dangerous spot with cheers coming from the crowd, but wasted so much time that it was virtually impossible to qualify for the finals, unless all the other handlers eliminated, which was unlikely.

Lisa came to the track. The current championship leader had been struggling through all the Qualifiers, and it was not her best weekend in the league. But Lisa seemed to have found her pace during the semi-finals. With high confidence, Lisa and Fire paid no attention to the judge's trap. Fire passed without even looking at the tunnel beside him, clearly due to Lisa's exceptional handling using a 180 degree turn with her body to the opposite side of the tunnel. She beautifully redirected Fire's vision as he climbed the dog walk without blinking, taking the team to first place without penalties and a time of 32:58.

After seeing Lisa's handling, while Sany was getting ready to go on the track, I ran to the side of the track to talk to Leo.

"Man, same exercise from Miami." I said worried.

Sany had started his run.

"Let's see how Sany does that exercise." said Leo.

Like Lisa, and with amazing confidence, Sany led Maximus through the difficult exercise without problem, climbing the dog walk and ignoring the tunnel. Time: 32:44.

"The more you try to help, the worse it will be." said Leo.

"What? What are you talking about?"

"The more you try to help her, and more time you stay there, the worse it will be."

"I still do not get it." I repeated, worried.

Mario entered the track for his run. Even much slower than the other handlers, Mario led Rex masterfully overcoming all obstacles. At the most difficult point of the track, approaching that damn tunnel that had eliminated several handlers, Rex looked and committed himself to the wrong obstacle and the elimination seemed obvious. Cheers from the crowd of "NO!", followed by a desperate scream from Mario. "REX!" shouted Mario preventing his dog from entering the wrong tunnel and saving the day.

Cheers and applause, Mario finished his run with no penalties but a high time of 33:15. It was quite possible that they could qualify for the final. It would be epic!

Amy was getting ready to start her run.

"Did you see how Sany and Lisa did it? Make the jump before the tunnel and run past the dog walk on the side, ignore the tunnel, and she won't even look at it." Said Leo.

Leo was right. Amy was on track and used the same strategy. She sent X through the jump just before the tunnel moving her body in the dog walk direction. X didn't even think about entering the wrong tunnel, climbing the dog walk correctly.

"Understood!" I said to Leo running back to the side of the track to prepare myself.

Amy finished her run beautifully and with the best time of the day. 32:39.

It was our turn! Leading the two Qualifiers on Saturday gave us the chance to go in last, after all the handlers, already knowing what time we had to beat.

I entered the track under cheers from the crowd!

I put Arrow on the start mark and walked away! Silence in the stands. I took a deep breath, straightened my cap out of my eyes. Raised my arm and Arrow lifted her butt off the ground getting ready to run. "OK," I released Arrow.

Arrow had been flying all weekend. The red clay surface was perfect for her. She was feeling extremely comfortable! 1-2-3-4, we passed the first obstacles! Seesaw, Arrow slipped a little sideways with one of her paws coming off the seesaw board, but nothing that compromised our performance. Two tunnels ahead, with a jump between them, smoothly done. Dirt flying from Arrow's paws as she took the turns. I could see her claw marks on the ground.

We were approaching the dangerous point. "Marquito, don't let what happened in Miami happen again", I thought. Jump! Immediately after the jump, I turned my whole body towards the dog walk, running 90 degrees in the opposite direction. "ARROW!" I screamed! Arrow immediately turned, completely ignoring the tunnel, and climbing the dog walk. I could hear the cheers from the crowd, screaming with our run. Three more obstacles ahead, A Frame and...DONE! Time: 32:29. Best time of the day!

Applause from the crowd! Screams! I looked to the side of the track at Leo who sent me the ok gesture.

Not only we were qualified for the final, but by that point we had finished every course of the weekend in first place! That round was mine! It had to be!

FINALISTS
Marcus & Arrow (32:29)
Amy & X (32:39)
Sany & Maximus (32:44)
Lisa & Fire (32:58)
Mario & Rex (33:15)
###
FINAL
Break while the judge prepares the final course. The crowd in the stands was going crazy and the reason was obvious, Mario in the final!

Mario was also enjoying that moment, a lot. Event organizers brought the microphone to him so he could speak to the fans in the stands, thanking everyone for coming and saying he would never qualify for that final without everyone's support. It was a really cool and emotional moment.

We entered the track to walk the last course of the day. No surprises. The track was complex but without high-risk elimination points, which made me even more relaxed. A few jumps with difficult angles, but nothing that any of the five competitors who made it to the final couldn't handle. It really seemed that the champion of that round would be decided on the clock, and not on whoever commits the least penalties.

Mario was the first to hit the track. Under a lot of excited shouts of his name and with a smile plastered on his face, he prepared Rex at the starting mark and walked away.

Whatever the result Mario gets at that moment, would be amazing for him. At worst he would finish in fifth place, and at best, why not a podium.

Mario released Rex and started his run. With a noticeably slower pace than the other dogs, he was doing his homework. The awkward angles of some jumps made old Rex's life a little difficult which ended up resulting in two bars on the ground. The team finished the run with a time of 39:24 with two penalties.

Lisa went on track with her partner Fire. Silence in the stands. Her fans were located more on the west coast and clearly Lisa wasn't having her best weekend, which was good for most of us. At this point, if Lisa wins one more round, the championship could be done.

Lisa had a consistent final. She was far from demonstrating the same speed she showed in the last two rounds but did enough to be faster than Mario. No penalties, and with a time of 38:52, she was up front.

Sany followed. No jokes, no teasing the crowd. Just seriousness on Sany's part now. I really don't understand why sometimes Sany behaves the way he does. When he's serious and paying attention to his run instead of looking for everyone's attention with ridiculous jokes, there's no doubt that he's one of the best handlers in the country.

What Sany did with Maximus in that final in Chicago was worthy of a standing ovation. Precise movements, blind crosses (which is when a handler makes a change of direction without looking at the dog, keeping the dog behind), and a lot of speed, lifted the crowd. Sany jumped into first position with a time of 38:41. Of course, old Sany had to show up when he looked at the crowd pointing to himself and yelling out loud "I AM SO GOOD". Oh, Sany!

Amy on track! If Sany did well Amy once again sent the message that she was there that year to repeat what she did the year before, winning the national title. Up until then no one had shown much skill in handling that course. In one of the moments, Amy made a move with the trunk of her body, which was enough for X to understand the message and seek a jump about ten feet away from him, without Amy needing to say anything. The sequence of slalom, tunnel and A frame was done with unparalleled precision, and they finished the run without penalties destroying the clock and setting 38:29. First position.

Our time! Up until that moment Arrow and I had won every run in that weekend. First place in Qualifier 1, first place in Qualfier 2, first place in the semi-finals. The confidence was there, and we were close to the perfect weekend, when a handler wins all four runs.

I got on track and put Arrow on the starting spot.

"STAY!" I commanded her and walked away.

I looked at Arrow in the distance. Silence in the stands that was broken with my shout: "OK!", releasing Arrow.

Now was the time to prove that I could be champion! First three flawless jumps, followed by a backside jump that Arrow made so perfectly almost touching the jump wing on the right side. Dog walk! Arrow passed so quickly that for a moment the obstacle's tripod that attached to the ground, lifted. Aggressive dive into the tunnel, puffing out the outside of the obstacle. "ARROW, UP!" I commanded. Without blinking Arrow climbed the seesaw sliding on the other side "BANG!", on the ground. Perfect, once again! Sequence slalom, tunnel, A frame rattling the chain that held the opposite sides together. Four more obstacles to the end, cheering crowd! This victory won't escape me! Now it's just...

Screams of "OHHHHH" came from the crowd. I looked to my right side where Arrow should be. "WHERE'S ARROW?" I wondered for a second. I looked back, Arrow was coming out of the tunnel! The wrong tunnel! WHAT? NO? IMPOSSIBLE! Arrow entered the wrong obstacle! I lost focus for a second, got careless! I could not believe it! We were out! My God! Again? The round was supposed to be mine, like in Miami! NO! NO! NO!

I crouched down to hug Arrow.

"I am so sorry!" I said to her down on the floor, three obstacles to the end!

Once again, I let it slip, I couldn't believe it!

RESULTS ROUND 6 CHICAGO

1. Amy & X

2. Sany & Maximus
3. Lisa & Fire
4. Mario & Rex
5. Marcus & Arrow

RANKING AFTER ROUND 6 CHICAGO

1. Lisa & Fire = 98 pts
1. Sany & Maximus = 98 pts
1. Amy & X = 98 pts

4) Marcus & Arrow = 92 pts
5) Mario & Rex = 30 pts
6) Joe & Jungle = 22 pts
7) Polly & Panda = 20 pts
8) Caitlyn & Target = 12 pts
9) Natasha & Sparky = 10 pts

###

That night back in my RV it was hard to swallow the disappointment. I couldn't believe it had happened again. Another victory thrown away. It had happened in Miami with an elimination in the last run, in Los Angeles when we knocked the last bar on the last jump, and now again, an elimination in the final in Chicago after being first the whole weekend.

Lying in the RV seat, I was watching my run on my cellphone and trying to figure out what I had done wrong, when someone knocked the door. I went to see who it was. It was Amy.

"Good evening!" said Amy holding a six pack of Brazilian beer.

"Hey." I replied sullenly.

"Can I come in?" asked Amy.

"Sure!" I gave her space and she entered.

Amy came in and placed the beer on the counter.

"I know you are feeling awful."

"Well, it's not one of the best days. But I will live."

"Brazilian beer?" – Amy asked passing me one of the bottles.

"Where did you find this?"

"Chicago. It was not hard to find a Brazilian place around the city"

We laughed.

"By the way, congratulations on your victory! Looks like you and Lisa are going to fight for the championship again."

"Thank you, but it's too early to celebrate. The first three are tied at 98 points and you're not far behind. I think this fight will go all the way to the last round."

"Maybe." I replied. "Good show for the public, right?"

I walked away and opened one of the cabinets.

"Spaghetti?" - I said chuckling.

"Why not, Marquito? Why not?", she replied giggling.

A few minutes later we were enjoying our traditional competition dish, and it was time to touch on a topic I had been thinking about for a long time.

"Amy, I need to thank you." I said wiping my mouth full of tomato sauce.

"For what?"

"For what you did for me. I never said anything to you, but I think I need to. I don't want you to think I'm not grateful for what you've done."

"What are you talking about?"

"I know you recommended me to the Planet Canine team."

"What?"

"I know you were the person who mentioned my name for the spot at the Planet Canine's team. Thanks for doing that."

"Marquito, I have no idea what you're talking about."

"About the spot on the team! Rich told me you were the person who recommended me for the team spot!"

"Rich? Who is Rich? I don't know any Rich.", Amy was confused by the conversation.

She looked right into my eyes.

"Did someone tell you that I was the one who recommended you for the spot at Planet Canine?" Amy asked.

My thoughts took over for a few seconds. In fact, Rich had never said it was Amy. Leo and I assumed it was her, but he had never said any names.

"Not really." I started to feel like an idiot. "But I got the proposal right after we met in Winter Park, and…"

Amy interrupted me.

"And that's why you thought I recommended you for the spot?"

"It wasn't you?"

"Marquito. First, I don't know anyone at Planet Canine. Second, I didn't even know you well. It was the first time I saw you competing. Yes, I thought you were a great handler, and cute too, but not enough to recommend you for a National League spot."

I was completely confused now. Amy started laughing in front of me. Out loud.

"I think you're thanking the wrong person!"

22

FACING THE GHOSTS

After Chicago, in early August 2007 I decided to face my biggest ghost.

I arrived at Florida State Penitentiary around 8:45 am, 15 minutes before visiting hours start. Outside, hundreds of people were waiting in line with plastic bags containing food, toiletries, and other items that families bring to prisoners.

I was nervous. I had never ever been near a penitentiary before. The entry process was not easy. Metal detectors and signing a visiting book with my name, and the name of the person I was going to visit, Mr. Renato Machado, my father.

Beside me, the prison officers were checking in detail all the bags that each visitor brought. I wasn't bringing anything. I just had my cellphone, my wallet, and my car keys. No gifts or food.

I passed through security and walked alongside other visitors to an open area with tables and chairs. I sat down. For a second, I felt nauseous, my stomach tightened, and I wanted to leave. But I had promised my mother. I had promised her.

The doors at the back began to open and some detainees

started to enter the communal area. I always thought visiting inmates was like in the movies, with that glass between the two people and everyone talking on a phone. But apparently not here. The detainees were going out through the door and spreading out in the common area, meeting their relatives.

No one was wearing orange like in the movies. Prisoners wore normal clothes but with a bracelet that identified who they were.

Several officers were around.

"No hugging!" said one of the officers beside me when one of the detainees approached to hug one of the family members.

I was tense. My hands were sweating. What the hell I was doing here? I wanted to leave.

That's when he appeared at the door. My dad. Much thinner and even more bald. He looked at me the moment he entered the room. He let out a smile and started to move closer. "What am I going to say?" I thought.

I felt a knot in my stomach. A rage mixed with fear slammed inside me. He walked over and sat at the same table, in the chair across from me.

"It's great to see you here!" he said with a smile.

I did not answer. I shutdown. Rubbing my hands between my legs to try to wipe away the sweat, and at the same time hide my nervousness. Hide my nervousness? It was impossible.

"Your mother didn't come?" he asked.

I just shook my head. I couldn't get a word out of my

mouth. A long silence settled. Until he tried to start a conversation one more time.

"I saw you competing with your dog. Arrow, right? Fantastic! Congratulations!"

More silence. I was trying to find the words to say something. My anxiety was growing and without noticing a tear rolled down my face.

"Are you okay?" asked my father. "Do you want me to ask for a glass of water? Please talk to me, Marquito."

Another pause until I finally managed to find the strength to open my mouth and let something out.

"Why?" I asked.

"What?"

"Why?" I insisted.

"Why what, Marquito?" asked my father leaning over the table.

"Why did you do that?"

More tears streamed down my face. I was angry crying. I was so angry. I looked at him and felt a rage that made my muscles tighten.

"Marquito. It's not that easy to explain."

"Really?"

I wiped the tears off my face and continued.

"Do you know what you put us through?" I whispered.

Even wanting to explode and yell at him, wanting to fly over that table and grab him by his neck, even wanting to punch him in the face, I whispered with fury building through my body.

"Do you know what you put mom through?"

"Marquito..."

"They took everything!!! We were left with nothing! Broken! Mom needing to work 80 hours a week to bring home food. Killing herself to pay the bills!"

"Marquito..."

"I'm not finished!" I interrupt him.

He lowered his head.

"We trusted you so much. Ed trusted you so much. I trusted you so much. You betrayed us. You lied. You destroyed our family, and for what? For money you couldn't even spend?"

I brought my hands to my face and took a deep breath.

"But mom asked me to give you an opportunity to talk to me. I am here. This is your opportunity to talk. So, talk."

My father leaned back in his chair.

"Marquito. I have no excuse for what happened. I won't even try to find an excuse to explain it. I was always afraid of reaching old age without money, without being able to give you, your brother and your mom a good life."

"And how did that go?" I interrupted.

Pause. Then my father continued.

"The only thing I wanted you to hear from me was that I regret a lot. There is no money in the world..."

He put his hand on his face and began to cry.

"...there is no money in the world that is worth it. Only today I see it. I know I betrayed your trust. You never deserved it. I made a huge mistake and there isn't a day goes by that I don't think about it."

He sat back in his chair, in tears.

"The only thing I ask from you is a second chance. I ask your forgiveness. If you can forgive me, I will be so grateful. My lawyer says maybe I can get out of here in two years. I would love to get back together with my family. With you!"

"You know it's not that easy. Do you expect me to come here, forgive you and everything go back to normal?"

"No! But you are here, right? I think this is a good first step."

I lifted my head and looked at him. Staring at each other for a few seconds.

"The only thing I ask, is come visit me more often and talk to me, that's all."

A dozen thoughts ran through my mind in that second. How could I forgive someone who did that to my mom and younger brother? Just forget? Impossible! But on the other hand, it was my father. And as angry as I was at that moment, I remembered the good times from my childhood when we went fishing in Windermere.

"So, Ed said you've been watching my competitions?" I tried to lessen the feeling of anger in my head.

"Yes, I watch all the rounds!" said my father smiling. "tell me more, how did this happen in your life? Tell me!"

I let out a small smile and wiped away the last tears on my cheek. Maybe I should talk to him.

23

NASHVILLE, TENNESSE
ROUND 7 NATIONAL LEAGUE
AUGUST 2007

The National League Round 7 was advertised in Nashville, but actually took place in Murfreesboro, about 40 minutes away from the city.

The location was the Tennessee Miller Coliseum, one of the largest fairgrounds in the country. It was known for hosting auctions, agricultural shows, and large rodeo events. Once a year it hosted a National League round.

Our arrival was smooth. Unlike Chicago and Los Angeles, traffic in Nashville was not that bad. Everything was perfect from the Nashville International Airport to our arrival in Murfreesboro.

The conversation with Amy after the last round left me confused. If she hadn't been the one who recommend me to the team, I had no idea who it could've been. I had completely discarded Sany. The guy hated me, since the first time we met at the local events in Florida, he always tried hard to put me down. Why would he recommend me for a spot in the National League? Not a chance!

The only person I could get that information from was Rich. Paula and Kurt would never tell me anything, but Rich, I think I could break him. I would need to speak with him personally and privately, but Paula was always around us.

On the ride from the airport to the Tennessee Miller Coliseum, Rich was in the car, but Paula was too. I had to wait for the right moment.

###

FRIDAY

Friday morning and cloudy weather outside. No problem, the arena was completely covered, and climate controlled by air conditioning. Perfect!

At the briefing, no surprises. Same things, rules, warnings, and more blah blah blah. I was beginning to understand why all the handlers hated the briefing. Always the same.

Steve had a side note.

"I would like to congratulate you all for the season!" Steve said in front of all the handlers. "We have three first-place handlers tied, and a rookie who is getting a lot of attention. Congratulations on the great season."

Amy was a few steps away. She looked at me and smiled.

"I just wanted to tell everyone that this tie ends today when I win the round! Hehehe!" said Sany.

A couple handlers laughed, the rest of the group was quiet and ignored him.

End of the briefing, we went down with the dogs for training on the track and surface adaptation.

The arena was gorgeous. Stands for 1500 people, large space with a roof that was extremely high! But the best part was the surface where we were going to compete. Again, the same clay surface that Arrow liked so much. The same one used in Florida local competitions, and just like in Chicago.

The training was good! Arrow was once again feeling great! The grip on the track was amazing! And Arrow was already demonstrating a motivation that I expected to see for the rest of the weekend.

After Amy and I finished our training, we went off track so Lisa could train. Lisa was clearly suffering with the surface. Fire skidded and slid across the floor. Amy and I watched from the side lines.

"I do not understand!" I said to Amy. "How can a dog slip so much on a track with such good grip?"

"Nails!" Amy replied.

"Nails?"

"On the West Coast 90% of the competitions take place on artificial grass, so they keep the dog's nails shorter. When the dog tries to run on dirt with short nails, that's what happen."

"Then why not let the dog's nails grow?" I asked.

"I heard rumors that after the Los Angeles round, they cut Fire's nail too short and now he is suffering for grip. Good for us, right?"

Sany and Polly had also gone in for training and unlike Lisa they didn't have any problems with grip. The dogs were running very well and Sany was pushing hard with Maximus. He would go full power to win the round and try to take the top spot in the overall standings.

"Do you want to go out for dinner tonight?" Amy asked, surprising me. "Have you ever been to Nashville before? Very good bars. A lot of music!"

"Never." I replied smiling.

###

That night we went to Nashville on an avenue called Broadway. One of the coolest places I've ever been. Several bars and live music. People playing guitars and keyboards on the streets.

We entered one of the bars near the Bridgestone Arena, where hockey games were played. We sat and enjoyed a good beer, talking.

"Do you know that a few years ago, the Nashville rounds were held here at Bridgestone Arena?" said Amy.

"Yes, I know. I remember watching it on TV. It looks amazing in there. Why is it not there anymore?"

"It was too expensive for the League. Then they transferred to Murfreesboro. Which is nice too."

"Yep!"

"So, did you find out who recommended you for the team?" Amy said laughing.

"No. I thought about Sany, but that guy always hated me. He's always treated me so bad, ever since I started competing in Florida. Why would he recommend me?"

"Well, sometimes people surprise us. You never know." said Amy.

"Nah! No chance. There's a former handler in Florida named Taylor…"

"Ah, yes! Taylor!", Amy interrupted me. "I remember her, how is she?"

"She is super good people!" I answer. "But I don't think it was her. She hasn't been in the League for a long time. I don't even know if she still has contacts there."

"I think she does."

A band continued to play country music in the bar. A few people began to line up, dancing some country music choreography.

"Are you into country music?" Amy asked.

"Not really my style. I'm more rock n roll!"

"Come on! Let's Dance!", Amy grabbed my arm.

"No! No! I have no idea how to dance that!"

"Let's go! I'll teach you!", Amy pulled me by the arm again.

It was impossible to fight her. Amy had already pulled me onto the dance floor, and we started dancing. She was totally comfortable and showing her skills as a line dancer. Me, a crazy person, who was already the highlight of the group for being the worst dancer. But I confess that after the first ten minutes I had already joined in the fun and even learned some steps. And it was a lot of fun.

Returning to our table, sweaty, tired, but with a renewed spirit, we went for another round of beer.

"I need to confess!" I said. "I had so much fun!"

Amy laughed.

"See? It's fun!"

As we were catching our breath, a man approached our table. Cowboy hat, with a glass of whiskey in his hand and totally drunk, he started a conversation.

"Hey, aren't you those dog competition people? Yes! You are! There's a dog thing this weekend, I saw it!"

The man almost lost his balance while standing, so drunk.

"Ah, yes! It's us!", Amy replied.

"Cool! Nice! Aren't you that foreign guy?", the man asked me.

"Hmm, yes!" I answer.

"You're Paraguayan, or Brazilian, some crap like that, right? Do not lie to me!", said the man.

Pause while Amy and I look at each other.

"I'll cheer for her!" said the drunk man to Amy.

"Thanks!" Amy replied.

"Not you! You don't even deserve to be in our country. Bunch of Latinos invading our country and taking the work of real Americans. Damn leeches. Go back to your damn place."

I tried to ignore him, but that kind of thing used to irritated me a lot. It wasn't the first time that happened, and as a child I had seen it happen several times with my parents.

"Sir, it's better if you go drink somewhere else!" I said getting up.

"Marquito, no! Please don't!", Amy also stood up.

The man, drunk, staggered once more before replying.

"Damn you, you leech!"

That's when the man threw all the whiskey that was in his glass in my face. The drink got into my eyes, burning. I was blinded for a few seconds, but with a defensive reflex I threw a punch that hit him right in the chin. In fact, I didn't even see where he got hit, but the man went to the ground.

"MARQUITO!" Amy yelled.

I put my hands over my eyes trying to see something, but it wasn't easy. I heard screams and saw people passing in front of me. That's when I felt a blow to my left eye. I didn't see where it came from, I just felt the hit and fell. Probably a punch.

The music stopped, some people screamed and ran. On the floor, I was stunned.

"Marquito, get up!" Amy reached down, grabbed my arm, and pulled me.

I couldn't see much but it looked like another fight started in the other corner of the bar. Amy led me out and we left.

"Are you okay?" Amy asked as we walked hurriedly down the sidewalk.

"I have been better!"

###

SATURDAY

I woke up on Saturday with a horrible headache. It wasn't a hangover. We hadn't even drank that much the night before. Amy got up from the bed beside me and looked at me.

"Damn!" she said looking at me.

"That bad?" I asked.

I got out of bed and walked into the RV's small bathroom, looking at myself in the mirror. I didn't look like Rocky Balboa after his fight against Apollo Creed, but a nice bruise had formed around my right eye.

"Nice!" I said taking a deep breath.

###

The arena was open! A good audience was gathering for the start of the competition. The place was packed with tickets sold out. Music, excitement, and people cheering! No competitors from Tennessee in the National League so the madness of Chicago and Las Vegas would not happen here, but the crowd in Nashville was extremely rowdy.

In one of the corners I saw, for the first time, a group of people waving at me. Wearing shirts with my name and Arrow's picture. It was the first time I had experienced the feeling of a crowd cheering for me. I waved back. It was cool!

Walking through the arena, I couldn't hide what was getting more attention that morning, my black eye.

"What the heck, Marquito? What happened?", asked Leo.

"It's all right! A small accident. Don't even ask."

Sany walked by and looked at me. He laughed out loud.

"Oh man! Somebody kicked your fat ass, huh?" Sany bellowed.

"Man, give me a break!"

"How many fingers do I have here?" Sany asked showing two fingers in front of me and still laughing.

"Got to hell, Sany!"

"Dude, hilarious!" Sany was almost crying from laughing so hard.

The judge was preparing the first Qualifier and Amy approached.

"Are you okay?"

"Yeah. Just a little headache."

"I am really sorry!" she said.

"Why? Was It you who punched me yesterday? I am asking because I don't even remember."

Amy laughed.

###

Time to run! Handlers ready for Qualifier 1. With three handlers tied for first place in the championship at 98 points, and me a little behind with ninety-two points, any mistake would mean the end. Only four rounds to the end. It was time to see who would really continue fighting for the tittle.

The first Qualifier course was quite challenging. That weekend's judge was famous for complicating things for the handlers. In all fairness, the course wasn't bad. It mixed good speed points with challenging exercises and elimination risk points.

The first handlers came to the track and put on a real show for the crowd. The first twelve handlers managed to finish their runs without penalties. Joe & Jungle were the first to suffer a penalty.

Natasha, Mario, Caitlyn and Polly all managed good runs and the times were close.

I was the first one from the top 4 to enter due to being fourth in the championship.

Even remembering Leo's words, which echoed in my mind, "FIRST QUALIFIER, DON'T PUSH TOO MUCH. FIRST COURSE IS JUST ADAPTATION", Arrow couldn't hold back. Extremely confident in that clay surface, Arrow drooled with every step, every command. Nailing and leaving her claw marks on the ground. The only thing I could do was try to keep up with her and be quick enough on my commands to keep her from going to a wrong obstacle. Time: 28:10, temporary first place accompanied by applause, whistles and screams from the stands.

Lisa followed, and showed a lot of difficulties in handling Fire around the arena in Nashville. Having the same issues she had in Chicago. Fire slipped around corners, skated over contact obstacles and could not reach the same strength from previous rounds. Even without penalties, the team ended the run with a time of 32:22, more than two seconds behind me, in fourth place, also behind Polly and Mario.

Sany on the track next and what a perfect run! Handling Maximus with perfect timing, Sany was gearing take the top spot. I was awestruck by Sany's handling. As Maximus passed the dog walk, shaking the arena, I could have sworn was the fastest dog walk I had ever seen. Inexplicably Sany didn't beat my time, falling short 0.02 seconds. I could see the disappointment on his face when the number 2 appeared in front of his name. He was trying to beat me. Time: 28:12.

The last handler to hit the track for Qualifier 1 was Amy, and she knew that those rounds where Lisa was struggling were a big opportunity for her to score more points than her main rival. Amy placed X at the starting mark and began her run. She wasn't holding the pace in the first qualifier. With Sany and I pushing a low time, she didn't want to be outdone. She ran, yelled at X in the middle of the track but it didn't help. Time: 28:25, and third place behind Sany and myself.

Once again I had won the first Qualifier.

The music volume went up! Partying in the stands as the judge started preparing the course for Qualifer 2. Sponsors tossing small packages with free dog food samples. Event organizers threw T-shirts to fans in the stands. A beautiful scene to behold.

In the break between Qualifiers, I went to talk to Leo.

"I know what you're gonna say! I can't risk that much in Qualifiers, but Arrow is flying. I can't contain her."

"I saw. All good! Your timing with her improved a lot. If she's asking for speed, give her speed!"

"I just don't want it to happen again!" I said worried. "I can't have another elimination at finals."

"Easy!" Leo said with his hand on my shoulder. "I don't want you to think about the final now. One thing at a time and each thing in its own time."

"OK!"

Unlike the first course, the course for the second Qualifier was perfect. Good speed points allowing dogs to develop a good pace, balancing slower points with risk of elimination. The judge in Nashville was doing an amazing job with these courses.

Dogs on the track and as I always say, when the course is good, the show is guaranteed! Dogs showing speed, and handlers being required to prove skillful to overcome the challenging exercises prepared by the judge.

Natasha, Mario, Caitlyn and Polly once again finished without penalties and very close times. The exception was Mario who got an exceptional run and practically guaranteed his place in the semi-finals.

Lisa on the track! Clearly Lisa was trying to find a solution to her grip problem. Fire had been fighting for grip since Chicago and every time he tried to develop speed, he slipped sideways. Lisa should chose a less aggressive and more conservative handling, even if it cost her time. And that's what she did! Balancing the run, she led Fire to the end without too many problems and with a high time.

Amy on track! With Lisa struggling, Amy came to the track just to qualify for the semi-finals. She didn't push X. Even so, she managed to be faster than Lisa, who at that time was only 4th, behind even Mario and Polly.

When Sany got on track, things changed. No conservative handling. Sany clearly wanted to send a message to the other handlers. "I'M HERE TO WIN", is what Sany's aggressive handling showed everyone in the arena. Lifting dirt from the ground, Maximus showed all his strength to the 150 people vibrating with his run. He finished the Qualifier 2 in first place, one second ahead of Amy.

My turn! We hit the track as the last team of the day. Arrow once again digging her paws into the clay, rattling the tunnels, and shaking the seesaw that exploded on the ground! BANG! Arrow definitely wanted more and I had to pick up the pace to keep from losing her on that challenging course. We crossed the last jump with an explosion of screams coming from the stands as the number 1 appeared on the electronic scoreboard next to our name, beating Sany by 0.3 seconds.

I hugged Arrow while out of the corner of my eye I saw Sany staring at the screen not understanding what had happened and how I could have beat him.

Once again we had won both Qualifiers and were dominating the pack, followed by Sany, Amy, Mario, Polly, Lisa, Joe, Caitlyn and two other handlers qualifying for Sunday's Semi-finals .

Walking out of the arena, after the end of the Qualifiers,

Leo was beside me and said that we needed to talk. We walked into my RV. Sweaty and with my clothes stained red due to the clay from the arena. I was thrilled.

"Man, perfect day! Sensational! Whooo!", I said.

"It was good but sit here. We need to talk."

Leo pulled out a chair and I sat opposite to him.

"What's up?" I asked.

"Okay, here's the deal. I have no doubts Marquito, that you are one of the best dog agility handlers I have ever taught, and I'm not just saying that to stroke your ego."

I sat, listening.

"Look what you did in Miami, Atlanta, in Los Angeles, and in Chicago! But you are still very inexperienced, and your inexperience is hurting you in some points. Miami, Los Angeles, and Chicago. What happened in those places?"

"I lost the final after leading the entire weekend."

"Exactly! And why did it happen?"

"I don't know. I was so confident those days that I thought I couldn't lose."

"And that's the problem. You're trying so hard, so hard, that you're losing yourself in the decisive moments. I want you to do something for me tomorrow."

I was paying attention to every word Leo said.

"The job, you already know how to do. But when you step onto that track tomorrow for the semi-finals and probably the finals, I want you to detach from the environment around you. Fans, other handlers, weather, everything. Think you're training in Plant City, having fun with Arrow. Forget you are running in a National League round. Relax!"

Leo pointed at my chest.

"You just need a little more of this here because you already have the technique. And believe me, you are better than everyone else in that."

I swallowed hard. Better than everyone? Leo was just saying that to make me feel calmer. But what he had said was right. I had to relax a little bit more, especially in the finals.

Leo got up and started walking towards the RV's door.

"And rest! Take care of that black eye. Eat something and go to bed early. You have a round to win tomorrow."

###

SUNDAY

I woke up on Sunday without a headache, but the black eye was still there. And it was going to stay there for the next week.

It was time for the semi-finals. Arena packed again! And this time I had more fans! The moment I entered the arena, I heard shouts of "MARQUITO! MARQUITO! MARQUITO!". What had started faintly on Saturday was now much louder. So cool! I waved back and got even more cheers and applause.

Being fourth in the standings, six points behind the first three placed, was forcing me to win another round. I had to win if I wanted to continue in the title fight.

Friday morning on the National League website commentators said that out of the four handlers with title shots, Amy, Lisa, Sany and myself, I would most likely be the first one to drop out of the fight because I was the least experienced.

IDIOTS! I wanted to show that I could go all the way, and maybe fight for the title.

The semi-final course was tricky. The most difficult point was a serpentine, when three jumps are placed in line and the dog has to make a sequence of jumps in the shape of a number eight. That was ok, the problem was that the judge had placed two tunnels, one at the entrance and the other one at the exit of the serpentine, so it was quite easy for a dog to get confused and enter the wrong tunnel instead of making the jump, ending up eliminated.

Because I finished leading the pack on Saturday, Sunday I was the last to go on track.

Of the first five handlers who entered the track, three of them fell into the judge's trap, leaving behind their dream of running in the final.

Lisa went on track still needing to find a solution to her grip problem. Backstage, some handlers saw Lisa splashing Coca-Cola on Fire's paws. An attempt to increase the grip of the dog's paws with the surface. It's not something forbidden, but at that moment it didn't seem it was doing much good. Lisa finished the run without penalties, but the 32:12 time seemed too high to possibly qualify for the final.

It got even more complicated for Lisa when Polly and Mario hit the track and finished their runs at 32:05 and 31:58 respectively, both faster than Lisa pushing her to third position with Amy, Sany and me still to get on track. If we were to make our runs faster than Lisa, which didn't seem difficult at all, she would be eliminated in the semi-finals.

Amy came to the track with X, already knowing about

Lisa's problems. She placed X at the starting mark the crowd broke its silence after she released him. Screams, applause and whistles echoed from the stands. Everyone cheering Amy! X seemed to slip a little down the track, but I knew X wouldn't have grip issues on that type of surface. Did the track grip worsen since yesterday? Amy was handling X looking for maximum speed approaching the serpentine prepared by the judge. X made the first jump and was supposed to turn left, but no! X looked at the tunnel in front of him and seemed committed to the wrong obstacle! "X!!!!" shouted Amy. With a perfect recall, X turned to Amy and finished the serpentine ignoring the rest of the obstacles. Amy finished her run with a time of 31:38, taking first position, and pushing Lisa to fourth.

Sany was next. Judging by Sany's runs on Saturday it was clear he was looking for a victory. Just like me, with only one victory in the league so far, Sany knew that if he could not win another round and if Amy or Lisa won a third time his title dream would be over.

Maximus on the initial mark! Sany released him and off went Maximus digging his paws into the red clay. Sany was showing his best. Aggressive maneuvers, Maximus with beautiful curves not wasting time in the transition between obstacles. It was clear that Sany wanted the first position. Maximus shuddered at the A Frame and stayed in the air for a few seconds as he went from the up point to the down point of the obstacle. Sany approached the serpentine sending Maximus to the first jump, made the move to the second jump but... MAXIMUS ENTERED THE WRONG

TUNNEL! A WHOOOO came from the crowd. Sany just collapsed on the ground, defeated. He was out of the final! Maximus approached Sany and as an act of apology, licked Sany's face. There was nothing else to do, it was the first time in the year that Sany was out of the finals.

I felt bad for Sany. He was having a great run, but this sport, like any other sport, can be pretty cruel sometimes.

Last on the track, it was our turn. Remembering what Leo had told me the night before, I tried to relax and make my run as smooth as possible. I felt a little nervous remembering our conversation the night before. And my legs were a little shaky. I decided to stop thinking. I just wanted to have a good run.

I put Arrow on the start mark.

"STAY!", I commanded her.

I backed away behind jump number 2. "OK!", I released her. From where I was, I could see Arrow turning her toes inward, digging her nails into the clay and launching herself forward. 1-2-3-4, the first four jumps were perfect. From a distance, "WEAVES!", I yelled pointing to the slalom that almost moved out of place due to Arrow's aggressiveness hitting the bars of the obstacle. dog walk, fast and accurate! I could have sworn the crowd was screaming, but I was just paying attention to my run. Seesaw, on the ground. And off we went for the serpentine sequence! Arrow jumped the first jump and didn't even consider the tunnel beside her. She was with me, eye to eye contact, practically asking me where to go at every obstacle. We finished our run: 31:22, taking first place in the Semi-Finals.

FINALISTS

Marcus & Arrow (31:22)
Amy & Fire (31:38)
Mario & Rex (31:58)
Polly & Panda (32:05)
Lisa & Fire (32:12)

Sany's elimination saved Lisa who had finished fifth, grabbing the last spot for the final. Mario was in and happy. Polly was loved and favored by the audience taking her little mix breed once again to a final.

###

FINAL

Time for the final! Five handlers, five dogs, five teams. Once again, as had happened in Miami, Los Angeles, and Chicago we were dominating the weekend with victories in both the qualifiers and the semi-finals. I had to remain calm. There couldn't be a repeat!

The final course was the most complex of the weekend. Right in the beginning, the judge had prepared a trap that I was sure someone would end up falling there. Right in front of jump 1, a tunnel facing the starting mark of the track. The dogs needed to go through jump 1, and do a reverse in jump 2, approaching the obstacle from behind, without entering the tunnel that was straight ahead, an extremely difficult exercise.

Lisa, Polly, Mario, Amy, and I were waiting on the pre-track. The tension was high and nobody was talking at all. Everyone was staring at the track, thinking of ways to overcome the trap set by the judge.

Lisa on track. It was now or never for Lisa who had only qualified for the finals due to Sany's elimination and was suffering from track grip. Lisa did her homework well. She was still suffering with the lack of grip, but due to her immense technical skills, Lisa was able to brilliantly escape the referee's traps and finish her run with a time of 38:45.

Polly entered to the delight of the crowd who once again demonstrated their support for the country's most beloved mix breed. Polly and Panda's dream didn't last long though. Polly placed Panda at the initial mark and when she released him, the little mix breed jumped the first jump and dove straight into the tunnel, falling into the trap set by the judge. They were out. Even disappointed, the crowd cheered on their feet as Polly took Panda on her lap and left the track. Polly waved, thanking the crowd. Another sad scene that afternoon in Nashville.

Mario on the track! Even with a slower dog, Mario was experienced enough to know that he needed to get Rex all the way to the end, even if that meant finishing the course slower. He had to get through those traps without penalties. And it was at times like these that the best and most experienced handlers appear. Mario did an exquisite run, and even though he was almost eliminated on another part of the track, he did recover Rex with an exceptional recall. The team finished the run without penalties with a time of 38:51, remarkably close to Lisa.

Amy and I waiting for our turn to run.

Amy got on track with X beside her. Shouts of "Amy, Amy, Amy" echoed. Amy placed X at the initial mark, walked away and called him! X started his run completely ignoring the judge's trap and facing the backside in jump 2 in a magnificent maneuver. Amy wanted and needed to win! A third win here could bring the title much closer. And she knew she had to take advantage of the fact that Lisa wasn't having a good weekend again. She continued to put speed into her run. She finished her run in 36:57, almost two seconds faster than Lisa, taking the first position.

Our time! Another final, another perfect weekend so far!

"On track Marcus & Arrow!" announced the speakers.

The crowd responded "MARQUITO! MARQUITO", "GO ARROW!", came screams from the crowd. There were people there cheering for us. But I remained focused. There was no room for errors! I took a deep breath and put Arrow on the initial mark!

"STAY!" I commanded and walked away.

With my body I tried to hide the entrance of the tunnel so that Arrow would not go to the wrong obstacle. "OK!", I released her. "BACK BACK BACK", I yell to Arrow who promptly complied and went around jump number 2, back siding and ignoring the judge's trap. 3-4-5-6, high speed sequence with dog walk and Seesaw on the way. Perfect! Running and extremely fast contact zones. Jump sequence, left, right! At each turn, a good response from Arrow that dug her claws into the ground and lifted the red clay leaving the marks of her claws wherever she had been. Jump..."ARROW!" I yelled and Arrow complied, ignoring a dangerous part of the course. Last jumps and DONE! No penalties! I bent down to hug her! I heard the crowd screaming and applauding! I looked out of the corner of my eye at the electronic scoreboard! FIRST! FIRST! FIRST! My God! MY GOD! WE WIN!

I hugged Arrow even harder and screamed! A scream of FINALLY! Our second win of the season!

RESULTS ROUND 7 NASHVILLE

1. Marcus & Arrow
2. Amy & X
3. Lisa & Fire
4. Mario & Rex
5. Polly & Panda

RANKING AFTER ROUND 7 NASHVILLE

1. Marcus & Arrow = 117 pts
2. Amy & X = 116 pts
3. Lisa & Fire = 113 pts
4. Sany & Maximus = 98 pts
5. Mario & Rex = 42 pts
6. Polly & Panda = 30 pts
7. Joe & Jungle = 22 pts
8. Caitlyn & Target = 12 pts
9. Natasha & Sparky = 10 pts

###

Later that day, the entire team celebrated my victory at a restaurant in Nashville. Everyone was there. Leo, Paula, Rich, Kurt Audian, Mario, myself, and the two dogs Arrow & Rex.

"A toast to the most important victory for our team!" Mr. Audin stood up with a glass of champagne in hand.

Everyone raised their glasses! "VICTORY!", they repeated.

I will not lie, I was delighted at the time. But those dinners and lunches with the team were never my favorite moments. I would be a lot happier eating spaghetti in my RV with Amy. Speaking of Amy, I didn't get the chance to talk to Amy after the round was over. Things got so crazy with Leo breaking into the arena and Paula and Rich coming to talk to me that I couldn't find her after the round.

"Marquito!" again Mr. Audian spoke, sitting across from me on the other side of the table. "I would like to let you know in front of everyone here to witness, that I have already have a contract renewal prepared for next year."

Leo and I looked at each other.

"Wow, Mr Audian! Thank you very much! I am very happy to hear that you are enjoying my work here."

"Yes, things are going very well. Now all that's missing is the title, right?"

Mr. Audian laughed, followed by Paula and Rich.

"There are still three rounds to go." I replied a little embarrassed. "A lot can happen."

"I have no doubts that you will continue to do an excellent job. Thinking about titles is totally normal at this moment."

Everyone was silent for a few minutes while swallowing another mouthful of food from their respective plates.

"Excuse me." Rich got up and left the table towards the bathroom.

I looked at Leo and whispered.

"Take care of Arrow!" getting up from the table.

"Where are you going?" whispered Leo.

"Just take care of Arrow for a few minutes!"

I followed Rich into the bathroom. Inside, Rich was using the urinal. I approached his side and started using one.

"Marquito, what a great run today!"

"Thanks!"

Silence and we went to wash our hands.

"Rich, I need to ask you something."

"Sure. What is it?"

"I need to know who recommended me to the team? Who talked to you and Paula about hiring me?"

Rich tried to change the conversation.

"Oh, Marquito! Forget it. Enjoy your victory. Look at the amazing season you're having. Why bother with that now? It's not even important."

Rich was walking out of the bathroom, but I walked in front of him.

"It's important! To me!" I said in a stronger voice holding the bathroom door. "Please, I need to know. Please!"

Rich took a deep breath, taking a long pause.

"Who do you think it was, Marquito? You know who it was."

"No, I don't know! I thought it was Amy, but she denied it."

"Amy? Of course not."

"So, who? Damn it, speak up!"

"Who's the only other handler from Florida in the League, Marquito?"

"Impossible! He hates me!"

"You sure?"

"The guy always treated me like crap, making me feel

horrible, teasing me. Always saying I was never going to get anywhere. And now you're telling me he was the one responsible for me coming to the National League? It doesn't make any sense."

"I think you and Sany need to have a talk. You might be surprised at what kind of person he really is. And not the character you see at competitions."

"I do not understand!"

"Just talk to him."

Rich left the bathroom, heading back to the table in the restaurant.

24

OLD FRIENDS, NEW PROJECTS

September 2007 coming out of training during the week, I decided to pay a visit to Rafi and his father, Mr. Monterey. I hadn't seen them since January that year when my life in the National League had begun.

I drove my car onto the Monterey's Ranch. The ranch gate was always open. I approached the house at the back and saw Rafi looking at me. I parked the car and Rafi came to greet me.

"Jesus Christ! Look who decided to show up!", Rafi shouted! "Son of a Bitch! MARQUITO!!! HAHAHAHA!"

Rafi walked over and gave me an enthusiastic hug, which I returned.

"How are you, my friend?" I asked.

"I can't believe you're here!"

"Why not? I know it's been a long time, but I'm here!"

"Brother, it's so good to see you!"

"And I'm not alone!"

I opened the car's back door and Arrow jumped out.

"Ah...ARROW! Future champion, huh?", Rafi bent down to pet her.

Mr. Monterey appeared at the back door of the house and approached.

"Hey, Marquito! Long time!"

"I know, I know!" I gave Mr. Monterey a big hug too.

"And look who's here!" said Mr. Monterey bending down to also pet Arrow.

"She's a big girl now!" I said.

"Yes, she is!" Mr. Monterey said. "Let's go in for a cup of coffee."

The four of us entered the main house on the ranch.

Minutes later, we were sitting at the kitchen table, talking, and drinking the coffee that Mr. Monterey ground himself using the beans planted on the ranch. Real coffee, not that horrible stuff that people drink at Starbucks.

"My God!" I exclaimed as I took a sip of that delicious coffee. "You have no idea how much I miss this."

Rafi and his father laughed.

"Man, tell me! What is it like to be in the National League?" Rafi asked excitedly. "We've been watching it on TV. So cool!"

"I won't lie, it's pretty cool! But you know, you don't have much time to do anything else. Training, traveling, competing, and repeating."

"Oh, shut up! All those cool cities you're traveling to. It must be really neat to visit all those places."

"Yes, but we never see the city. I don't know anything

about those places. From the airport to the arena, and from the arena to the airport."

"Stop complaining!" Rafi said. "Do you want to come back and work here again?"

"I would do that!" I answered.

We laughed.

Mr. Monterey poured some more coffee into my mug and brought out some cookies that he baked himself. Since the death of Rafi's mother, he's done everything there. Of course, Rafi always helped.

Off to the side, on top of a counter, a picture of Rafi and his parents, all together. At that moment I had some thoughts about Ms. Monterey. Always treating us so well. I missed her.

"Mr. Monterey, I came here to tell you something." I said.

"Ok."

"I came here to thank you."

Pause. I took another sip of my coffee.

"Without you, none of this would have happened in my life. I didn't have money to buy a puppy and that day you gave me this dog here, (I pointed to Arrow at my side). It was the most important day of my life. The day everything changed. And I thank you for that. From the bottom of my heart."

Mr. Monterey took a deep breath.

"I really appreciate your words. But Marquito, I didn't do anything. I've sold hundreds of puppies and none of them have become a champion in major competitions. It was you! Only you! You dedicated yourself, you trained..."

"I know!" I interrupted. "But without a dog, how was I going to do all that, right?"

Everyone laughed, I continued.

"So, thank you! Thanks for what you did for me. I will never forget."

"Don't make me cry, okay?" said Mr. Monterey.

The three of us laughed.

"I have a few more puppies here! Want to see them?"

"I thought you weren't breeding Border Collies anymore?"

"I changed my mind!" he replied smiling. "Do you want to see them, or not?"

"Of course, I want!"

We left the house and walked to the old kennel in an outdoor area. A litter of six Border Collie puppies were there ready to move to a new home. About nine weeks old. Arrow got excited, and she was very curious about the little puppies.

"Your cousins Arrow!" Rafi said.

"They are really beautiful!" I said. "Is business going good?"

"Well, you know. I'm not a famous breeder so people look more for those sport breeders, instead of me. They pay a fortune for those puppies."

"Wait a second! But this place, is where Arrow came from! How many people could be interested in puppies like her."

"Marquito, I've never advertised using Arrow. I would never do that!", said Mr Monterey.

"And why not?"

"I don't know, I wouldn't use your dog as marketing to sell puppies."

"But Mr. Monterey just look at the sales opportunity you have. Look, right here!", I pointed to Arrow. "You have a puppy that is fighting for the National League title, who came out of your kennel. You are the breeder!"

"I told him that." Rafi interrupted. "But he never wanted to do that!"

"I'll fix it now!" I said.

I logged onto my social media account using my cellphone and took several pictures of the litter.

"Do you know how many followers I have now? Millions! Get ready because your cellphone will start ringing in a few minutes."

Rafi and Mr Monterey looked at each other.

I quickly posted pictures of the litter on my social media account with the words: "COUSINS OF ARROW FOR SALE IN PLANT CITY, FLORIDA! CONTACT KENNEL AT..." and used Mr. Monterey's phone number.

"By the way, what about the old warehouse at the back?"

"It's still there!" said Mr. Monterey.

"Let's take a look!"

At the back of the property was the old warehouse that no one had used for anything in years. The same one where Rafi and I used to play when we were kids.

A lot of dust, things thrown on the floor, and a lot of junk.

"This is a mess!" said Rafi.

"We don't use this warehouse for anything!" said Mr Monterey.

"I have an idea." I said. "Let's clean this mess. Remove all the garbage, renovate it and set up our Dog Agility training center here."

Mr. Monterey was listening, curious about what I was saying.

"Look..." I continued. "After we finish renovating the warehouse, we will put an artificial grass surface in here and bring some dog agility obstacles. Jumps, tunnels, A frame, dog walk, everything. Leo can train some students here. This will bring a lot more people to the property."

Rafi and Mr. Monterey remained quiet.

"Outside the warehouse, we can set up another training track. This one will be natural grass, with another set of obstacles. Let's renovate the kennel too. Let's build masonry kennels. More people coming to train here and seeing the puppies in a nice, well-kept kennel. And then, with Leo's students, we'll pass a percentage to you, Mr Monterey. What do you think?"

"Marquito!" Mr Monterey said. "It sounds expensive."

"Don't worry about that. A few weeks ago the company told me that if I needed to improve my training facility they would help. It's time to collect the offer."

Rafi had already cracked a smile. His father still looked reluctant.

"It seems a little too much, Marquito!"

"No, it's not! I will start preparing everything! Let's make this place buzz with people!"

A cellphone vibrating interrupted the conversation. It was Mr. Monterey's cellphone.

"I think you better answer that!" I said.

"HELLO?" Mr. Monterey answered the phone.

Pause.

"Yes, this is the kennel where Arrow came from! Yes, we have six puppies ready to move to a new home."

Another pause. Mr. Monterey looked at me with the cellphone to his ear.

"How much per puppy?" he said on the phone.

I looked at him and whispered, pointing my finger up:

"Whatever you ask, they will pay!"

25

CHARLOTTE, NORTH CAROLINA
ROUND 8 NATIONAL LEAGUE
SEPTEMBER 2007

Three rounds to the end of the season, and I was now the championship leader. Surreal! That was the only word that came to my mind. From the beginning of the championship, from the moment I signed the contract with the team, I wanted to be competitive. I wanted to win rounds. But imagining that I would make it to the last three rounds leading the pack, insane!

Things were still very even. Amy was in second place and only one point behind me. Considering that each victory is worth twenty-five points, one point difference is a technical draw.

Lisa was third just five points behind me and four behind Amy, also with full chances of fighting for the title. And Sany, after his elimination in the semi-finals in Nashville still had 98 points, the 19-point gap to the leader was already causing him concern. After all, he had to recover in Charlotte to stay in the fight.

###

We arrived at Charlotte International Airport on Thursday around 2 pm. Upon arrival, I could already see what this round would mean to the people, when I saw a giant poster of Amy in the airport lobby. It was the round where Amy would compete in front of her fans, and probably with the crowd pushing her across the track during the weekend.

The round would take place at Cabarrus Arena & Event Center, about 40 minutes' drive from the International Airport.

We arrived outside the arena around 4 pm on Thursday, with all the RVs and teams already there. From the outside, the place didn't look like much, it looked small. We wouldn't know until the next day if the facilities inside were good or not.

During the night, I decided to go to Amy's. I knocked on the door and she didn't take long to answer.

"Hey!" I greeted Amy.

"Hey, how are you?"

"Good! Come in!" She said.

I went into the RV and Amy was preparing her uniform for the competition.

"Have a good trip?" she asked.

"Yeah, all good. Quiet. You?"

"Me? I live twenty minutes from here!"

We both laughed.

Since my victory in Nashville, Amy and I had been talking a lot through texts and video calls. Without even seeing each other between rounds, talking to her was very natural as we chatted so much online.

"So, I just stopped by to wish you good luck this weekend and bring you this!"

I took a Princess Leia pendant from my pocket and handed it to her.

"Aww! How beautiful! Thank you!"

"I bought it at Disney Springs in Orlando. When I saw it, I thought of you."

She hugged me and gave me a kiss.

"Well, I think I need to go back. I'll let you rest for tomorrow." I said, already heading to exit the RV.

"You can stick around tonight if you want."

She smiled in a naughty way.

"OK!" I answered.

"But just to make it clear, if you beat me here in Charlotte, I'll literally kill you." she laughed.

"I'd like to see you try."

###

FRIDAY

Friday morning briefing. All handlers there, including Sany, of course. After what Rich told me in Nashville, I needed to get the story straightened out with Sany. Why did he recommend me to a League team? The guy always spoke very badly about me, and now he is the one responsible for the greatest opportunity of my life. I needed to get this cleared. But it had to be in private and not among all those people.

Sany was quiet. No jokes, no silly games. That weekend was life or death for him. If Sany had some bad runs and by any chance he didn't qualify for the finals, it would be the end of the championship for him. And with only two rounds to go, mathematically he would no longer be able to fight for the title.

Maybe this was the right time to play a little joke on him. Revenge for always trying to distract me, trying to make me small. No, leave the guy alone. He must be under immense pressure from the team. He almost didn't renew his contract for this season because last year was bad for him. This year things at least got better for him. Round eight and he still had chances to become champion.

"Sany quiet today, huh?" Mario asked, sitting next to me in the briefing's room.

"Yeah. I think the pressure is hitting his ass."

"Probably. Looks like this weekend he doesn't feel like being the funny one."

"Do you think there is any chance that he will be without a team for next year?" I asked Mario.

"I think there are a lot of teams that would like to have him. The guy is good. Kind of an idiot, arrogant, but he's a good handler." answered Mario.

"What about you? Won't you miss all this?"

Mario laughed softly.

"My friend, I can't wait to wake up whenever I want on Sunday mornings!"

We both laughed.

###

After the briefing we went down to finally look at the

arena and the track. Time to take the dogs out for surface adaptation and see how they behave.

Entering the arena, I confess, I was a little surprised. The place wasn't that big. In fact, compared to everywhere else we competed before this, it had the least capacity. Around seven hundred people.

The stands were so close to the track, I could already imagine that the elevated pressure on the handlers would be brutal. And without a doubt, Amy would be being supported by 100% of the fans there.

The best part was when we got our feet on the track. To my delight, it was the third consecutive round using a clay surface. Same as the one used in Nashville and identical to the one used in Chicago.

When we hit the track, I could see a little bit more of what had happened in Nashville and Chicago. Arrow absolutely feeling at home on that surface. Her training had been perfect. Speed, precision, and a great grip gave me a confidence boost for the next couple of days.

Amy and Sany were also extremely comfortable. Their training had gone well. Both X and Maximus also exuded confidence and a lot of physical strength. Lisa still seemed to suffer a bit with Fire. Even though she looked better than in the last two rounds, it was still visible on Lisa's face that she wasn't happy.

As soon as her practice was over, everyone listened when she commented to her team representative:

"The League now only makes rounds on this type of surface. Horrible!" complained Lisa.

In fact, she was right. Artificial grass flooring has always been the ideal for dogs, but the high cost created barriers for all rounds to be carried out on that type of surface. And besides, with rounds happening more frequently in large fairgrounds where agricultural events also take place, laying artificial grass floors would be stupid, so the clay was still the most used, to Lisa's disadvantage.

###

SATURDAY

We woke up on Saturday to a beautiful sunny day in Charlotte. It was not a hot day. The temperatures in mid-September were beginning to drop in the northern United States.

Outside, I could already hear the screams and the noise of the crowd coming from inside. The moment I set foot inside the arena, I got scared. The place was completely taken over by Amy's fans. They were screaming, singing, whistling, and stomping their feet against the stands making the whole place shake.

"AMY! AMY! AMY!" would be the chorus heard all weekend. The small arena caused a claustrophobic feeling for the handlers who found themselves surrounded by fans on all sides. Poor Lisa, who without a doubt, would be the main victim of the crowd that weekend.

###

QUALIFIER 1

Another AKC judge that weekend, and we already knew what that meant: opened straight line courses with no significant risk of elimination points. In Qualifier 1, we had practically a beginners course with three long straights lines and only one change of direction. A lot of running!

The track offered a lot of speed to the competitors, but no point of potential elimination risks. Lots of spaces between obstacles which would result in a footrace for time, rather than a course that would test the technical skills of the handlers.

With the first handlers and dogs on the track and no eliminations, every handler started to keep an eye on the clock.

Mario was suffering, evidently. Every advantage he could have with a technical but slow dog, disappeared on a course like that. Joe, Caitlyn and Polly made good times, with Joe standing out half a second ahead of everyone else. But that didn't last long because when Sany hit the track, super serious and focused, he took everything he could out of Maximus in the first Qualifier and destroyed Joe's time. A very solid run from Sany, taking the temporary first position.

Lisa came next and honestly, I felt bad for her. If I thought the crowd in Las Vegas was loud, my God, the crowd in Charlotte nearly brought the arena down with so much noise. Boos, screams, whistles and the crowd still stomping their feet on the metal bleachers making a deafening noise and literally shaking the ground throughout the arena. Lisa didn't care, still smirking as she walked onto the track.

The speakers said something that was impossible to hear over the noise. It was something like "Silence! Respect the handlers", in vain! Lisa started her run under the biggest booing and screaming I've ever heard in a dog agility competition. But, she didn't get discouraged by the boos.

Clearly Lisa and Fire were much better than in the previous two rounds. Probably because Fire's nails were finally long enough to improve his grip on the clay surface. Without penalties and with a lot of personality, Lisa took Fire to the end of the course, but it wasn't enough to beat Sany's good time, temporarily taking second place.

Amy on track! "AMY! AMY! AMY!", were the screams coming from the crowd! The home handler took to the track for the first time that weekend to an explosion of applause coming from the stands. Smiling and looking serene, she placed X at the starting mark and began her run in front of a crazy crowd. Incredibly X slipped approaching one of the obstacles and dropped a bar. "OHHHHHH!" was heard from the stands. Even with the best Qualifier time, Amy was trailing Sany and Lisa.

Our turn! We hit the track as the last team in Qualifier 1. No booing for us, and not much cheering for support either. We were quietly applauded on our walk to the starting mark. Arrow ready and off we went for the first run of the weekend. Arrow, as always, feeling great on the clay track but something also happened to us. At the same point where X slipped and dropped the bar, Arrow also slipped and dropped the same bar. Unbelievable. A good time but not enough to be faster than Amy which left us in fourth position.

At the end of Qualifier 1: Sany, Lisa, Amy, Marcus, Joe, Caitlyn, Polly and Mario led the group.

###

"What happened at that spot on the track?" I asked Leo.

"I don't know. Maybe a hole or something out of level."

"Arrow and X! Same bar! What the hell???"

"Calm down. It was just the first Qualifier."

###

QUALIFIER 2

In Qualifer 2 the judge didn't change his strategy much. He just reversed the direction of the course. What was jump number 1 before, now was the last jump and vice versa. A little lazy for a judge, but what can you do?

Amy was not happy with the judge's courses. And I heard when she spoke to the person in charge of her team.

"So much running!! Why do something like that?", said Amy.

Off we went once more on another wild running course.

Another one who was disappointed with the courses in Charlotte was Mario. Unable to be competitive with Rex on such fast courses, and unable to use any of his technical skills, Mario entered the track already defeated, and even managing a run without penalties, the high time would certainly eliminate him from the semi-finals. A horrible weekend for my teammate.

Polly was the highlight of the second Qualifier. "The most beloved mix breed in the country", as he was called, had achieved another great run without penalties and the little Panda had taken the lead in Qualifier 2, to a standing ovation from the crowd.

It was my turn! And what I wanted most was to recover from that fourth place in the first Qualifier! And so, we did! With Arrow showing her best, and a lot of aggressiveness, precise contact zones and so much speed, we drew applause from the crowd. Also, a slalom so fast that Arrow broke one of the PVC poles of the obstacle. We took the provisional lead on Qualifier 2.

Our run had been so good that even with all the support that Amy received from the crowd, she wasn't able to beat our time.

Amy got on track after us and tried hard to get a good time. In fact, during her run I had no doubts that Amy would beat my time, and when she didn't, I was surprised. Was Arrow once again the fastest dog on that weekend?

Amy wasn't happy at all. In her own home she had not managed to win any of the Qualifiers. And the crowd cheered her as she walked out of the track, crestfallen. "GO AMY!", "YOU CAN DO IT", were screams that echoed through the stands.

Lisa took to the track under a lot of boos! A lot of boos! Shouts of "GO BACK!", and when the crowd began to stump on the metal bleachers, the noise was deafening again. But Lisa didn't care, at least she didn't seem to. She came to the track without looking to the sides and gave everything she could. Fire slipped again and Lisa had to help him with an even more conservative handling, wasting time.

Screams rang out from the stands as Lisa finished her run and a giant number 3 appeared next to her name. We were still in first, followed by Lisa and Amy.

Sany was the last to go on track in the Qualifiers. This was another Sany. Since the day before at the briefing, Sany had not been seen with his usual behavior, making jokes, or making fun of everyone. Closed expression and focused on what he had to do. After the elimination in Nashville at the semi-finals, it was all or nothing for Sany and Maximus. And he did it again! Perfection in his handling and perfect responses from Maximus took them to the top of the chart. Sany celebrated with a loud scream and a punch in the air, which lifted the crowd. Sany was still, very alive.

At the end of the Qualifers, the eligible handlers for Sunday's semi-finals in order were Sany, me, Amy, Lisa, Polly, Joe, Natasha, and three other handlers.

Sany was dominating the weekend. I was fine, and I knew I could fight for the top spot. Both Amy and Lisa were showing shaky presentations. Lisa was clearly out of her comfort zone with both the surface and the track style. And Amy, maybe the pressure of competing at home was affecting her performance.

###

I watched as Amy walked out of the arena with X on a leash beside her, heading back to her RV. I ran to catch up with her. I wanted to talk to her.

"Amy!" I screamed.

She could clearly hear me but continued walking without looking back.

"Amy!" I called again, getting even closer.

No reply. Right next to her, I called her again, touching her shoulder from behind.

"Hey, Amy!"

Amy turned around.

"Not now, Marquito!" she replied in an assertive tone.

"Are you okay?"

"Not now! Sorry. I need some time. Please give me a break."

"Yes, of course!" I answered. "If I can help with anything, just let me know."

"OK!"

Amy turned away and continued walking towards her RV.

###

SUNDAY

Once again, the arena was completely full. Things were on fire there. Loud music and dancers from the Charlotte Academy of Dance performed to entertain the crowd as the judge prepared the course for the Semi-Final.

The mood was heavy among the competitors. Sany, Lisa, and Amy, all frowning, focused. No "good morning", "how was your night?", or any other attempt of interaction between handlers. It was the toughest environment among competitors I had seen since the beginning of the season. And I had a feeling that until the end of the season things were only going to get worse.

After Charlotte there would be only two more rounds to go, and we all knew that the race for the title had already started, there in Charlotte.

###

SEMI-FINALS

The massive surprise of the day was the Semi-finals course. The complaints coming from some handlers the day before had made a difference, because the semi-finals course was nothing like what we had seen the day before. Lots of potential elimination areas and incredible four backside jumps, a record in the season.

During waking course, it was visible that the handlers were happier than Saturday. The question people always ask is: "Why would a competitor be happier with a more complex course than with a simpler course with long straight lines and with minor risk of elimination?"

It's an easy answer. When you prepare a dog to be a high level competitor, you prepare them to be used to more challenging courses, they must be ready for the worst. Wide open courses with long straight lines make dogs lose focus, losing their stride and making handling difficult.

First dogs on track! The applause from the loudest fans of the season so far, and all handlers doing a sober job on that tricky course. Natasha and Joe ended their runs with one penalty each, dropping one bar on one of the backside jumps.

Polly made the arena go crazy when she took "the most beloved mix breed in the country" in, with one of the most beautiful runs I have ever seen her do, going to the top of the chart, and practically securing, once again, a place at the final. Time: 29:12.

What a wonderful job Polly was doing with Panda. For a long time, mix breeds were discriminated in dog agility competitions. In fact, until ten years before, strays could not compete at all. It was necessary to present a pedigree and a certificate of pure breeding to compete. As the rules changed, some mutts were starting to show up in competitions, but no one had ever reached the level of Polly & Panda. Now, with so many impressively positive results in the National League, a door had opened for, who knows, more mutts to start showing up.

Lisa on track! Noise, boos, crowd stomping in the stands. "GOING TO ELIMINATE!" I heard people shouting from the stands. Honestly, I thought it was becoming disrespectful. I agree that the fans are there to cheer, but this was wilder than in Las Vegas.

Even though I, of course, rooted for Amy (and for myself), the fans had to respect Lisa, one of the biggest winners of the national dog agility.

The best way Lisa found to silence that noisy crowd was with an astonishing performance on the track. What a run! What a technique! With a more technical course than on Saturday, Lisa managed to demonstrate why she is one of the most incredible handlers in the country. And Fire, MY GOD! what a well-trained dog and what DRIVE! Even though he slipped twice, one of the times falling on his side and touching his flank to the ground, he still managed to finish in first position with a time of 28:49. No doubt they would have been even faster if it had not been for Fire's two slips.

Quiet crowd. The beautiful run Lisa & Fire did lower, a little bit, the fire that emanated from those stands.

It did not last long, because when the speakers announced: "On track Amy & X!"

The crowd woke up and the screams, now of motivation, started to explode again! "AMY! AMY! AMY!" "GO X," "X! X! X!" were some of the screams emanating from the fans. One of the fans had a piece of cardboard that said: "THE X MARKS THE SPOT"!

We were all watching as Amy entered the track, adjusting the brim of her cap down, hiding her eyes, and fixing the little ponytail behind her head. X at the initial mark and off they went with the crowd in the stands pushing them at every obstacle. One by one, X was overcoming them all, and leaving behind the judge's traps without taking any chance of making a single mistake. Beautiful handling by Amy, who got a standing ovation when X passed the last jump and the number 1 appeared next to her name with a time of 28:38.

It was clear the relief Amy felt at that moment, removing a gigantic weight off her shoulders. I could see her taking a deep breath and huffing as she walked off the track.

It was my turn to hit the track for the semi-finals.

No booing, but also not a lot of cheering. In the distance I could hear someone shouting: "LET'S GO MARQUITO!" I got on track with Arrow and put her at the starting mark. Was it possible to beat Amy's time? I pulled away and looked at Arrow. Lifted my arm and Arrow moved from a sitting position to standing. Mouth open, drool slipping from the corner of her mouth. She was ready.

"OK!" I released her!

Arrow threw herself over the first jump and almost dropped the first bar when her left rear leg touched the jump wing and the crowd let out a "WHOOOOO" My heart jumped in my throat, but I had to swallow and continue. Three first jumps with perfect first backside jump. Aiming for the slalom and, as always, entering aggressively and making the bars of the obstacle bend from so much pressure she was putting on it. A frame ahead and Arrow climbed the board so hard that I could see one of the corners of the obstacle sinking into the red clay. Right turn, another backside, perfect! Seesaw...BANG! On the floor! Tough left turn with Arrow skating as her paws lifted clay from the ground. Final sequence of obstacles and DONE! I looked at the electronic scoreboard: 28:35! Yes, we beat Amy by 0.03 seconds.

I heard boos from the crowd! Not as many, but some boos came from a few areas of the stands. I did not care. I looked at Amy outside the track. She was serious, staring at the track.

Sany was the last one to enter for the Semi-finals. Having dominated the entire weekend so far, I personally thought that Sany was the favorite to win the round. He had arrived in Charlotte to put himself back in the title fight.

Sany entered the track with a silent crowd. It looked like the crowd was starting to realize that Amy might not be the favorite to win that day too.

Sany placed Maximus at the starting mark, backed away, and called for his dog. Many years after that day, I would still remember one of the most iconic scenes I had ever experienced in my life in Dog Agility. Maximus jumped the first jump, and without explanation made a left turn towards a tunnel that was there. The tunnel was not close, it was not a risky point on that course, but Maximus for some reason saw something in that tunnel. Sany tried, yelling "MAX!" "MAX!" But it did not help. Maximus made one jump and turned into the tunnel to his left, entering the wrong obstacle. They were out. One jump! Only one jump was what they managed to complete on that course.

Sany dropped to his knees. The fans, understanding Sany's despair and understanding the situation, sympathized, and stood up, applauding him.

Sany was not just out of the finals in Charlotte. It was the end of his dream of being champion. With only two rounds left, there would be no more mathematical chances for Sany to try for the title. I felt bad seeing that scene. It was sad. And I am sure the other handlers felt that way too. We wanted to win, and for that, others needed to lose. We all understand that, but it was hard not to feel bad for Sany at that moment, devastated.

FINALISTS

Marcus & Arrow (28:35)

Amy & X (28:38)

Lisa & Fire (28:49)

Polly & Panda (29:12)

Natasha & Sparky (29:42)

###

FINAL

The atmosphere remained tense. Out of all the rounds played so far, I had never seen anything like it. Anticipation and stress emanated from the pores of the competitors, especially from Lisa, Amy, and I.

With Sany now out, only the three of us had a chance to fight for the title of the season. And now, it was kill or be killed. Each of us dealt with that stress in whatever way we could.

The final course followed the same pattern as the semifinal course. Complex, challenging and with a few points that could easily take the less attentive handler by surprise. The main highlight of the course was the slalom's entry. Coming from a tunnel under the dog walk, the dog would need to exit the tunnel and enter the slalom without any help from the handler, who would be trapped behind the dog walk.

Distance exercises are not simple, and most handlers have problems with them. First, because the dog needs to be extremely independent to move forward without having the handler at its side. The second problem being how to indicate the correct obstacle being so far away from the dog.

The apprehension was around the fans too. Even though they still wanted to believe in Amy's victory, they were having doubts because everybody had expected Amy to dominate the weekend, just as Lisa had done in Los Angeles and Las Vegas.

Natasha & Sparky were the first on track. The team did not have a good run ending eliminated after the first few obstacles, not having time to reach the most challenging point of the course.

Polly & Panda came next and under a lot of applause they managed to go all the way to the end although with a lot of difficulties getting through the slalom. On the first attempt, Polly gave the command to Panda who was confused when he realized that his handler was on the other side of the dog walk coming back in Polly's direction, refusing the slalom. Polly tried again and Panda, not understanding, refused once more. It was only on the third attempt that Panda understood the command, made the slalom and the team managed to go all the way, but with an extremely high time and two penalties.

Lisa on track! Boos, yells, and more stomping on the metal bleachers, with the crowd once again making deafening noise in the arena.

Lisa ignored it. She started her run with Fire showing once

again a sharp and consistent technique. In the most difficult part of the course, Lisa yelled "WEAVES!" from behind the dog walk and Fire without blinking, and beautifully, entered the tunnel on one side of the dog walk exiting on the other side and diving into the slalom perfectly. It was beautiful to see. In any other arena, Lisa would receive a standing ovation, but in Charlotte that morning fans just keep silent. A brutal silence where you could even hear Fire's footsteps running across the arena finishing his run in first position and silencing everyone in the stands.

Amy on track! And things were not as good for Amy or me. Lisa's run had been perfect, and she had put enormous pressure on us. The crowd had felt it and were looking for strength to push Amy onto the track.

"AMY! AMY! AMY!" The crowd screamed and sang.

Amy began her run, with X launching himself through the first jump and picking up speed with every stride, every turn. The seesaw exploded to the ground with X sliding down the plank. More jumps, perfect! Looking from the outside, the timing between Amy and X was absolutely perfect. Amy approached the most challenging point on the course, sent X into the tunnel and remained on the opposite side of the Dog Walk. "WEEEEAVESSS!" Amy yelled desperately as X exited the tunnel to enter the Slalom. Everything looked perfect until X turned back for a second looking for Amy. "WEEEAVESSSS!" Amy commanded a second time and X lifted his head looking for the slalom and diving into the correct obstacle. Screams of relief from the crowd, applause, as Amy finished her run and no one knows how, but she managed to finish first.

Amy hugged X tightly while still on the track, on her knees, as if thanking God for that run.

Ecstatic fans in the stands. But I still had to go on track.

At that moment, the world was in Amy's favor, and it was no surprise that I was booed when I hit the track. After what Amy had done seconds before, no one inside that arena wanted to see someone else win.

I put Arrow in the initial mark and walked away!

"OK!" I released Arrow.

With clay flying from her rear legs, Arrow began her run chasing me down the track. Two sequences of high-speed jumps followed by a straight-line tunnel that Arrow passed very forcefully.

The crowd no longer booed. Just watched it, in silence.

A frame! Arrow climbed the first part of the obstacle so powerfully that she descended on the other side sliding with her nails scratching the surface of the obstacle. We approached the challenging part of the course. I commanded Arrow through the tunnel yelling: "WEEEAAAVEEESSS" I yelled to Arrow who was still inside the tunnel, hoping she would find the right path. On the opposite side of the Dog Walk, I saw Arrow coming out, head held high, looking for the Slalom. Everything moved in slow motion for a few seconds! Arrow continued forward until finding the slalom and entering correctly! "MY GOD! WE DID IT!!" I thought for a second. I continued running towards the last obstacles and we made it through the final jump without penalties.

Silence!

I looked at the monitor and the NUMBER 1 appeared next to our name! "WE WON???" "SERIOUSLY???" were the first thoughts that came to my mind.

The silence coming from the stands confirmed it. Yes, I had won my third round in the National League. The second in a row. I could not believe it. I looked outside the track where Leo was jumping and celebrating. I was in shock. The crowd was in shock. I won in Charlotte, at Amy's house.

I put the leash on Arrow and in the distance, I saw Amy leave the arena, her head down. Leo approached me and hugged me! I pushed him away and ran, trying to catch up with Amy.

"Amy!" I screamed.

That time she did not ignore it. She turned to me, she had tears in her eyes.

"Marquito!" Amy yelled. "What did you do?"

"Amy..."

"You beat me at home! What was that?"

Amy was sobbing with tears coming down her eyes.

"Amy, what did you want me to do? Lose on purpose?"

"You're an asshole! An asshole!"

Amy pushed me with both hands in the middle of my chest, nearly knocking me over.

"Get out of my way! I do not want to talk to you! Go celebrate your victory! I hate you!"

I was speechless! Amy turned around and walked away.

Leo was behind me watching everything.

"Marquito!" said Leo. "Leave her alone. There is nothing

you can do right now. There is nothing you can say. Nothing will make this situation any better. Let her think about it."

Leo was right. I walked back to the arena.

RESULTS ROUND 8 CHARLOTTE

1. Marcus & Arrow
2. Amy & X
3. Lisa & Fire
4. Polly & Panda
5. Natasha & Sparky

RANKING AFTER ROUND 8 CHARLOTTE

1. Marcus & Arrow = 142 pts
2. Amy & X = 134 pts
3. Lisa & Fire = 128 pts
4. Sany & Maximus = 98 pts
5. Mario & Rex = 42 pts
6. Polly & Panda = 42 pts
7. Joe & Jungle = 22 pts
8. Natasha & Sparky = 20 pts
9. Caitlyn & Target = 12 pts

###

Feeling somber that night back in the RV, I spent half an hour looking out the window at Amy's RV. The light still on, not far from me. I thought about going over there and knocking on the door, trying to talk to her. But I knew it was the best to let the dust settle. In fact, eventually she was going to have to understand that we were just competing.

I worried that she would take all of it personally and would never speak to me again. "DAMN IT, MARQUITO!" I thought. I did not regret giving everything to win the round, but I felt bad for her.

Still looking out the small window of my RV, I watched as Sany got out of his RV with Maximus on the leash and a backpack on his back. He was leaving, and this was my chance to talk to him.

I opened the RV door and got out, walking towards him.

"Sany!"

"Hey, little dwarf!" Sany replied ironically and clearly mentioning my short stature.

"Sorry about today!" I said.

"Really? You sorry? Why? Now you have one less competitor to worry about."

I was quiet for a few seconds.

"Look, I have a flight to catch! So, if you'll excuse me, I need to go."

Sany started to walk away.

"Why did you recommend me for the Planet Canine team?" I asked as Sany walked away.

Sany stopped and turned around.

"Looks like someone got their tongue-in-cheek, huh? Who was it? Paula? Rich, right? Goofballs!"

"It doesn't matter. Why did you recommend me to the team?"

Sany did not answer. I continued speaking.

"You know, I was your fan before I met you in person. I was rooting for you in past championships, and the first time I meet you in person you treat me like crap. Then you recommend me to a team in the National League. I just want to understand."

Sany started to laugh:

"Marquito! Marquito! So naive. You have no idea how a competitive environment works, do you? It's not just a matter of winning on the track, my young Padawan. It's a matter of winning here!" Sany pointed to his head. "It's a mind game. It starts outside the track. Learn that, and maybe it'll help you!"

Sany walked away again.

"Then why recommend me? If you thought I was a threat to you, why bring me to compete against you?"

Sany stopped again, paused, and turned around.

"You know, before you showed up there wasn't anyone in Florida able to compete against me. I was the king, always was. This made me lazy, no challenges. So why train hard and improve my handling?"

Sany took a deep breath and continued:

"When you showed up and almost beat me in Florida, I knew I needed to get better. Train more, refine my handling. You helped me. You helped me be a better handler. And bringing you to the League was part of the plan. I won rounds this year. I was almost always in the finals. I wanted to beat you. You pushed me to be better."

Sany paused again. I tried to find the words to say something, but I could not.

"Congratulations on winning today! And please win this championship. Enough of those girls winning."

Sany turned and walked away.

26

CONSEQUENCES

Mid-October 2007. After returning from Charlotte and still trying to process everything that had happened with Amy, I went to my mom's house. Sitting at the table on the porch on a pleasant autumn afternoon, with a glass of apple juice in front of me, staring at nothing.

"Hey!" My mom approached me, opening the kitchen glass door, and sitting beside me.

"Hey!"

"A penny for your thoughts." my mother said smiling.

I smiled back.

"It's nothing, mom! It's all good."

"Hmm. I don't know if I believe that."

"I think it's just the pressure of the end of the season."

"No, I don't think it's that either." my mother said. "I think it has to do with that other competitor that you are having a little thing with."

"Mom!" I replied surprised. "How do you know that?"

My mother laughed and replied.

"Mothers know everything. And, Leo has been telling me some things."

"That rat!"

We both laughed.

"So..." my mother insisted. "Tell me what happened."

"We had a pretty serious fight this last round."

"Let me guess. She was mad at you because you won the competition where, in her opinion, she should have won."

I smiled.

"You are unbelievable!" I said.

"Don't forget. Mothers know everything. Always!"

We laughed once more. She continued.

"Well, have you tried putting yourself in her shoes? Maybe she really got mad because she hoped to win there. Maybe you would also be mad if this happened in Florida, with people rooting for you."

"I know. I get it. But what did she expect? That I would lose on purpose?"

"I think she's just mad at the situation. And not at you."

"I don't know. Last time we spoke she seemed pretty mad at me."

"Give her a break. Let things settle down. You'll talk again, you'll see."

"I don't know, I think she'll never want to talk to me again."

"Well, if she really likes you, she will. But if she don't, it's because she doesn't really like you. And then maybe it's the best for you both to follow different paths."

I lowered my head and thought. Maybe that was it. Maybe

she didn't really like me, and all that happened just because we were in the right place at the right time.

"I know it's hard, but you need to stop thinking about it. Think about your training. By the way, I heard that you guys are building a new training facility in Plant City?"

"Oh mom, how do you know everything?"

"A mother always knows!"

###

In Plant City, construction on our new training center had already begun. The old warehouse had already been cleaned and was being painted.

Leo, myself, Rafi, and Mr. Monterey were there supervising the work.

"My God! There is much more space here than I thought!" I said inside the warehouse that was now empty.

"I know!" answered Mr. Monterey. "I didn't even remember how big this place is."

"Marquito, I think we'll be able to put a complete set of obstacles in here." Leo said. "And, we'll still have space for a crating area, and a small office."

"Great!" I answered.

"We had a minor problem with the warehouse's bathroom." Rafi said. "But they are already changing some pipes and it will also be good to use."

"And we already have a list of eight people who want to come here to train their dogs." said Leo, excited.

We were all happy with the initial results. The warehouse would fit a bigger training track than we expected, and the high ceiling would help with the ventilation and cooling system for the hot Florida summer days.

"Let's see the new kennels!" I said.

"Yes, let's go!" Rafi said.

We started walking out of the warehouse towards the back of the house, where the old kennel no longer existed and now two employees were working building the masonry walls that would form the new kennels.

"And that litter, Mr Monterey?" I asked.

"They're all gone, Marquito!" answered Mr. Monterey excited. "Five days after you posted on your social media, they were all gone."

"That's what I said, remember?" bragged, Rafi.

We approached the area where the new kennels were being built and looked around. On our left, the house where Rafi and Mr. Monterey lived. In the background, the entrance to the property. Behind us, the warehouse that was being renovated.

"Yeah, I think we have a beautiful future ahead of us here." I said smiling. "I don't know, maybe even our own future dog agility team, huh?"

"Calm down!" Leo said. "That's dreaming too big!"

Everyone smiled.

"Marquito, I wanted to thank you once again for all this." Mr. Monterey said.

"Mr. Monterey, we're past the thanking moment. No need to thank. I want to see this place growing!"

27

BOSTON, MASSACHUSETTS
ROUND 9 NATIONAL LEAGUE
OCTOBER 2007

The league's website had written a huge story about me. The only rookie who won two consecutive rounds was now, the favorite to win the National League.

With an eight-point lead over Amy, and with a fourteen-point lead over Lisa, I knew that if I win in Boston and neither of them finished above third place, statistically I would be the champion.

In the article, the writer mentioned that it was the end of the era of fighting between Amy and Lisa, and the beginning of a new era with a talented young handler running with a very well-trained dog ready to be champion in his rookie year.

I tried not to pay too much attention to those articles, mainly because one day they portrayed you as a God, and the next day as nothing. So why bother with that?

I couldn't lie, I was euphoric with our results. Winning two consecutive rounds, in Nashville and Charlotte, was without a doubt the most important thing I had ever achieved in dog agility. But I knew I hadn't won yet, and a slip in the last two rounds would mean the end of the dream.

Lisa and Amy were much more experienced handlers than I am, and they would come with everything for the last two rounds.

Since our discussion in Charlotte, Amy and I hadn't spoken again. We stopped texting each other and no more video calls. Lost contact completely. Even on her social medias Amy was gone. Hasn't posted anything since the end of the Charlotte round.

Her last post, right after the round, said: "I WOULD LIKE TO THANK EVERYONE WHO ATTENDED THE COMPETITION IN OUR HOME TODAY. I WAS VERY SAD FOR OUR RESULT AND EXPECTED TO GIVE YOU ALL A LITTLE BIT MORE. BUT IT'S NOT OVER YET. LET'S FIGHT TO THE END. THANKS!"

After that, she was gone.

I was feeling bad. I miss talking with her. I miss the jokes, the laughs. I didn't know how things were going to turn out between us. Everything was new to me. Maybe Amy really was an unbalanced person as many said. Maybe she was one of those people who would do anything to win. But in a competitive environment, weren't we all like that?

Round 9 in Boston would take place at the Topsfield Fairgrounds, about 40 minutes from Boston International Airport. Once again, a place that hosted agricultural events, rodeos. Even destruction derbys had taken place there.

I was honestly excited about the place before I even arrived there. I got information that the surface of the track was once again made of clay, which was a gift from God to us. The last two rounds we had won happened on clay, and clearly it was a big advantage for us.

Late Thursday afternoon we arrived at the site. No surprises. From the outside, it looked like a lot of the places we'd competed in all year.

The competitors' RVs were already there, including Amy's, which I could see parked not far from mine. The arena, next to the RV parking lot looked great from the outside and impressed me. No doubt much bigger than the arenas in Nashville and Chicago. But I would be able to look inside the next day.

Now it was time to rest, because the next few days would be intense.

###
FRIDAY

On Friday morning I got scared when I left the RV around seven in the morning to take Arrow for a pee. A cold, sharp and intense wind hit me full on. And I, wearing only shorts and a T-shirt, was caught off guard.

It was cold. For a Brazilian raised in Florida and used to 104 degrees Fahrenheit it was freezing. The temperature of 50 degrees Fahrenheit didn't seem to affect most other handlers who also started getting out of their RV's taking their dogs for morning needs.

Amy got out of her RV a few seconds later. Already in her team cap and hair in a ponytail. She looked at me but turned her head to the opposite side. A few seconds out and she brought X back inside her RV.

I didn't have a good feeling about this weekend.

The morning briefing was tense. No one in the room spoke. A doleful silence took over the environment. Mario was at my side as usual. Lisa, silent in a corner of the room. Amy, on the other side of the room, was also quiet.

Steve did his routine, explaining some protocols for the weekend, getting on and off the track, accessing results, and all the usual. At the end, he made his mention of the title dispute.

"We have three handlers competing for the title in these last two rounds. Let's fight for the title with respect, and put on a show for the audience, ok?"

Nobody answered. The silence remained, until Sany opened his mouth.

"Whoever laughs first will lose!"

Everyone laughed, including me. Sany had to be the one to break the ice in that tense moment.

Briefing finished and we walked down the stairs to the arena. It was time for training and adaptation to the track's surface. I was excited. Another track with a clay floor, the same one we always ran so well on. Couldn't wait. Could we win another round?

I stopped dead in my track as an electric shock went down my back. As I entered the arena for the first time, I saw the surface had been changed!

The gigantic arena, with capacity for over 1000 people, and large stands around it was gorgeous, however, the surface that was traditionally used in the competitions at the site had been replaced by artificial grass.

No one but me looked so shocked. Apparently everyone already knew that the surface of the track had been changed, except me. Lisa, just ahead of me, plastered a huge smile on her face as she first stepped onto the floor. She crouched down, passing her hand over the brand-new artificial grass, as if she were petting a fluffy rug, and smiled.

Sany passed by me.

"Amazing, right?" Sany said.

"They said the floor was clay." - I said.

Sany laughed.

"Some people still have a lot of influence inside the organization." Sany said nodding to Lisa.

Our training hadn't been bad. On the contrary, Arrow was actually running well on that surface. Slipping a bit here and there, but in general the grip of the track was pretty good.

The surface was brand new and had been put on a few days before the competition.

Amy was fine too. X showed a lot of grip doing corners and maneuvers. She was ready to recover in the championship.

On the first day, the team that was catching everyone's attention was Lisa & Fire. Clearly in a much more comfortable environment, Lisa demonstrated incredible precision in her training. Using back sides, blind crosses, rear crosses, and diverse moves. Lisa was also prepared for the weekend, and Fire, was getting the attention of all the other handlers during practice.

The next day, with the arena packed, things would start to get interesting.

###

SATURDAY

I woke up on Saturday to more excruciating freezing day. Forty-one degrees Fahrenheit was on the display inside the RV indicating the outside temperature.

I put on my team uniform jacket and we left. In the distance, it was already possible to see the movement of cars parking and the public entering the arena through the main entrance. Competitors entered through the back entrance and as soon as I set foot in the arena I knew it would be another interesting day.

The arena wasn't fully packed, but it was one of the most beautiful sites I had seen during the season. Now with all the lights on for the first time, you could get an idea of the grandeur of the place. A large electronic scoreboard at the top was ready to announce the results. Two screens showed videos of competitors from the previous rounds, including Arrow and I winning in Charlotte. The grandstand that surrounded the track in 360 degrees added a beautiful feeling to the environment.

Music rolling, people excited in the stands, each one rooting for their favorite handler. "MARQUITO! LET'S GO MARQUITO!", I heard coming from the crowd. I waved back and was rewarded with more applause.

It was time to think about the courses.

For the weekend, the organization had brought in a European judge.

Dog agility is very popular in Europe, and some of the best handlers and judges in the world are from there. But there was an important difference between the courses made by American judges and European judges. Competing in a course judged by a European judge meant competing on tracks with a high risk of elimination and multiple traps. And that's exactly how the Qualifiers started.

###

QUALIFIER 1

The Qualifier 1 course caused tension among the handlers. Sharp corners, jumping at difficult angles, tunnels strategically placed at points on the track that posed an intense risk of elimination were just some of the problems handlers needed to be concerned about.

It's important to say that even with all those challenges, it doesn't mean that the course was bad. On the contrary, the course offered the dogs speed points and low speed exercises without breaking the flow of the runs. It really was a good and challenging course.

The first victims didn't take long to appear, with three of the first five handlers who entered the track being eliminated. The second dog to hit the track that day fell on one of the jumps and literally broke the jump support in two, causing concerns among handlers and fans. Pretty ugly thing to see, but the dog didn't suffer any injuries.

A few minutes of break for the organization to bring a new jump onto the track and the runs continued.

At that point, the highlight of the first Qualifier had been

Natasha and Polly, both with great times and running without penalties. Polly with Panda once again standing ahead.

Mario came to the track and, like usual, on challenging courses that didn't require so much speed that Mario showed his talent with old Rex. Best first Qualifier time without penalties. I remember watching Mario running and thinking what an exceptional handler he is. There were already rumors that Mario was training a new six-month-old puppy and that he had plans to return to the National League in a few years. He always denied it and said that for him the National League would end this year.

Mario was at the top of the table until Sany went on track to destroy the clock and set the best time of the day. With no chance of being champion after the elimination in Charlotte, now Sany had nothing left to prove. Well, he still had no contract for next year, so technically he was still trying to prove he could come back for next season. Would Sany come back or not? Nobody really knew.

Lisa took to the track right after Sany for her first Qualifier and was the first one to rouse the crowd, which until that moment had been relatively quiet, but now completely freaked out. That was the Fire we had seen in Los Angeles and Las Vegas, and that was the Lisa we had also seen before. Extremely aggressive handling, too aggressive for a first Qualifier but Lisa took Sany's time down by more than a second. Crazy crowed standing, applauding Lisa and Fire. It was clear that Lisa was venting all the bad results from the previous rounds. And with the artificial grass surface, she was in the fight to win in Boston.

Amy came right after and also pushed as much as she could on her first performance of the weekend. Handling very aggressively, Amy was clearly struggling to beat Lisa's time. Yells for "AMY! AMY!" echoed in the crowd and she finished her run with a time very close to Lisa's, but still not as fast.

The last one to get on track in Qualifier 1 was me, being the leader of the championship, I got on track last in the first Qualifier.

After watching Lisa, Amy, Sany, Mario and all the handlers being really aggressive on the first leg of the day, I had nothing else to do but follow the same strategy and try to make a good time on the first Qualifier.

Things were going well until at a certain point in our run I lost connection and contact with Arrow who went at a difficult angle in one of the jumps, knocking the bar. The noise of the bar hitting the ground discouraged me and again making me lose the connection with her, giving the JUMP command too late, and another bar came to the ground.

We finished the first Qualifier with two penalties and a higher time than Lisa, Amy and Sany.

Walking with Arrow off the track, I passed by Amy. I looked at her and was ready to say something, but she just turned her face away.

###

Break between runs. The music rose as the judge prepared the course for Qualifier 2.

I went to the side of the track to talk to Leo.

"What was that man?" asked Leo.

"I lost the connection with her. I don't know what happened, I just lost connection with her!"

"Listen! Don't let these "extra competition" things enter your mind!"

"What are you talking about?" I asked.

"Marquito, don't let this thing between you and Amy interfere with your handling..."

"Leo!" I interrupted. "It has nothing to do with my thing with Amy! I lost the connection with Arrow, just that!"

Leo scratched his forehead.

"Okay. If it was not that, let's pay attention to Qualifier 2."

"Okay." I replied sort of ignoring Leo.

I wasn't even thinking about Amy when I was running Qualifier 1. Was it somehow affecting my performance? Impossible. "LET'S GO TO QUALIFIER 2 AND QUALIFY FOR SEMIS," I thought.

###
QUALIFIER 2

Qualifier 2 course followed the same patterns as the first Qualifier. Lots of jumps at difficult angles, tunnels at tricky points on the track begging for elimination, and a demand for extreme attention from handlers.

Handlers started to enter the track and began, one by one, to be eliminated. Joe, out! Natasha, eliminated! Caitlyn, out! After several handlers left the track, many of them not even making it halfway, Polly was the first to be able to finish the course.

Under applause and shouts for "PANDA! PANDA!", the "most beloved mix breed in the country" managed to secure his qualification for the semi-finals amid many handlers disappointed with their performance.

Mario took to the track to show how it's done. With a good time on the clock, Mario lifted the crowd in the stands finishing his run without penalties, taking the temporary first place in the table and guaranteeing his position for the semi-finals.

After Mario, it was my turn. Even with two penalties in Qualifier 1, I knew I didn't need to be as fast to qualify for the semi-finals. After so many eliminations by the other handlers before me, whoever finished Qualifier 2 without penalties would practically be given a spot in the semis.

I started my run trying to balance my handling. Arrow wasn't uncomfortable on the artificial grass, but clearly she wasn't as comfortable as in the two previous rounds we'd won. But her DRIVE was still there. Arrow ran strongly, putting speed where the course allowed, and making good turns with the good grip of the track. But once again for a brief second, I lost the connection with her and when I tried to help her in one of the jumps, I ended up walking in front of her, and she touched the bar, knocking it over. One more penalty! And now, I was concerned about our situation in Boston.

Sany, Amy, and Lisa followed to run Qualifier 2.

All finished their runs without penalties. Sany was doing the basics, and doing the basics for Sany means finishing his run without penalties and always in the TOP 3.

Amy and Lisa battled for every tenth of a second in Qualifier 2. Both were aggressive, accurate and had the audience watching on their feet. It was a good show for the crowd! Nobody could beat their time.

The dogs, X and Fire, were flying, and it looked like no one could beat them that weekend. It was the old fight between Amy and Lisa at its core in Boston.

With 0.03 seconds difference, Lisa was ahead of Amy.

Saturday's rounds over, the qualified for the semi-finals on Sunday, in order, were Lisa, Amy, Sany, Mario, Polly and me, but in 7th place.

I needed to change something for Sunday or there was a chance of losing the lead of the championship in Boston.

###

Over the course of the day I had run into Amy several times. But it really seemed like she didn't want to talk to me. Every time, she turned away and ignored me. So I decided I wouldn't even try anymore. My Saturday had been pretty terrible and I needed to focus to get better. Maybe Leo was right and without even realizing it, I was allowing my feelings to get in the way. Something much bigger was at stake here in Boston, and I couldn't let anything get in the way of my performance.

###

SUNDAY

Sunday, and the arena was even more crowded. The empty seats I had seen on Saturday were gone. Loud music, cheering, and event sponsors throwing free samples to fans. The arena was partying!

###

SEMI-FINALS

The semi-finals course followed the same pattern as what had been seen on Saturday. The European judge was really forcing the handlers to show their best.

The highlight of the course was an exercise that used four tunnels in a straight line forming a square in the middle of the track. At a certain point, the handlers needed to make the four tunnels in the sequence, however, avoiding jumps that had been placed between them. In other words, the risk of a dog getting confused and heading to the jump instead of the next tunnel was immense. It was a high speed sequence that would demand a lot from handlers and dogs.

The first two dogs to enter the track were unlucky, and both ended up being eliminated in the challenging four-tunnel exercise the judge had prepared.

The biggest problem with the exercise was that the tunnels were in a straight line and the dogs were pushing for a lot of speed, leaving the handlers behind them. When the dog needed to head to the next tunnel there was a jump ahead, and the handlers were not well positioned to bypass the jump and direct the dogs to the next tunnel.

Leo yelled from the side of the track and I ran to him.

"What's up?" I asked.

"Pay attention! You can't let her get too far ahead of you! Before reaching that sequence of tunnels you will need to be one or two obstacles in front of her. Otherwise she'll go out in front of you and that's it. DONE!"

"OK!"

Leo was right! The big secret to getting through that exercise without eliminating was to stay ahead of the dog. If

Arrow got out of the tunnel without me ahead, there would be no chance. She would look for the nearest obstacle, which would be that jump intentionally placed there by the judge. And bam! Out!

Due to the bad result in Qualifers we were already the next ones to enter. Until then, no dog had survived the course.

I walked with Arrow to the starting mark. I could hear shouts of "MARQUITO! GO MARQUITO!", coming from the stands. Yes! I had fans!

"STAY!" I commanded Arrow, as I walked away.

"I HAVE TO STAY IN FRONT OF HER ALWAYS", I told myself!

"OK!" I released Arrow.

Arrow lunged for the first jump. I could see small pieces of rubber sticking out of the ground as she jumped the first obstacle in the course. Two jumps and we went to A frame. Arrow hit the surface of the obstacle and rattled the chains holding it to the ground. We approached the slalom, no problems. Great entry, with strength and precision. Arrow was looking for grip grabbing the ground while her claws came out of her paws and with her pads slidding along the surface. Two more jumps and we're off to the dreaded sequence of tunnels. I ran hard! I felt a little twinge in my calf but kept running.

With my right arm outstretched, I pointed to the first tunnel. "TUNNEL!!!", I yelled loudly! And there was Arrow diving into the first tunnel. In two seconds she was through the first tunnel but I was ahead. Bypassing the dangerously placed jump and "TUNNEL", I yelled again! Arrow dove on the second tunnel, lifting rubber off the ground.

Once again I ran like crazy now diagonally, looking for the third tunnel. But Arrow was already out of the second tunnel, side by side with me. Again, we went around the jump that was there just to make life difficult for the handlers. "THIS WAS CLOSE", I thought. And now I raised my left arm "TUNNEL" I shouted for the third time and Arrow with a lot of speed entered the third tunnel. There's still one more! My God, I was behind!

I ran fast towards the fourth and final tunnel of this endless exercise! I am not going to make it! Arrow exited the third tunnel about three feet ahead of me and looked at the jump. The jump that could wipe us out. There was nothing to do, it was all or nothing! I yelled "TUNNEL" again, hoping that Arrow would bypass the jump and enter the last tunnel, and so she did. She entered the tunnel, we continued our journey, and ended it with the best time so far! What a relief! What madness was that course! But we got it!

Only when I finished the run could I get an idea of the scale of what we had done. Applause, cheers, and whistles from the crowd! Now it was time to wait for the other handlers, but I think we are in the final!

Without a doubt, it had been the most physically challenging course I had ever run in my life. I returned to my chair and sat down breathless. Mario was there and approached:

"Man, that was absolutely beautiful!"

The next two on track were Mario and then Polly.

Handling Panda, Polly had problems with the tunnels. She

was not eliminated and managed to finish the run, but on the approach of the fourth tunnel she lost connection with Panda who did not enter the tunnel and got a refusal. Even so, she still managed to recover and finish with only one penalty.

Sany took to the track oozing confidence and, why not, arrogantly, shamelessly copied my plan, using the same lead by keeping two to three obstacles ahead of Maximus. He finished the run without penalties but with a slower time than mine.

Stepping off the track, he passed by me while I was sitting in my chair still catching my breath.

"I like the plan!" Sany said laughing in my direction!

I did not answer. "SON OF A BITCH" I just thought.

There were still Amy and Lisa to hit the track for the semi-finals, and oddly enough I was leading the pack at that point, followed by Sany, Mario, and Polly.

Amy took to the track, and the crowd was very supportive. Silently I was also rooting for her.

She placed X at the starting mark, backed away, and began her run.

"COME ON AMY!" I thought. What is this crazy feeling? I wanted to win but I still wanted Amy to win too! What a weird feeling!

X was flying on the track! With precise contact zones and a slalom that earned sighs and exclamations from the crowd, Amy approached the exercise with four tunnels and sent X into the first tunnel.

"LET'S GO AMY!" again I thought. Damn it! Yes, I was rooting for her!

Surprisingly, when X ran into the first tunnel, Amy didn't

run towards the second one, but to a spot on the track right in the center of all four tunnels!

"WHAT ARE YOU DOING, AMY???" I thought! "THAT'S CRAZY!". My first impression was that she would be eliminated. But no! Without moving and standing in the center of all the tunnels, Amy commanded X from a distance, circling the jumps in a precarious position and taking the tunnels, one by one, without any mistake. One of the most amazing runs I've ever seen a handler do in my life. They finished the run, taking the first position with a faster time than mine! It was just beautiful.

As she exited the track, she glanced at me. I didn't say anything, just a subtle nod of my head, which she returned.

Lisa on track! The handler who had dominated all the Qualifiers so far had a pretty tough job to do now, beating Amy's impressive run.

Lisa started her run with Fire barking as she passed the first jump. Lisa's handling was very similar to Amy. Slightly different but very similar. It was difficult at that moment to tell which of the two was going to be faster. But when Lisa approached the exercise with the four tunnels, it became evident that it was impossible to beat Amy on that track. Using the same handling as Sany and I, Lisa got past the dangerous spot on the track and finished without penalties, but with a slower time.

Amy led; I was second. Once again, we would fight to see who would be the winner.

FINALISTS
Amy & X

Marcus & Arrow
Lisa & Fire
Sany & Maximus
Mario & Rex
###
FINAL

As in Charlotte, the mood was tense among the five handlers who were in the final. Everybody focused and fixed on the track as the judge prepared the final course.

In the crowd there was no tension or stress. Music, dancing, and celebration. I preferred the crowd behaving that way. There were no Boston area handlers competing and people were watching for fun and not specifically cheering for any handler. People were there to watch a show!

Handlers walked the final course without even looking at each other. It was easy to explain the reason for such concentration, the final course brought another complicated challenge.

Again "playing with tunnels" the judge this time had placed two tunnels in the shape of the letter "C" facing each other, and the handlers needed to pass with the dogs between the tunnels, looking for a jump on the opposite side, without allowing the dogs to enter any of the tunnels. It was like going through a narrow corridor with tunnels on either side and not letting the dogs go in. Pretty hard.

Teams lined up on the pre-track! Pressure! I had Lisa in front of me and Amy behind me in the pre-track line. Right now you've got to only think about your run. Forget who's on your side. You have a final course to run ahead of you, and nothing else matters.

Mario was the first one to hit the track. If there was a handler who had the dog in his hand, it was Mario. Rex was a slow dog, but in exercises that require the dog to focus on the handler, Mario & Rex were unbeatable. They passed the exercise prepared by the judge, with a high time of 35:14 they managed to finish the run without penalties.

Sany was next! I was curious to see how Sany would survive that exercise.

Sany started his run with Maximus drooling down the track and leaving a trail of rubber as he ran. All perfect obstacles. Slalom! Seesaw! A frame! Dog walk! "DAMN, WHAT A GOOD DOG MAXIMUS IS", I thought. They approached the dangerous exercise created by the judge. Sany quickened his pace and raced away from Maximus, about four meters ahead of his dog. Wasting no time and making it look simple, Sany ran through the tunnels and called Maximus who didn't even look around. They finished the course with a great time of 31:39 in the temporary first position.

Lisa on track for another final! She had to take advantage now to recover in the championship. After poor results in Chicago, Nashville, and Charlotte she had to win one more round if she wanted to continue in the fight for the title.

I confess, I was rooting for Lisa & Fire to be eliminated. I know, it's a horrible thing to say. Wishing for a sporting colleague to do poorly. But at that moment I couldn't help that I wished they were eliminated. But it didn't happen! On the contrary, Lisa led Fire absolutely beautifully, going through the dreaded drill with the tunnels and still beating Sany's time. Time: 31:29.

It was our turn! I entered the track with Arrow walking to the start mark under a lot of applause and cheers for support from the stands. Everyone that weekend was being applauded. No boos, no bad words. It was a very cool crowd in Boston.

I put Arrow in the initial mark:

"STAY!" I commanded her.

I walked away to start my run. Thoughts of being national champion crossed my mind. Winning that round and practically guaranteeing the champion trophy. Fourth or fifth place in New York on the last round and I would be champion. Calm down! We have to do right here in Boston!

"OK!" I released Arrow!

Arrow was doing well, very well. Her grip was good, just a little slip at the start. Arrow made good turns and at all times kept eye contact with me waiting for the next command. Mouth open, drool splashing everywhere as she ran. A perfect A frame! Dog walk so fast that it shook the ground and elicited sighs from the crowd. We approached the dangerous point of the track. "WE HAVE TO PASS BETWEEN THOSE TWO TUNNELS, I JUST HAVE TO KEEP MY BODY STRAIGHT, DON'T TURN OR I WILL POINT THE TUNNEL OUT TO HER", I knew what I had to do.

We entered the exercise and I heard a loud noise, a noise that resembled the noise of a dog entering a tunnel at full speed. I looked back! Arrow had entered the wrong tunnel! NO! NO! An "OHHHHHH" came from the crowd. We were out. My God! Eliminated! I put my hands to my face and Arrow, not understanding what she had done wrong, sat beside me, and looked at me, confused.

There was nothing to do, I crouched down and hugged her "IT WAS NOT YOUR FAULT! IT WAS MINE". We started leaving the track under cheers of support from the crowd and the only thought I had in my mind at that moment was "DID WE LOSE THE CHAMPIONSHIP? WE WILL HAVE TO GO ALL OR NOTHING AT THE LAST ROUND".

Amy was entering, the last handler of the day! I was devastated. I was probably feeling like Amy in Charlotte. No, Amy was probably feeling a lot worse than me. It was her house.

Amy started her run!

With Lisa in first place, she had to be faster and more accurate than her rival. X dug her paws into the artificial grass of the arena, lifting rubber off the ground searching for the best grip he could find.

Again, I'll be honest. I was rooting for Amy! Technically speaking it would be much better for me if Lisa won because she was only third in the championship while Amy was second, much closer to me. "GO AMY!", "WIN THE ROUND", I thought, while watching from outside as Amy handled X.

X aggressively climbed the seesaw, sliding down the plank and throwing his body forward. The seesaw exploded on the ground, scattering rubber and X's drooling everywhere. Amy commanded X to enter the slalom and he did it so aggressively that the first pole egged so much that I thought it was going to break.

They approached the dangerous point of the track, Amy

running way in front of X probably using the same handling as Sany and not allowing the dog to look to the side where the tunnels were. It worked out! Amy passed! A few more jumps and DONE! They finished the run without penalties.

Everyone looked at the electronic scoreboard waiting for the final result. A few seconds and the number 2 appeared next to Amy's name. Time: 31:34, 0.05 seconds slower than Lisa.

On the other side of the track, Lisa screamed, celebrating! She had won the round in Boston, with Amy in second.

From a distance, I saw Amy leashing X, head down, and stepping off the track. I thought about going to her and saying something, but in that moment, I knew the best thing to do was stay silent.

RESULTS ROUND 9 BOSTON

1. Lisa & Fire
2. Amy & X
3. Sany & Maximus
4. Mario & Rex
5. Marcus & Arrow

RANKING AFTER ROUND 9 BOSTON

1. Lisa & Fire = 153 pts
2. Marcus & Arrow = 152 pts
3. Amy & X = 152 pts
4. Sany & Maximus = 113 pts
5. Mario & Rex = 54 pts

6. Polly & Panda = 42 pts
7. Joe & Jungle = 22 pts
8. Natasha & Sparky = 20 pts
9. Caitlyn & Target = 12 pts

###

With the victory in Boston, Lisa took the first position in the table. But Amy and I were only one point behind her. It would be all or nothing at the last round in New York.

28

DECISIONS

November 2007 and the weather in Florida was already starting to get cold. The heat was already behind us.

"That was absolutely fantastic!" my dad said with a smile on his face and punching the table.

I was visiting my dad again, a week after I got back from Boston. I still felt uncomfortable in that place, but talking to my dad was going much better.

He could not hide his happiness at seeing me as I entered the large communal area. I was happy to see him again too.

It's so easy to judge someone without knowing their motives, their life story, or their aspirations. I am not defending my father, far from it. I think he made a serious mistake in life, but at least he was paying for what he did.

It was visible in his face, in his body, how much that prison had punished him. How hard it was for him to go through all that, away from his family. As much as he deserved to pay for what he had done, I could see real regret in him. The price he was paying was high. And being there just twice visiting him, I could already believe that he could go out and be a better person. But there was still time for him to pay for what he did. Time. A little word that means so much, and we only realize its importance after we've lost it. Remembering how much more we could have enjoyed it.

"I know! I didn't believe it either!", I replied smiling.

"So let me see if I understand. There is only one more round in New York."

"Yep."

"And you are only one point behind the leader of the championship, that's Lisa."

"Yep."

"And this Amy, who by the way you like a lot..."

"Ah... Dad!" I replied laughing and turning my head.

"I know! I know! You two are just one point behind this championship leader Lisa."

"Yep."

"So, any of you three who win the last round, or finish ahead of the other, will be the champion."

"Yep."

"That's crazy!"

I laughed.

"It seems like never before in the history of the League that they had three handlers so close on the last round."

"And you think your dog is ready? Do you feel ready?"

"I am fine. She is fine. We don't change anything from what we normally do. We are training as usual. Studying the judge to try to be prepared for the exercises he could prepare. Trying to sleep well, eat well. All normal."

My dad took a deep breath and leaned back in his chair.

"I'm very proud of you."

"Thanks."

Pause.

"I would like to see you there." I said.

"I would like to be there. But I want you to know that I'll be watching, and I'll be there with you even though I'm away."

My dad placed his hand on my arm. I put my hand over his hand.

"I know. I will do my best not to embarrass anyone."

"Relax, there is no chance of that happening."

We both smiled at each other.

###

I heard the horn of the black Suburban in front of my house. It was Kevin, coming to pick me up to take me to the airport.

My mom was with me inside. I grabbed my backpack and put it on. I connected Arrow's leash to her harness and stood up. My mom walked over and put her hands on my face.

"I don't have much to tell you." my mother said. "Just good luck. You are already the champion."

"Thanks for always supporting me. Even when it seemed like a stupid hobby."

"It was never a stupid hobby."

We hugged each other tightly. Another honk coming from outside.

"I need to go!" I said walking away from her.

"Have a good trip, God bless you! We never know the

surprises that will happen in our lives.", my mother said before I walked through the door.

Unlike some other people, my mom never questioned me, never judged me, and never made any jokes since I started competing with Arrow. On the contrary, she always supported me even before she truly understood what this dog agility thing was all about it. After everything she did to help us through our family's most difficult time, I know now I had the opportunity to give back to her a little bit of what she had done for us.

The title I was going to fight for in New York was not just a dog agility title, it was my declaration to the world, and even to myself that I was not just another regular person living in this world with a regular job and paying my monthly bills. I could do more, I could make a difference in someone's life. The same way my mother had made a difference in my life since everything that happened in our family.

This was my chance. And I would do everything I could to not let this opportunity pass.

###

"You are quiet today, my friend!" said Kevin steering the Suburban.

"Oh sorry. I think I'm a little distracted."

"Ok, I understand. Title fight this weekend, right?"

"Yep" I took a deep breath.

Pause, then Kevin continued.

"Ah, I need to tell you something. Remember my daughter, the one who was annoying me for a Border Collie after seeing you competing in Miami."

"Yes, of course! I remember."

Kevin touched his cellphone, attached to the car's dashboard, and a picture of a girl with a Border Collie puppy popped up. I smiled happily.

"Man, that's cool! Very cool! How old?", I asked.

"Five months." Kevin replied. "And she already said that she wants to start training for agility."

We both laughed.

"See, the problem you caused me?" Kevin said.

"Look. Because I "caused" this problem, I am going to do something for you. Call me next week after I get back from New York, and we're going to Plant City together to my new training center. Let's train this puppy, ok? On me."

"Serious?" Kevin said with a big smile. "Wow, thank you very much!"

"It's ok! Thank you for the great conversations, always!"

29

NEW YORK
ROUND 10 NATIONAL LEAGUE
NOVEMBER

Ten rounds, three competitors, only one title. In three days, we would all know who it would be, Lisa, Amy or me. Only one would win the title.

Under freezing weather and some small snow flakes, I arrived at my hotel. No RV's that weekend. The chaotic city of New York doesn't have space for large Rv's. We would all stay in hotels.

I looked out the hotel window and started to admire the "wild" landscape of that insane city that never stops for a single second. Cars, taxis, horns, police cars and ambulances. What a noisy place.

Not even at night was there a second of peace. The noises continued; the cars did not stop passing by. People continued walking along the sidewalks.

Two o'clock in the morning, lying in bed I turned back and forward trying to close my eyes and fall asleep, in vain.

There was no way to relax my body and turn it off. I would be running for the National League title, can you imagine that?

I got out of bed in the darkness. I opened the window curtain and the glare of the city lights entered. I looked out. 2 am and cars and people still going by. "BUNCH OF IDIOTS, GO TO SLEEP", "IT'S ALMOST 3 IN THE MORNING", I thought.

From the window I could see Penn Station, and a little further behind, a gigantic building, a huge dome were it said Madison Square Garden. The arena where the final would take place.

###
FRIDAY

After a few hours of sleep, I got up around eight in the morning. The briefing would be at the convention center of the hotel where we were staying.

I arrived at the lobby and most of the other competitors were already there. We were lead to a side door that gave access to the convention center.

We sat down and spread out around the place. Steve started his briefing as usual, talking about the competition and the ground rules we already knew.

"And finally, I would like to thank you all for the sensational season. Congratulations on the disputes and thank you for keeping the League competitive and exciting. Thanks to you, we signed a contract with two more big sponsors that will allow us to make an even better season for next year."

"They could use a little more of that money to invest in the arenas!" Lisa said in the middle of everyone.

"That's what we do, Lisa." Steve replied.

"I know, but we can no longer compete in arenas with little infrastructure that still use those red clay surfaces that pose a risk to dogs and handlers."

"I don't think they pose a risk to anyone!" Amy interrupted.

The atmosphere started to get tense.

"Amy, I'm sorry but there are no doubts that the future of the sport is in artificial grass. You can argue against it, or just accept it. Look what they do in Europe."

"I think the surfaces where we competed this year were pretty good, with little exceptions." Said Amy.

A silence took over the place.

"FIGHT! FIGHT!" shouted Sany.

Everyone laughed, including me. Lisa and Amy, of course, remained quiet. Steve continued.

"Lisa, we always work to offer the best infrastructure for our competitors. Our intention is to continue using different types of surfaces, thus offering different possibilities, and increasing competitiveness."

Lisa just went quiet and didn't respond. Looks like Amy had won the first round that weekend.

End of briefing and we were leaving the room when I tried to approach Amy.

"Hey!" I said.

"Hey!" she answered.

"Are you alright?"

"Yeah, fine. you?"

"All good."

Awkward pause.

"Well, good luck to you this weekend." I said.

"You too." Amy replied with a shy smile.

She walked away from me.

###

We arrived at Madison Square Garden with the dogs after lunch for training and for the dogs to adapt to the surface of the track.

The process of entering the Garden took about twenty minutes. From the entrance gate we made our way to a long hallway. We walked through the corridors of the building until we reached a room where our uniforms were prepared and waiting for us.

After that, another long walk through corridors and we finally set foot inside the arena. I was completely dumbfounded by what I saw. The place was gigantic. The bleacher's lights were not yet fully lit and it was not possible to see from inside the arena where the bleachers ended. They just disappeared into the top, into the darkness. At that time I had no idea how many people could fit in there, but I started to imagine that place full, once the arena opened to the public for the weekend.

After my amazement at the arena it was time to check out the track and enter with Arrow for the first time.

Was I surprised? No! It was expected that the surface used in the final round in New York was made of artificial grass. Of course Lisa was happy about it and, in theory, Amy and I were at a slight disadvantage. But really, that wasn't bothering me one bit. Especially after I put Arrow on track for the first training.

That surface was so good! What a sensational grip! The dogs were sticking to the track and the training showed that all dogs and handlers would be able to use full speed without fear of slipping.

Slightly different from the artificial grass used in Boston, the material used in New York was shorter, like a thicker carpet with more rubber and therefore more grip. The surface was like a good bathroom rug that clung to the floor and didn't let anyone slip.

With 100% of the competitors happy with the surface, we were now depending on the judge, and what he had prepared for the competitors.

###

That Friday night the fatigue really hit. It was around eight o'clock at night and I was exhausted. I ended up falling asleep in the loveseat in the hotel room when someone knocked on the door.

I jumped up quickly thinking maybe it was Amy, and opened the door, it was Paula.

She looked me up and down, sizing me up with a not-too-happy face.

"Aren't you ready yet?" Paula asked.

"Ready for what?" I asked.

"For dinner."

I had completely forgotten that there was a dinner at a restaurant with the team. Even Mr. Audian would be there.

"Damn it, I completely forgot."

"Then get dressed. We are waiting.", Paula said.

"Paula, I'm not going. Honestly, I'm so tired and tomorrow is one of the most important days of my life. I need to rest."

Paula, still at the bedroom door, looked over my shoulder as if searching for somebody inside my room.

"Are you alone?"

I took a deep breath before answering her.

"No, there are three hookers here. We're having an orgy. Do you want to participate?"

Paula stared at me.

"Paula, I'm alone. I didn't sleep well last night. I am just really tired, and I need to sleep. Please."

"Okay. I'll talk to Mr. Audian."

"Thanks."

I closed the door and looked at Arrow lying in the middle of the room.

"You think I am going to regret that, right?"

Arrow turned her head to the side as if answering me.

"Well, if we win the tittle, I'm sure everything will be fine."

###

SATURDAY

Arrow and I arrived at the arena around 10 am. By car, we entered through the side gate. Regular people were entering the Garden through the main gate.

As we walked through the corridors the noise from the music was echoing in the background. The arena was already opened to the public.

We arrived at the locker rooms that were normally used

by NBA Basketball teams. Surreal feeling to be using one of those locker rooms. Life is very surprising.

Music and clapping echoed everywhere. There was no doubt that an excited audience was already waiting for us in the stands. Mario was with me in the same room and noticed that I was acting a little more nervous than usual.

"Hey kid, all good?" asked Mario.

"I'll tell you in a couple days."

Mario laughed.

"You are going to do just fine!" said Mario.

We were ready! We walked out of the locker rooms and started walking through the tunnels towards the arena. The noise got louder, and I saw the end of the tunnel that led to the arena.

Amy, Polly and Joe rushed past me with their respective dogs. I was still walking with Arrow at my side. That long walk helped to put my nerves at ease. Yes, I was nervous. It wasn't quite common for me to get nervous like that. The only exception, without a doubt was the round in Miami, my first. After that, especially after the victory in Atlanta, things calmed down and I learned how to deal with it. But today, things were different.

When I finally reached the end of the tunnel and entered the arena, my legs shutdown. I looked around that gigantic, crowded place.

All the lights were on and for the first time I could see the grandeur of Madison Square Garden. To see the last rows of seats I had to look up, almost as if looking to the sky, the place was huge.

"Holy Mother of God!" I said out loud to myself.

A giant screen at the top of the arena showed videos of past rounds. They were showing Lisa's victory in Boston. It was there that the results would be announced. The first row of seats had been retracted and there was now an area for crates and team coaches.

Still stunned by the immensity, I remained standing at the exit of the tunnel, unable to move my legs.

Sany ran past me, entering the arena and looked quickly at me.

"Welcome to Hell!" Sany said laughing.

After almost five minutes, I finally managed to move and ran into the arena.

Leo was in front of the first row of seats, just behind the area where the crates were.

"Impressive, huh?" Leo asked.

"I've never seen anything like this in my life!"

"Welcome to the adults playground!"

The judge for the final round would be the same one who judged in Miami. Yes, the same one where I was knocked out in the final, throwing away my first win. He was known for his unpredictability. His courses ranged from treacherous tight ones to very open ones, with long lines and lots of speed. We didn't have a clue what he was up to for the weekend.

###

QUALIFIER 1

The answers to our questions started to appear in the first Qualifier.

An open course with a lot of straights lines and only one

elimination risk point. But overall, the first course prioritized speed. Three tunnels in straight lines, followed by the slalom with the entry also in a straight line. Two backside jumps and contacts also with frontal approaches. It was going to be a lot of running.

The first handlers entered the track and it was clear what the judge was trying to do. Placing a course with so many straight lines to significantly reduce the number of eliminated dogs, making the crowd even more excited about the competition.

Everybody was finishing their runs. A few bars on the ground and some refusals, but nobody was being eliminated.

Every handler on the track had their name showing in bold letters on the electronic scoreboard on the roof of the arena. It was really cool! The architecture was something I had never seen before in a dog agility competition.

Polly took to the track with the unconditional support of everyone in the stands. She waved to the crowd and finished her first run without penalties and with the provisional first place in the table.

Mario followed shortly thereafter but couldn't beat Polly's time.

Sany was next and got on the track smiling and enjoying the moment. He bowed to the fans who loved it and returned it with many shouts of "MAX! MAX! MAX!", an ode to his dog Maximus. Sany decided to put on a show. With a perfect run, he put more than a second on Polly, drawing applause from everyone. Sany even sent kisses to the crowd that went crazy.

There was no doubt that Sany was enjoying the moment.

The last three handlers were the ones fighting for the title and there we were, side by side, on the pre-track ready to go. Amy, myself, and Lisa.

Amy walked X onto the track. Serious, with her well-known low cap style, almost covering her eyes and with her ponytail sticking out from behind the cap.

I wanted to root for her. I was rooting for her. But I was also there to win that championship.

Amy destroyed Sany's time! Using the perfect grip provided by the surface, she didn't spare X. At that moment there was no longer that "the first Qualifier is just to adapt to the track" thing. It was clear that the three of us would give everything we had from the first run until the last. It was the final!

On the way out, after a run that bordered on perfection and with the crowd crazed, Amy sent Lisa a look that could melt steel.

"On track Marcus & Arrow!" announced the speakers.

Still nervous, with sweating hands and wobbly legs, I stepped onto the perfect arena surface, positioned Arrow for our first run of the day, and off we went. There was no reason to be conservative, it was win or win. And on that course with so many straight lines and so many tunnels in straight lines, Arrow's speed was so intense, it was impossible even to think about being conservative.

Our first run was awesome. It wasn't perfect, but it was decent. We beat Sany's time, but not Amy, which seemed unbeatable.

To end the first Qualifier, Lisa took to the track with her

partner Fire on the leash. She gave a little peek to the electronic scoreboard, presumably to check the times, put Fire in the starting position and left.

The screaming audience, motivating Lisa just as they were motivating all the handlers. You could see T-shirts and banners throughout the stands cheering for specific competitors. Lisa, Amy, Sany and even Mario, Polly and me.

Lisa was playing hard. She yelled at Fire on the track trying to get everything out of her partner who obeyed every command from his handler without flinching.

Lisa crossed the last jump finishing the first Qualifier but failing to beat Amy's time on the first attempt. The times were close, and after the end of Qualifier 1, it was Amy who was at the top followed by Lisa, me, Sany, Polly, Mario, and Natasha.

Pause to rest.

The volume of music rose in the arena. Cheerleaders came in to do their stunts and hype the crowd. I went to the side of the track to try to talk to Leo. The sheer volume of the music and the applause from the crowd following the rhythm made communication difficult.

"Man, I gave everything I had. They are both flying." I said to Leo.

"You three are very close. Impossible to say who will be faster. But don't worry, at this point you are totally in the fight."

"OK!"

###

QUALIFIER 2

The Qualifier 2 course was already prepared, and all handlers entered the track to walk it. This time the judge had balanced the course very well. There were two high-speed points with sequences of five obstacles in straight lines, but one very tricky low-speed point with a trap that, for sure, would eliminate some handlers.

My thought did not take long to be proven. The first three handlers who entered the track ended up eliminated. The big challenge for that course was that there was a very abrupt transition between a high speed point with two jumps and a straight tunnel, to a low speed point formed by two backside jumps and the slalom. It was forcing handlers to abruptly reduce the dog's speed. Those who couldn't do it, ended up watching their dog diving into the wrong obstacle and get eliminated.

Joe, Natasha and Caitlyn, survived the course without being eliminated but with penalties. Polly and Mario managed to finish their runs without penalties and had secured themselves in Sunday's semi-finals.

Sany was next! And the crowd was in love. With nothing to lose and completely relaxed, running with no pressure, Sany took to the track again bowing to everyone. He put Maximus on the starting mark, backed away, and started his run.

Sany, as always, showed a lot of skill handling Maximus. Perfect contact zones, turns with a great response from Maximus, who never hesitated accepting Sany's commands and a lot of speed led Sany & Maximus to make the best time of the day, but with a penalty when Maximus slipped down the dog walk not touching the contact zone.

The next ones were myself, Lisa, and Amy, the three who were fighting for the title. It was our turn! I had a plan! Use the same strategy that gave us the victory in Charlotte with aggressive handling, always running ahead of Arrow and always giving commands with two to three obstacles ahead.

It worked very well! Arrow was showing her best form and complying with every command masterfully. From the jumps in a straight line, through the tunnel at high speed, to the abrupt speed reduction to the two backside jumps, entering the slalom and ending our run beautifully, drawing cheers and applause from the crowd as well as "GO MARQUITO! GO ARROW!" that I could hear coming from the stands.

"I want to see them beat this time!" I said to myself, looking at Arrow.

I was pretty sure neither Amy nor Lisa could beat my time. But Lisa shut my mouth by handling even more aggressively with Fire, and ending her run with a lower time than mine. The difference was a mere 0.04 seconds, but she had made it.

"That's just impossible!" I said again to myself, still with Arrow beside me on the leash, outside the track.

Amy was the last one on track, and after winning the first Qualifier it was clear she had enough motivation to pursue the "perfect Saturday" by winning both Qualifiers. Amy put X at the starting mark and left! It was possible to see patches of artificial grass rising from the ground as X ran across the track. "AMY! AMY!", was heard coming from the crowd.

I could see Amy's expression. Teeth bared and the vein on her neck sticking out. She was giving absolutely everything she had. X was responding very well, listening to all Amy's commands and throwing himself at obstacle after obstacle without fear. Amy finished her run and everyone looked at the screen searching for the result. It was a number two that appeared next to her name. Lisa had won the second Qualifier.

The numbers were unbelievable. Lisa: 32.08, Amy: 32.09 (amazing 0.01 seconds behind), and me 32.12 (0.04 seconds from Lisa and 0.03 seconds from Amy).

What an incredible competition! What an amazing show the audience was witnessing that Saturday afternoon in New York.

"I do not believe this!" I said to Leo. "I thought I had the perfect run and those two still beat me! Unbelievable!"

"It's close! The difference is zero! You are still in the fight."

Yet what I did know was that Amy had won the first Qualifier and Lisa the second. And I had finished third in both. I had to change that, or the title would go to one of them. I needed more!

No parties, no restaurant dinners. After the final of the Qualifiers on Saturday, I went straight back to the hotel. I had dinner there and went to my room.

###
SUNDAY

Sunday's runs were scheduled for 1 pm. An unusual time, because the competitions usually take place in the morning. I didn't really know what the reason was, but probably because the event was being broadcast on TV and the afternoon was better for the audience.

Even so, we had to be at the arena at 10 am, which is

also quite late because we were used to arriving at the arena around 7 am. No problem, I used the extra time to rest and arrived promptly at 10 am in the locker room.

While I was getting ready beside Mario, Paula walked into the room.

"Good morning!" Paula said.

"Good morning!" Mario and I responded.

"Marquito, I need you to follow me for a second." said Paula.

"Paula, I'm getting ready to go on track. I don't want to go anywhere, with all due respect."

"I think you won't regret it." Paula said smiling.

Unable to say no, I followed Paula through the corridors that led to the arena. No handlers around there yet, and the people in the stands were still settling into their seats.

Paula continued walking through the crating area and it was only then that I saw them. My mother and brother, sitting in the front row, next to Leo! My heart jumped into my throat! I desperately ran to them and hugged them!

"My God! What are you all doing here???", I asked unable to contain my emotion.

"We came to cheer for you!" my mother said.

"That's right, bro!" said my brother. "Now you'll have to win!"

"But how? How?" I asked.

Paula interrupted.

"We thought it would be good for you to have your family around at this important moment. So, we brought them on a flight this morning from Orlando."

I ran and hugged Paula.

"Thanks! Thank you very much!"

Paula smiled and gently pushed me away.

"I'm so happy you guys are here!" I said.

###

SEMI-FINALS

No doubt now with my family in the stands, I had gained more motivation. It was the first time they were present watching me competing, and it was the last round.

Cheerful crowd in the stands! Lots of music, dancing, and people having fun!

"Ladies and gentlemen, welcome to the National League! Who will be the champion?", announced the speakers.

The crowd responded excitedly. With shouts and choruses of motivation to their favorite handlers. It was a beautiful party that was taking place in the stands.

The judge really decided to complicate things for the handlers as the semi-finals course was, as expected, the most difficult of that weekend so far.

The judge had prepared one of the most difficult exercises handlers can find. In the midst of a course that was already complex throughout its length, the judge even prepared a surprise for the handlers.

With a "C"-shaped tunnel, he placed the entrance of the slalom within the circumference of the tunnel. For the dogs to be able to enter the slalom correctly, they would need to run towards the tunnel and at the last possible second turn to the left entering the slalom, without entering the tunnel. A nightmare for handlers.

One of the most interesting things at the time was observing the difference in the handlers' mood. While Polly, Mario, Caitlyn, Sany and the other handlers who weren't fighting for the title, were having fun with the music and making fun of the crowd, Amy, Lisa and I were serious with our eyes fixed on the track looking for solutions to survive the course, and looking for ways to pass that complicated exercise created by the judge.

When handlers started to enter the track for their runs, the joy began to fade from some handlers' faces. Several were eliminated in that dreaded slalom inside the tunnel's circumference.

Among them, Caitlyn, Joe, and Nastasha. One by one, eliminated. The crowd was having the most fun you could ever imagine. After every elimination, a shout of "OHHHHH!" followed by clapping and shouting for the name of the handler and dog.

Polly came to the track and managed to survive the course. As she approached the slalom, she ordered Panda to stop with a strong "STAY" command. Poor Panda kind of freaked out, dropped to the ground and then Polly led him into the slalom correctly. The untraditional handling cost Polly a long time on the clock, but she managed to get the dog all the way.

The unlucky one was Mario, who fell into the referee's trap and said goodbye to the season. The crowd gave him a standing ovation when Mario took Rex on his lap and said goodbye, leaving the track for the last time. Without having qualified for the final, his time in the National League ended there.

Sany came next. Even though he'd been joking since he'd arrived at the arena, it wasn't hard to see the change in his face as he hit the track with Maximus. He got serious and focused. He stared at the track and placed Maximus at the starting mark.

Rocked by the crowd supporting his dog. "MAX! MAX! MAX! Sany was able to finish his run with mastery and leave behind the dreaded exercise prepared by the judge, finishing in the provisional first position.

Amy, Lisa, and I were the next ones to get on track for the semi-finals. Following the next day's reverse ranking order, I would be the first to enter. Amy and Lisa, who had dominated the Qualifiers on Saturday, would enter after.

I got on track with Arrow on the leash beside me. I heard the shouts of "GO MARQUITO!", "GO ARROW", coming from the crowd. Through all that noise, I couldn't hear my mother and brother in the stands, but I knew they were there cheering me on.

I felt a twinge in my stomach and a shiver. One mistake and that would be the end of it.

I put Arrow on the start mark! "STAY!" I commanded!

Arrow sat up and I removed her harness. I walked away! Two, three, four meters from her. I looked over, immediately she got up waiting for my command to start running.

"OK!" I screamed!

With silence in the crowd for a second, I could hear Arrow's paws scraping the artificial grass. Pieces of plastic flew back. Arrow launched herself over the first obstacle and our run began. 1-2-3-4, first straight line done to perfection. We approached the A frame which shuddered as Arrow aggressively threw herself over the obstacle. Two more jumps done with precision. Turn to the left, a slight slip after landing from one of the jumps. Nothing that affected our time. dog walk! "GO GO GO", I screamed! Arrow ran over the dog walk taking the supports off the ground and swinging the entire obstacle. We approached the slalom. It was now or never.

If I got too close to the entrance of the slalom, my body could point the tunnel to Arrow. So, I decided to stay away. I stopped running about five meters from the slalom and yelled: "WEAVES!!!!!!", Arrow continued towards the tunnel. "WEAVES!!" I yelled again and she understood. She turned to the left and entered the slalom correctly, claiming cheers and applause from the crowd. We finished the course! And what a run! No penalties and the best time among all handlers so far.

I dropped to my knees as I hugged Arrow, who happily played with her leash on the way out of the track. I looked at Leo, my mother and brother beside him. They were applauding, like the rest of the arena. We did it! It was still possible.

Amy was already getting on track as I left. She placed X at the starting mark and started her run. And what a run! X drew sighs from the crowd! Amy was performing the run of her life, using every bit of energy in her body, and every obstacle was done perfectly, including the slalom and the tunnel. Amy crossed the finish line with X but was unable to beat my time. Amy was in second.

The last handler to enter the track for the semi-finals was Lisa. There was nobody in the stands sitting. Everyone was standing watching the incredible battle between Amy, Lisa, and myself.

Lisa started her run with Fire and, as expected, she wasn't holding anything, but Fire barked at Lisa's every command, as if arguing with her. But Lisa was perfect. Fast, accurate and I had no doubt she would be the fastest in the semi-final. Fire with monstrous skills went through the slalom without even hesitating and risking entering the wrong tunnel. Lisa ran, passing the end line and everyone looked at the electronic scoreboard to check the result. Inexplicably a number 3 appeared next to her name. What??? Third??? How is that possible???

I didn't know how to explain that, but the reality was that I was first in the semi-finals. And now I was trying to relax a little bit, because in a few minutes we were going to the final, to decide the title.

FINALISTS
Marcus & Arrow
Amy & X
Lisa & Fire
Sany & Maximus
Polly & Panda
###
FINAL

A lot of excitement in the crowd! The whole arena in celebration and it was time to prepare for the grand finale. Who would be the champion in such a competitive season?

I returned to the side of the track where Leo and my family were.

"Well, now is the time!" I told Leo.

"I have nothing to tell you right now. You know what to do. Regardless of what the judge prepares for the final course, I know you are prepared."

"Son, do your best!" my mother said. "What you've done it's amazing. We are very proud of you."

"Yes, we are!" said my brother. "Just win the thing!"

We laughed.

I returned to the track to walk the final course. The final course! The one that would decide who would take home the champion's trophy. More than just a trophy, but the title of National League Champion.

The judge decided to play with tunnels once again! What an obsession this judge had with tunnels! It was expected that the course would be complicated, and it was. And the big highlight was, just like in Miami, a tunnel under the Dog Walk. Only this time, the two entrances were pointed to the same side, and the dog would have to go up the Dog Walk, without entering either sides of the tunnel.

Polly with Panda was the first one to go on track! Of the five that were playing in the final, Polly was the one that certainly showed the least technical skill. But seeing Panda running on that track with the whole crowd saying "WE LOVE PANDA", was without a doubt one of the greatest moments of the entire season.

The job Polly had done with that little mutt was outstanding, and she deserved to be in that final. One of the most epic scenes in dog agility history.

Watching those two running that course, I just wish more

people could train dogs from different breeds so they could compete in dog agility shows. Who knows, maybe I would do that in the future?

Despite having a few problems and dropping some bars, Polly managed to take Panda to the end without being eliminated, surviving the challenge created by the judge.

Sany was next. Even with no chance of being champion, Sany wanted to prove that he could have been. What would happen to Sany next season nobody knew. His team had not announced any contract renewals and apparently Sany was without a team to compete for next year. I honestly hoped to see him. I think a handler of his quality should not be left out of the League.

Speaking of quality, Sany ended up falling for the judge's trap. Completely unexpected! Sany was doing a spectacular run. Unfortunately, he was too late to give Maximus the command so he got confused and ended up entering the tunnel to the left of the dog walk, being eliminated.

Sany was upset and that was understandable. But he didn't lose his good mood. He waved to the crowd, bowed, and blew kisses. The fans loved it! It was the end of the season for Sany!

Lisa, Amy, and me. The moment of truth.

Unlike when we were competing in the semi-finals, I wasn't nervous. On the contrary, I was calm. I felt peace. Across from me, Amy looked nervous. She kept moving, touching her hair, petting X. She was restless.

"On track Lisa & Fire" announced the speakers.

Lisa hit the track for her last run of the year. The last of the season. She placed Fire in the starting position and released him. Both ran out doing the obstacles one by one, in sync in away that felt more like a dance than a dog agility competition. With every move Lisa made, every verbal command or sign, Fire moved with a synchronicity enviable by any dog agility handler in the world.

Silence in the stands! People stopped screaming for a few seconds to admire the Lisa & Fire show. Approaching the dog walk and Lisa with one arm pointing upwards and shouting "UP!", made Fire look up, forgetting about the tunnels and climbing the dog walk with an unparalleled simplicity. A champion simplicity! Lisa ended her run with a burst of cheers and applause! The perfect run, first place in the standings and a giant headache for Amy and I, who would be next on the track.

"On track Amy & X" announced the speakers.

Amy walked X onto the track and got ready. A little fix of the ponytail and a deep breath. Amy was not so calm. "OK!", she released X who quickly dug his claws into the ground, lunging forward.

Beating Lisa's time wouldn't be easy, but Amy was one of the best in the country, and if there was anyone who could do it, it was her. X was full of confidence and barked while running with long strides and perfect jumps.

The seesaw exploded on the ground echoing through the arena, X lunged for the slalom, bending the bars forcefully. They approached the dog walk with the tunnel underneath. Amy made a movement throwing her body against X's body, angling the curve better, directing X exactly in the perfect line towards the dog walk. X simply ignored the tunnels and climbed the obstacle correctly.

The crowd cheered! They had passed the most precarious point on the track. After the dog walk just three more jumps and that's it. X looked at Amy and barked. Amy stretched out her arm pointing at the last two jumps and X... TURNED TO THE OPPOSITE SIDE AND WENT INTO THE WRONG JUMP! NO! WHAT HAPPENED?

The crowd was silent. A horrible silence. People didn't believe what they were seeing. Amy had been eliminated at one point on the track with absolutely no risk of elimination. X just turned to the side and made the wrong jump.

Amy was on the floor, on her knees. Across the track, Lisa celebrated! Her biggest rival was out.

Slowly, Amy gathered the strength to get up and start leaving the track. Hands over her eyes, probably full of tears. The crowd started to applaud and shout her name "AMY! AMY! AMY!". She waved back and more applause came.

It was my turn. I started walking to the track while Amy was coming out. Yes, her eyes were full of tears, I could see it now. I wanted to hug her and comfort her.

She approached, we were side by side, I was entering the track and she was leaving it. She looked me in the eyes, those eyes filled with tears:

"Just do it!" she said to me in a split second as she left the track.

"On track Marcus & Arrow!" announced the speakers.

It was our turn. The last one of the day to go on the track, the last one of the season to go on track. Amy was out and now it would be Lisa or me.

I took a deep breath, closed my eyes as I walked to the starting mark. I put Arrow on the starting mark and walked away.

I took one more deep breath clearing my mind. Everything was silent, everything stopped. I thought about my family in the stands. I thought about my father. I thought about my friends. I thought about how lucky I was just to have the opportunity to be there.

"OK!" I released Arrow who started our run.

The world went in slow motion. I would tell that story for years to come, and many would not believe me. How the world at that moment became slow and quiet.

SEESAW!

Gently, fluidly. I felt myself not running but floating at a perfect pace.

TUNNEL!

One more obstacle behind us! I looked at Arrow who returned eye contact. I pointed to the next obstacle.

SLALOM!

Another on. So smooth! Even though for years to come people would tell me how fast I was running in that final, I could not feel the speed.

A FRAME!

I felt the lightness and connection between me and Arrow. The most amazing partner in my life.

JUMP, JUMP, TUNNEL!

One more sequence made. We approached the Dog Walk

with the tunnel underneath. The same exercise that we had eliminated in Miami in the first round!

"UP!" I commanded Arrow! She lifted her head in search of the dog walk, and quickly found it. Without threatening any error, Arrow climbed the dog walk leaving the tunnel behind as well as my ghosts.

JUMP, JUMP, JUMP!

Three more obstacles and that was it...DONE! We finished our run without penalties. I bent down and hugged Arrow, not looking at the electronic scoreboard. I didn't know what our time was. I just hugged Arrow there on the ground.

I heard the crowd screaming, cheering, applauding. Someone had won, but who?

I looked forward to my family in the stands. My mom was hugging my brother, jumping, and screaming. Leo, jumped the fence and ran down the track. That's when I knew.

I looked up at the electronic scoreboard where the number 1 was next to our name.

WE WON! WE ARE THE CHAMPIONS OF THE NATIONAL LEAGUE!

I started to walk with Arrow off the track, still without the weight of what had happened. As soon as I left, I received a strong, tight hug. It was Amy! She hugged me in a way I would never forget. Still teary-eyed, she looked into my eyes, and we hugged, our foreheads touching.

"You deserve it!" she said. "You deserve it!"

Amy kissed me on the cheek and walked away. There was no time for me to respond. Leo jumped on top of me hugging me and screaming.

"We won! We won!"

In less than three seconds Paula and Rich appeared from thin air, hugging me.

"Ladies and gentlemen let's congratulate National League Champion Marcus & Arrow!" announced the speakers.

Lisa walked over and held out her hand toward me.

"Congratulations, Marquito!" Lisa said. "What a great season you had. And congratulations to Arrow. She is an amazing dog!"

"Thanks! That means a lot coming from you!"

Sany also approached:

"Congratulations, dwarf! Very Cool!"

"Thanks man! Let's see if you respect me a little bit more now!"

Sany smiled.

"Never!" he walked away.

Amid the mob that formed around me, I ran away with Arrow on the leash, running to the front row in the stands, towards my family.

I grabbed my mom and brother in a joint hug, the three of us. No one said anything, just a long, tight hug. Words weren't needed.

RESULTS ROUND 10 NEW YORK

1. Marcus & Arrow
2. Lisa & Fire
3. Polly & Panda
4. Sany & Maximus
5. Amy & X

RANKING AFTER ROUND 10 NEW YORK

1. Marcus & Arrow = 177 pts
2. Lisa & Fire = 171 pts
3. Amy & X = 162 pts
4. Sany & Maximus = 125 pts
5. Polly & Panda = 57 pts
6. Mario & Rex = 54 pts
7. Joe & Jungle = 22 pts
8. Natasha & Sparky = 20 pts
9. Caitlyn & Target = 12 pts

###

Hours later, after all the madness, I went back to the hotel. I needed to take a shower, change clothes and we were all going to dinner to celebrate. Me, the team, and my family.

I walked into the hotel lobby with Arrow on the leash beside me, and the giant champion's trophy in my left hand. People congratulated me.

I got in the elevator and pressed the number five. The elevator went up and when the doors opened on the fifth floor I ran into Amy.

Wet hair like someone who had just taken a shower. Backpack on her back and X on the leash beside her.

"Hey!" I greeted, surprised!

"Hey!"

Pause. I got off the elevator and we stared at each other for a few seconds. I was looking for the right words.

"Are you leaving already?" I asked.

"Yes, my flight is leaving tonight."

"Ah, I understand."

Another pause.

"Big trophy, huh?" she said.

"Yes! Did you see it? Beautiful, right?"

One more pause.

"Are you going to do any local events in the next few weeks?" I asked.

"Oh, no. No. I need a vacation. At least two months without Dog Agility."

"Vacation? Florida?", I asked.

She smiled.

"Perhaps."

"I don't know if you know, but Orlando is really cool this time of year!"

"Really?" smiling.

"Yep! It has theme parks, all kinds of restaurants, shopping, pleasant weather, not cold, and the beach is not that far away."

Amy smiled. That beautiful smile I liked so much.

"And now, I have my own place, you know?"

"Oh, really?" Amy now had a big smile.

"Yeah. It's not big but it's a pretty cool place. It has a large backyard for dogs and is close to the tourist area of Orlando."

Amy looked at me for a few seconds.

"I'll call you when I get to Charlotte."

"OK."

Amy passed me, got into the elevator, pressed the button, and the doors closed.

###

Back home in Orlando, the following weekend we were celebrating with the typical Brazilian barbecue.

Friends were there. My family, Leo, Rafi, Mr. Monterey. The people who were part of my life.

Leo was bragging as he was doing tricks with Arrow. Balancing treats on her nose.

I was on the grill, preparing the meats. My mother was pacing around bringing things from the kitchen.

The big trophy was full of ice and beers.

Beside the grill, my phone vibrated. I picked it up. "NOTIFICATION FROM THE NATIONAL LEAGUE WEBSITE".

I clicked on the link, which opened the news:

"PLANET CANINE DOG TEAM CONFIRMS SANY BASTOS TO BE MARCUS MACHADO'S PARTNER IN THE NEXT SEASON"

My eyes widened:
"HOLY...!!!!"

competitors table

HANDLER	DOG	CITY	BREED	DOB	TITLE
Marcus	Arrow	Orlando FL	Border Collie	2004	2007
Sany	Maximus	West Palm FL	Border Collie	2001	2003
Amy	X	Charlotte NC	Border Collie	2002	2004, 2006
Lisa	Fire	San Francisco CA	Border Collie	2000	2002, 2005
Mario	Rex	Chicago IL	Border Collie	1998	2001
Polly	Panda	Atlanta GA	Mix	2003	None
Caitlyn	Target	Denver CO	Border Collie	2005	None
Joe	Jungle	Charleston SC	Border Collie	2004	None
Natasha	Sparky	San Diego CA	Border Collie	2005	None

ABOUT THE AUTHOR

MARCO MAGIOLO is a Doctor of Veterinary Medicine graduated from the University Anhembi Morumbi in São Paulo. Originally from Brazil he is also a behaviorist, dog trainer, and former dog agility handler. For nearly 20 years, competing in many countries around the world. Canine Legends is his first novel, and is inspired by real events from his competitive life, in a fictional world.

Website: www.idtcdogtraining.com
Facebook: Marco Magiolo
Instagram: marcomagiolo
Twitter: @Marco_Magiolo
YouTube: youtube.com/marcomagiolo

Positive reviews from wonderful readers like you help other readers feel confident about choosing this book. Sharing your happy experience will be greatly appreciated. Please leave a review on Amazon!
I hope you enjoyed CANINE LEGENDS: A DOG AGILITY STORY.
Thank you!
MARCO MAGIOLO

www.ingramcontent.com/pod-product-compliance
Lightning Source LLC
LaVergne TN
LVHW021756060526
838201LV00058B/3113